Courage and Conquerors

Hadassah Pomeroy

ISBN:1508475393
ISBN-13: 978-1508475392

"From the powerful depths of humanity comes a collection of unique, soul-stirring short stories so fascinating you'll find their adventures irresistible."

~ Hadassah Pomeroy

ACKNOWLEDGMENTS

I can never thank you enough, Juanita. Indeed you are an outstanding editor. My gratitude and sincere thanks.

1 ANAK

Long before the white man came far north of Canada, the Inuit roamed the vast wilderness. They moved with the seasons, always returning to the same hunting ground.

Caribou hooves thundered across the land on their migration. On the hill, a pack of wolves howled, sweeping eagles screeched and the sun blushed through the clouds.

Kalua, wrapped in coarse sealskin, went hunting early. He looked round at the villagers, snug in their tepees. The large wooden frames were covered with layers of skins to protect them against the Arctic wind; driftwood and seaweed with stones to secure them at the base.

Snowflakes fell with a hush and patted his face as he walked towards the ocean. Camouflaged in the snow, he waited as two seals emerged from under the blow hole, shaking their flippers. Swiftly, he thrust his long spear and impaled the larger one. The second seal bellowed, splashed and dived into the deep.

Kalua carried the seal back to the tepee on his shoulders. The red blood, dripping behind him as he walked, left a trail against the pure white snow. The warmth of it melted circles into the icy surface. Reaching the camp, Kalua hung his catch between two stakes. The dead game now meant life for Kalua and his family.

He entered the tepee through the front flaps. "I smell a storm coming," he said to his wife, Nunavut who was breastfeeding their six-week-old son. "I must trap more walrus. There are many on the ice flow. Their blubber will keep us warm and we need more oil for cooking. I will wait until one rolls up on the beach."

Kalua approached his wife and rubbed his face against hers, then kissed the infant. "The boy has your beautiful mouth," he whispered, and then he left again.

Kalua climbed the hill and scanned his hunting ground of walrus below. The cold wind whistled between the high snowdrifts that almost covered the sparse pines. The snow whirled in a storm around him, before the wind stilled and it fell in heavy sheets.

The sound of blood chilling screams reached him from not too far away. He dug into the snow behind the tree, crouched and lifted his head to see a male bear attacking a female and her cubs.

Bellowing, the beast bit into a cub with his sharp fangs and flung him aside. Kalua watched in horror as the monster stood on its hind legs and reared over the female. The black mark on his lower back stood stark against his raised fur.

With ivory claws outstretched, he pierced her throat and ripped open her chest. A second frightened cub ran from where he'd snuggled against his mother and hid behind the rocks.

Kalua was terrified the male would catch his scent and come after him. Fortunately the wind shifted to blow in the opposite direction. Numbed with cold, he crouched and kept an eye on the cub. He was all too familiar with the ferocious behavior of bears towards their mating females and offspring. He'd witnessed it for years and it baffled him.

The raging bear's face was now covered in blood and he rubbed his head in the snow before shuffling away. Far in the distance a pack of wolves howled. The wind dropped and a hush fell across the frozen land.

The little cub returned to sniff at his mother's body. He snuggled against her fur, whimpering as the heat of her lifeblood drained away.

Kalua had never before been in such a predicament. He followed his natural born instincts and crawled on his stomach towards the golden cub so as not to frighten him. He stopped short of the body and mimicked the mother bear's purr. He dragged himself across the snow, ignoring the cramps that attacked his stiff leg muscles.

Kalua rested for a while, and then crawled until he was only a few feet away from the young cub. He made purring noises until he saw the tired and confused cub's ears prick up. Although he knew he could outrun the cub, his intuition prompted him to extend his hand and gently touch the tiny, soft paws. Both man and animal purred, and the bond of a lifetime was sealed.

Kalua's tears melted the snow beneath his chin. He picked up the young cub and tucked it inside his warm seal skin. With haste, he headed back to camp.

His call shivered between the tribal tepees. The natives rushed out and the huskies barked. All held their breath when Kalua took out the cub.

"I'll take him inside. Bring your axes and knives. I'll show you where the mother lies. Wait for me."

Startled, Nunavut gazed at the trembling little creature.

"He can share your milk with our son. I'll also cut tiny pieces of the fresh seal I caught this morning," Kalua said.

The woman sat cross-legged and held the cub. She extracted rich warm milk from her breasts and squirted it into his mouth. He opened his eyes and closed them again, resting his tiny paws in the folds of her bosom, and fell asleep.

An hour later, the hungry baby wailed. Nunavut placed the cub on the layers of soft skins beside the crib and suckled her son, Tayal. Feeding time alternated between the infant and tiny cub.

The tribe returned with the mother bear's body and skinned the pelt. Kalua received the honor of the magnificent coat. The tribe and huskies shared every morsel of meat, as did the Arctic fox who lurked behind a snowdrift. It waited until the natives left and then he snatched the remains while scavenging birds pecked the bones clean.

* * *

By some incomprehensible, miraculous law of nature, the golden cub clung to Nunavut. She was his mother now. He loved the warmth and shelter of her breasts, thrived on her life-giving milk and the meat from Kalua's seals.

"He never stops licking Tayal's face." Nunavut laughed. "A wonderful bond."

"He will grow enormous and quickly," Kalua said. "It's important the huskies get used to his presence. Dogs don't like bears. I'll chain them a short distance away from our camp. This will be extremely difficult. I will take the cub and teach him to hunt, starting first with small hares. The wilderness is his true home, he must trust it without fear."

"What do you think of Anak as a name?" she asked.

He glanced at her. "Anak...with mischief," he muttered. "I love it." Kalua was thrilled.

"I am going to make myself warm shoes from his mother's large paws," Nunavut said.

Nunavut thrived with her new menagerie, cooking for her large family, and busy feeding Tayal and Anak, who had a voracious appetite. She was happy. Anak followed her around constantly. At night, he sprawled beside Tayal's crib on his back with his legs in the air.

Nunavut brushed her face against her husband's chest, whispering, "A bear entered our lives. Thank you for saving him. My heart pounds with happiness. I love Tayal, Anak and you, Kalua. I could never live without you."

Kalua caressed her body as he held her close. "Listen to the noisy pair. What a bundle. Tayal gurgles and Anak snores. Let's get some sleep, beloved."

* * *

Kalua's parents and his brother, Okpatok, dwelt in the tepee next to them. Okpatok brushed the window flap of the tepee aside and gazed out at the grey sky. The sun filtered weakly through the low clouds. He turned away and sighed, then sat cross-legged beside his mother. His obsession and exasperation with Nunavut bordered in insanity.

"For years I have pleaded with her to be my wife." He rested his head on his mother's lap. "I have loved her since we were children playing in the snow." Okpatok loved and hated with extreme.

"She belongs to your brother. You cannot change that, my son."

"They taunt me, her skipping around like the Arctic fox and him laughing at me, mocking me. I can no longer tolerate watching her with him, bearing his children. I hate my brother for it."

"Hate is strong, Okpatok. It consumes you. You are like a restless wind."

His mother wrapped the soft hide around her shoulders.

"Mother, you give me courage to live. You are close to my heart, but I must leave. I can take no more." His tears trickled onto his hands. "I must venture into the silent white wilderness and follow my destiny. Nunavut's blood flows in my veins, put there by the blood bond we made as children when I made a small incision on her thumb and mine. We are joined forever. All I've ever wanted is her." Okpatok's tears fell on his mother's gnarled hands. Her eyes were filled with despair as she stroked his thick crop of hair. He lifted her hands and kissed her palms.

"Please...stay home," she pleaded, her body trembling with sadness.

"Wherever I go, Mother, you will be the invisible wind following me all my days," he whispered. "I might find a lonely friend like the Arctic fox, a beautiful creature."

"Why the fox?" she asked, smiling.

"Champion of the survivors, solitary and excellent hunters. They blend with the stark white, their bushy tails like a brush sweeping the air, their eyes intelligent and piercing." He gazed at his mother's sad face. "Cunning, they appear and disappear within moments with their young, avoiding the dangerous predators."

The wind rose as his father spoke. "It's a lonely world out there in this savage land," he said, a man of few words. "Take the dogs and sled. That's all we have to give."

Okpatok's farewell swelled in the humble tepee. He hugged his parents. "I'll see you in the Spring.

His mother clutched him to her bosom. Heartbroken, she couldn't let him go. He kissed her gaunt cheeks. "When you see a fox, I will be there and you will be my invisible wind."

Okpatok's eyes were bathed in tears as he stepped out into the fog. The solitary black sheep, manacled to Nunavut's destiny, vanished with the sled.

* * *

When Anak was a year old he was no longer able to enter the tepee because of his size. He pushed, nearly crushing the entrance as he tried to squeeze between the flaps. Taller than the tepee, traumatized and confused, Anak reclined against it and bellowed a forlorn call. The bear remembered how as a cub, he'd pillowed his head on Nunavut's soft breasts. She'd loved him like a mother. Now he was surrounded by howling dogs and dark cold nights.

The bear felt resentment, alienation. Nunavut, holding her son, rushed out to the distressed Anak. Both snuggled against him. The bear licked Tayal's face. How could he understand?

"I'll sleep outside beside the furry one until he gets used to the change," said Kalua. "He'll keep me warm."

"I can't bear seeing Anak so unhappy. His pain is my pain," Nunavut cried.

"He will grow even more, a giant," said Kalua. "Every night we'll take turns to stay with him. You stay a few hours and I will spend until morning. We'll continue for a month and see how he settles." He stroked her hair gently. "I'll take him out with the kayak. Bears are excellent swimmers. They cover great distances and their sense of smell is acute. I'll introduce him to the walruses and seals on the ice flow, teach him to stalk. He will soon learn to hunt and forage for himself." Kalua ran his fingers over Anak's face. Their bond was strong as ever.

When darkness fell Nunavut came out of the tepee. Yawning, Kalua stepped back inside.

"Anak, my precious Anak," she murmured as she lay his favourite dish of seal flippers and a chunk of blubber before him.

He purred his pleasure and slobbered over his food as he consumed it with a hearty appetite. Nunavut kissed his nose and eyes. He returned the affection by resting his head against her bosom as he had when he was a cub.

"You are too big now. It's all this milk of mine and Kalua's game. You understand why you are unable to go into the tepee." She stroked his ears. "You understand, my hulk." Nunavut hummed to him soothingly as she huddled into the shadow of his great arms and fell asleep.

At midnight, Kalua woke her, cradling Tayal in his arms wrapped in fur. "The cold is good for his lungs. One day he will grow to be a great hunter." Nunavut placed Tayal in the crook of Anak's thick, muscular neck. The bear licked the little boy's hands and cheeks affectionately and tears rose in Nunavut's eyes. "You will see Tayal every day," she whispered. "He is learning his first steps. Soon he will run with you."

At each mention of Tayal's name, Anak's eyes opened wide. He understood, and brushed his rough tongue against her face. Nunavut lifted her son from where he snuggled against the sad bear.

Anak stretched his large paws and clasped Kalua close to his golden fur. Warmth rose from the magnificent creature and Kalua felt a tug at his heart. He stroked the gentle brute with his fingers and Anak purred happily. A breathtaking aura of content grew around them.

* * *

The following morning from the beach Kalua watched the bear's movements, overwrought with excitement. Anak trampled up and down the ice, slipping several times and sliding on his bottom. Growling, he raised himself until he found his footing. He stood on his hind legs, lifted his head and flared his nostrils. Sniffing the air, he bellowed.

Alert, the bear's natural instincts took over. He shuffled a short distance, rubbed his nose on the ice and stopped. The fishy scent of the seals guided his nose. He listened with his ears pressed to the ice. Anak heard swishing and flapping noises. Excited, he stamped again and again, digging into the ice with his powerful paws then leapt, crashing through the frozen layer. He plunged into the seal's breathing hole and with a quick swipe, grabbed one. Anak was ready to survive the boundless cold wasteland.

Every day after that Kalua, Nunavut, Tayal and Anak combed the long beach. The colossal beast's scenting skills were remarkable. A short distance away, he spotted a fox chewing on the remains of a whale carcass washed up on the sand.

Anak chased him, but the cunning fox eluded him as he detoured here and there before the bear lost sight of him. Anak returned to his family, panting heavily.

Tayal poked a finger against his leg as the beast purred. "Don't harm the foxes. They are beautiful."

"Anak is a hunter. That's the way he will survive. He is free and we cannot interfere with nature." Kalua ran his fingers through his son's thick hair.

Nearing the chain of rocks, the walruses spotted the bear approaching. They splashed into the water, followed by their pups. Hungry, Anak dived in and caught one. The mother's call was one of distress as Anak held the squealing pup. Swiftly, he choked it and silence fell on the ice.

Tayal looked at his father. "He was so little."

"Yes, my Tayal. Anak must fend for himself. One day you will understand. It is the way of nature. We are all animals though we do not behave like the four-legged ones. In the animal kingdom, only the strongest survive."

* * *

Spring arrived with a profusion of colours. Huskies gave birth to puppies and ignored Anak. He was part of the surroundings and yelped all day.

Mating walruses fought on the rocks, seals and calves slithered on the beach and above, mewing gulls flew.

Tayal stood near Anak, reaching above the bear's knees, trying to grasp them with his small hands. Nunavut's tears of laughter streamed upon her high cheek bones. Ten foot tall Anak and little Tayal—she realized how much the bear had grown.

She watched the beast take giant strides on his paws, carving his sharp claws on the sandy beach. Her son followed trying to keep pace but tripped, whimpering. Anak turned and gently picked the boy up by his pants. Tayal laughed and stroked the bear's eyes.

Of late, Anak was restless. Kalua smiled. "It is spring, the mating season. Soon, he'll leave us to find a mate but he will be back."

As if understanding Kalua's words, Anak cuddled the boy against him and purred. He dropped Tayal gently near Nunavut and trampled away, bellowing. Nunavut understood.

"Where did Anak go?" ask Tayal, confused.

"He's gone off to find you a present, a surprise," she answered. The bear stayed away for several weeks.

* * *

Kalua caressed his wife's soft belly.

"I wonder where Anak is. We must leave for the great hunt; catch enough game to last the winter. Timing is crucial. Last year was a short summer, the geese left early." Kalua rubbed his face against his wife's abdomen. "The child is in a hurry, knocking in your womb. I love you, Nunavut." His sad voice rose above the wind.

Shivering, Nunavut stood close to her husband. He held her. "We'll be back before the heavy snow," he murmured and picked up Tayal. "Help your mother feed the dogs. Each must have the same amount. I cut sufficient of meat. At night, make sure you fasten the tepee's entrance well. Protect your mother." Kalua glanced at his wife, smiling.

"When will Anak come home?" Tayal asked.

"Soon, soon." Kalua's throat felt dry. His heart pounded. "Anak has two homes. Hunting seals across the ice and our home which he loves."

Kalua hugged him. "Anak will protect you for the rest of your life," he said and left.

Kalua, head of the team, never whipped the huskies. Hearing his raucous voice, they pressed on. He scanned the timeless splendor. Perhaps Anak would appear. They followed the trail of migrating caribou. They pawed to reach vegetation in the snow with their front hooves.

"We'll intercept them on three sides. Four crawl up that ridge," he indicated. "Two men and I will hide between the willows and to the west there is a steep mound, an excellent spot to spear them," he said.

The hunt was well-coordinated with several caribou slain. A wounded animal sprinted for a few moments then dragged, the spear hanging from his right front leg. He frothed at the mouth and neighed in agony.

"Follow him and put an end to his misery," Kalua shouted to the other men.

A tribesman pursued the desperate animal. Kalua spotted wolves prowling around their rocky den. The reindeer collapsed near it. He retreated fast. It was the caribou or him.

The ravenous pack attacked, tearing the animal to shreds. On the ridge, a tribesman leaned too far. He slipped and rolled towards the stampeding herd. Forking their antlers at the man's intestines, they hurled him in the air. The mass advanced, crushing him to death.

The cold wind rose as the Inuits huddled in the lee of the sleds.

The dull hoot of the snow owl filtered above the infinite dark theatre.

Kalua's throbbing heart longed for Nunavut, Tayal, his unborn child and the splendid Anak.

"At dawn we'll retrieve our friend's body," said Kalua. "Before the eagles and vultures pick him clean. Then we'll steer to the valley of the elk. Aim your spears with accuracy at the temple or heart, a quick death. I dislike seeing them struggle." Kalua bit his lip. "Some limp for miles, find a hole and die from their injuries. Two men will stalk the elk," added Kalua.

At first light, Kalua's keen eyes surveyed the wilderness. He cried out, "There are three elk at the edge of the valley, more scattered above. We'll make it a clean sweep, no risks."

The men held their weapons. Several magnificent elk pawed for sedges and lichen. With the shifting wind, they pricked up their ears and snorted. The spears zoomed across the plains and five giants fell.

Axes and knives in hand, the men cleaved and sliced chunks of meat from the animals then sheathed them in oiled skin bags to load onto the sleds. The eerie howl of the wolves echoed across the plains. They headed back with their game.

The dogs barked as a colossal bear sprang towards the dogsleds. Kalua sighted him from behind the trees. "Anak," he stammered with joy.

The hunters watched the giant with wonder. Spectacular, five-year-old Anak weighed over nine hundred kilos and stood ten feet tall. Shaking his head, the wind ruffled his golden fur. Anak brushed his large paws on Kalua's back. He lost his balance and stumbled. Beast and man danced with joy at finding each other again.

All of a sudden, the bear stood on his hind legs, snarled and turned. Kalua spotted another bear approaching at a distance.

Anak growled. He sensed the enemy facing him was a threat, a dangerous predator, and he had to protect his beloved people. Anak swerved down the slope and gave chase. The dogs were nervous. Terrified, Kalua watched as

Anak leapt at the monster. He dug his teeth deep into the bear's throat then ripped its chest wide open. Kalua gasped as he recognized the large black mark on the lower back.

Tableaus of memories from five years before played in his mind. He remembered this bear killing Anak's mother, leaving the shivering cub hiding in the snow. Ironic how Anak had butchered his father the same way. Kalua stripped the dead bear's coat to take back. Victorious, Anak followed the hunters along the coast back to the camp.

The giant slept outside the tepee with Tayal curled up against his thick fur. The bear wrapped his warm paws around the boy's cold feet. Both were the same age. Kalua snuggled beside his wife and listened to the whistling wind.

* * *

Several months later, the smallpox pestilence carried by the transmigration of animals and birds ravaged the wilderness. Many fell victim to the contagious disease. Dying, they crawled into snow holes and froze. Food was scarce. The wind shrieked, the heavy snow fell with a hush, only the desperate dared venture into the blizzards to plunder from the dead in the neighboring tepees.

Kalua felt a dark premonition and shuddered. He checked the game hanging on the stakes. There was ample food for the family and his parents in the next tepee. Like a black shroud, the epidemic pervaded the land. Kalua and Tayal were spared. Nunavut was plagued with high fever and pustules puckered her face and body. Kalua's parents were stricken as well. Daily, he shuffled between the two tepees with loyal Anak constantly by his side.

Tayal bent over his mother and sponged her forehead with snow.

"I am going to the medicine man close to us to ask him what to do and save Mother. The wise man listens to the Great Spirit. I'll be back in a short while. Trickle some water into Mother's dry mouth."

Kalua ran outside and Anak trampled behind. He returned a little later panting. "The old man urged me to gather seaweed." He grabbed a large seal skin bag and rushed outside once more. His heart raced.

Anak bellowed, his instinct warning him Nunavut was not well. The scent of her slow decay reached him as followed behind his master.

Short of breath, Kalua pulled seaweed as fast as he could. "Nunavut," he said to the bear.

Anak understood and pawed at the weeds to help. When the bag was full, Kalua slung it on his back and staggered home. The bear poked his nose into through the flap of the tepee. Tayal approached and kissed his nose then sat beside him. Together they watched Kalua as he warmed some fat and smeared it over Nunavut's weeping sores. He covered her entire body and face with a layer of seaweed to ease the pain and reduce the inflammation.

Kalua watched Tayal sitting dazed in the corner and heard Anak's distress. Tayal's tears fell on the bear's nose and he licked them away. His cries howled and echoed across the savage wasteland.

Throughout the day, Nunavut raved in delirium. Kalua was preparing the evening meal when he heard her scream. It chilled his spine. Between her splayed legs, the fetus expelled with a gush. Weeping, Kalua wrapped the little one in skins and placed it at his wife's breasts. Exhausted, she fell asleep. Kalua put the stillborn in a bucket of snow.

For a whole week, the morbid disease racked Nunavut's frail body. Day and night, Kalua fed her with nourishing walrus soup. The seaweed slowly healed the poisonous pustules.

Tayal fed the huskies and cleaned the tepee. He took Anak to the beach to distract the sad bear. At daybreak, Anak crawled out from his sheltered snow-hole and stretched.

On that sixth morning, Kalua brought the stillborn to Nunavut. He knelt and felt his beloved's brow. "The fever has gone. I love you, Nunavut. I'll take the little one to the rocks now," said Kalua, devastated.

Nunavut trembled as she touched the lifeless babe. "He is cold." She wrapped her shawl around the child.

Tayal approached his mother. "When you are well, we will all play together with Anak. He hasn't seen you for many days. The bear is lost without you and I miss your seal cutlets." He leaned against Nunavut's shoulder and brushed a hand over the silent bundle.

Clutching the tiny stillborn to his chest, Kalua walked out with Tayal. Together the three travelled to the tribe's burial place a fair distance from the village. They climbed the maze of slippery rocks hewn like catacombs. Kalua buried the lifeless bundle in the narrow niche between two rocks and sealed the makeshift grave with a heavy stone.

The wind rose as he mourned the loss of his child, his pain almost unbearable. With tightness in his chest he cried, "Why? Why?"

Tayal cried as he buried his face in the fur on Anak's hind leg. The bear bellowed his shattered, forlorn call and it shivered above the galloping waves.

"Nunavut, my Nunavut," Kalua called as he rushed home with Tayal an Anak. "Open the tepee entrance flap," he said to Tayal. "I want Anak to see your mother." He lifted her into his arms and held her up to Anak. The bear purred as he licked Nunavut's feet and hands, flicking away the seaweed in all directions. "Nunavut must rest now. You will see her tomorrow." That night, sitting beside Nunavut, Kalua said to the boy, "Your grandparents won't last long. Their life is fading away," said Kalua to Tayal. "There is nothing I can do to help. They are old, weak, sick and stiff from the cold and cannot eat the food I have cooked. Soon they will be released from all pain and fly with the Great Spirit."

* * *

Almost a year had passed since Okpatok left home. He was a survivor, a wanderer. He slept in the open, surrounded by his dogs. In winter, the solitary man erected a small tepee wide enough for the few huskies to share his hermitage. He huddled against them for warmth. Now, hungry and chilled to the bone, he crawled out and scanned the bleak waste.

In the dogsled, he kept dried seal meat and nutritious strips of seal sinew. Some were strapped around his neck which he chewed. In sealskin bags, he stored skins, bows and arrows and hung them off the sled. The Arctic fox followed him, friendly enough to often share his meal. Fascinated, Okpatok watched as the fox crouched down and lay still. He'd spotted his relished rock ptarmigan. Below in the ditch, the hen waited. Concealment and coloring were the bird's defense against predators. Four chicks hid within her tousled feathers. One sneaked out. The mother spread her wings and swept it back under.

Suspense hung in the air. Okpatok dared not move. As the snow whistled across, the rock ptarmigan's plumage turned white to match the surroundings.

The fox jumped, confused at the sudden disappearance of the bird. He turned right. The bird ran left and hid in a clump of willow, scratching out snow around her. A curious chick took a peep. The flustered mother shoved it beneath her. Okpatok laughed. He wanted to hug the fox, who retired from sight.

Okpatok loved the rhythm of life in this savage, beautiful land—winds, snow and brilliant colours, trapping white hares, stalking caribou and hunting seals. The peril of being exposed to danger, a predator against the defenseless, the forlorn call of the animals touched his soul across the harmony of seasons. All this excited him. Most of all, he'd found a friend— the Arctic fox.

Okpatok gazed up at the Northern Lights, his heart swelling. Creation, the ineffable cloaked in mystery, was beyond his comprehension. Who was the painter with his brush creating such dazzling colours? Where did he hide in the endless darkness between the multitudes of stars?

Okpatok heard a faint, distressed voice. He shuffled a few paces. Dismayed, he saw a man crawling through the snow, his face covered with weeping sores.

"Don't touch me. Don't come near. It's deadly. The devil's everywhere," he said as he collapsed.

Okpatok's tongue cleaved to his mouth, he shuddered and fled. Okpatok remembered that during the hunting season the old, young and sick always stayed behind along the coast, in the refuge of their tepees, waiting for the men to return with game.

"Nunavut, Mother!" His screams rolled above the littered corpses. He secured the dogs. The dogsled pitched and heaved. Hours later, darkness sneaked up on him as he raced towards the coast.

The luminous splendor of the northern lights spread across the heavens. Okpatok arrived at the settlement. He hid behind a six foot snow drift. Spear in hand, he stalked. Like the Arctic fox, he waited.

Anak was fidgety and kept growling. Concerned, Kalua stepped out into the swirling snow.

"What is it?" Kalua stroked the bear.

Anak snarled. The beast felt danger.

Okpatok recognized his brother's voice. With chattering teeth, he fumbled in the dark, hearing the bear trampling towards him.

"Who's there?" Kalua shouted.

Anak sniffed, stood onto his hind legs and bellowed.

Okpatok dropped his spear. Terrified, he watched the monster hurling down on him. The raging animal chewed his hand right off to the forearm with razor-like canines and flung the man behind his parents' tepee. Okpatok staggered to the dogsled.

Kalua did not pursue the intruder. It was too risky to leave Nunavut and Tayal. He heard the huskies flee. Anak stayed outside all night guarding the tepee.

Within a short distance, Okpatok alighted from the dogsled. He acted fast, knowing how fatal his injury could be. To ease the pain and reduce the blood flow, he covered the mangled stump with snow then wrapped a tourniquet of dry sinews around it, tightening them with a small knife. He pressed his forearm in the snow, slumped back in the sled and fainted. The huskies followed the familiar scent home. Okpatok, with his power of endurance, survived.

He shivered with cold, his stump throbbed and he raved, driven mad by the pain. He sprinkled snow on his wound, trying to numb the ache.

"Nunavut!" he screamed. He despised his brother for snatching her from his life to spend long, lonely days in despair. She should have been his wife, borne his children. He was an excellent hunter and would have provided well for her and her family.

How he longed for Nunavut's laughter rolling above the morning breeze. He remembered how, as a boy, he'd chased her through the snow pulling her ribbons from her hair. Kalua had stolen his happiness and Okpatok's hatred boiled in his heart.

Nunavut had taunted him to the point of madness, and her loving his brother had poisoned his mind with thoughts of revenge against Kalua.

"You understand, don't you?" Okpatok spoke to the fox that rested his head against the Inuit's foot. Piercing eyes consoled him. He loved this

18

solitary animal, a splendid tame sphinx resting beside him.

* * *

At dawn, Kalua spotted the severed hand, unaware it was his brother's. Anak kicked at the lifeless fingers. Kalua assumed it belonged to a desperate robber, come to plunder food during these hard times. Tayal slipped outside and saw Anak sniffing at the limb, sickness rising in his stomach. "Look," he cried, picking up a spear. "Is it from the thief who fled last night after Anak attacked him?"

"Yes. We'll get rid of it but first we must check on your grandparents," his father said.

Together they walked to the next tepee where they found the grandparents frozen, lying side by side. Tayal touched his grandmother's face. Grief-stricken, he and Tayal wrapped the grandparents in walrus hides.

"Does it take long for the body to freeze?" Tayal asked with the curiosity of a child who does not comprehend the full sadness of death.

"For the old and weak it is swift. The heart stops pumping blood and freezes quickly in their narrow veins. Death is painless. They simply go to sleep," Kalua reassured his son. "The young, who shelter in the snow holes when caught in blizzards, can last a few hours after their food supply is gone. They huddle together for warmth for as long as they can." Kalua's voice flooded his son's world with fear, but the boy bravely helped his father bury the grandparents in the burial place beside Nunavut's baby. They set fire to the tepee to destroy the disease and the severed limb was cast into the sea.

* * *

Crowning the horizon, orange sky touched the dark blue sea. Happy, Anak bellowed. He loved Nunavut, Kalua and Tayal.

Day by day, Nunavut regained her strength. She sipped small amounts of seal soup and ate morsels of walrus blubber strips. The pestilence shroud lifted and vanished.

Kalua often took his son out in the kayak. He glanced at Anak swimming alongside and said, "Look at the magnificent iceberg rearing from the icepack, like a rising white god. Eventually, they split with rumbling thunder and break, floating to the unknown. Fearsome, spectacular, might of nature."

Tayal knit his brow. "What lies beyond?"

"Remote worlds. Perhaps one day I shall navigate far to the end of the horizon where it touches the sea. I wonder like you, Tayal, what is beyond. You are a thinker. It's chilly. Let's go home. I'll prepare the evening meal. Mother is still not strong enough on her legs to cook."

Walking back to the tepee, Kalua thought of his son's future. Half the natives in his village had perished. Now he visualized Tayal as a great leader, a warrior who would unite with other tribes to save his people. He would be a wise, compassionate and fair master guiding his tribes, a backbone of this wild, spectacular land.

* * *

Not far from where they walked, Okpatok sat cross-legged while the fox chewed strips of dried sinews. He touched his stump. Over a year had passed and it was still tender. He looked at the fox.

"Though you can't speak, your eyes do. You understand whatever I say. I will not rest. In life and death, Nunavut is my destiny. My body is eaten away with hatred and revenge and I am choking on it. There will come a time when I am no longer beside you. Find a vixen, my friend."

The fox lifted his head and howled as Okpatok brushed his soft pointed ears.

Later, Okpatok raced towards the settlement. He pitched the dogsled between two hillocks and tunneled inside a burrow to spy on his brother's movements for several days. He fed the dogs every few hours to keep them quiet. At sunrise each day, Okpatok sighted Kalua, the boy and bear shuffle to the beach and disappear in the kayak. They returned hours later.

* * *

At first light, Nunavut cut walrus cutlets cooked in blubber. "Smells delicious," said Kalua, kissing her.

"Tayal insists to take the kayak again. Anak, of course, agrees." He chuckled. The boy dipped his fingers in the swimming blubber. "Mother, I love your cooking." Tayal licked the dripping fat from his fingertips.

The blushing sun rose. Far out in the field, two icebergs emerged.

"The white gods are covered with gold this morning. They are travelling to the end of the horizon and will vanish. It's an omen." Kalua murmured, a chill running down his spine.

Tayal was mesmerized. "They might float forever. Can we take the kayak every day?" he asked, excited.

"Of course, until the change in weather. The sun will soon hide for several months."

* * *

Dawn skirted the skyline. Okpatok waited as the kayaks disappeared then he leopard-crawled towards the tepee. Inside, Nunavut was patching Tayal's trousers. She lifted her head as he entered through the flap. Okpatok raised his stump.

Nunavut was numb with fear and revulsion. "It was you...the bear..." She did not finish the sentence.

"Yes. You will pay for this. Both of you will be punished."

She tried to stand but he kicked her hard in the groin, spitting as he rubbed his mangled hand in her face. He frothed at the mouth, his madness complete.

Kicking her again, he pinned her down, spread-eagled.

"My seed will grow in your womb. I will haunt you for the rest of your days."

"No, no!" She fought, digging the sharp bone needle into his chest, clawing at his face with her fingernails, ripping at his coat and pulling out chunks of his hair.

He bit into her neck like a vampire thirsty for blood, for revenge. "Kalua can't kill me. Without you, I died years ago," he screamed. "I have always loved you! Hating me will only torment you."

* * *

On the rocks, two elephant seals with pendulous snouts wrestled. The raucous calves in the labyrinth grunted. "Leopard seals are much smaller, prodigious hunters, pursue in packs," said Kalua.

Anak, hidden behind the kayak, spotted a huge walrus on the ice flow.

"They are unpredictable," Kalua continued.

Enchanted, Tayal gazed at the horizon with wonder. "The fog has spread over the white pillows."

Suddenly a walrus slipped beneath the kayak, lifted and tilted it forward. Kalua and Tayal were flung out into the icy water.

The walrus rammed his upper tusks into the canoe and it capsized. Tayal's head ducked in and out of the water. Panic-stricken, Kalua cut through the water to his son with strong strokes. "Hold onto my back," he screamed.

Anak saw the walrus chasing the pair. The raging bear slashed his powerful legs like oars and plunged headlong towards it. With an iron grip, Anak fastened onto the walrus's throat, gouged out his eyes and flung the body aside. He paddled to Kalua and Tayal where he pulled the boy onto his shoulders with his strong mouth. While Tayal clung to his muscular neck, Kalua clutched his fur as Anak waded to shore.

On the beach, the bear lowered them safely to the ground, shook himself vigorously and sneezed. Father and son rushed to their tepee, shivering with cold.

"Change quickly and sit by the fire," Kalua said to Tayal.

Nunavut sat on a stool in the corner behind a screen of seal skins. Kalua rummaged for dry clothes and threw them to Tayal.

"I'll tell you all about the morning's ordeal, Nunavut. It's never happened before. We'll have some food first."

Nunavut remained silent, surprising Kalua. Usually when they returned from their daily trip, she ran to greet them excitedly.

"I don't feel well." She coughed, struggled to rise, and then collapsed.

"Mother!" Tayal screamed.

Kalua jumped up. He picked her up and carried her over to lay her on Anak's mother's warm coat. Alarmed, he saw the deep cuts on her neck, the bruises on her arms and legs. Nunavut's moist eyes were veiled with despair. It wrung Kalua's heart. Near the stool was evidence of hair and ripped coat shreds.

Kalua smeared walrus blubber over her angry lacerations. He did not question his wife. She slept all afternoon. In the evening Tayal gave her seal soup mixed with special seaweed.

Kalua knew who did this to his wife. He recognized Okpatok's coat. Throughout the night he sat beside Nunavut and stroked her cold hands. He was silent as he felt the agony she'd endured lately—the smallpox, the loss of her child and now, the unforgiveable act that stripped her of her soul and dignity.

"Anak will kill him for what he has done to you," he whispered through his tears as he kissed her hands gently.

"Who would want to hurt Mother?" Tayal cried, bewildered.

"When you are a man and become a great hunter, pursue and kill your game for only one reason—survival. Through the curtains of years to come, I see you in my mind, a champion leader. Banish the evil and their blood stains on this wilderness. It's my fault. I shouldn't have left your mother alone. Next time we will take her in the kayak with us." He hushed the whimpering Tayal.

"I am taking Anak with me at first light," said Kalua, facing his son. "Block the entrance inside. Lie near it, spear in hand. You are old enough and well-experienced to handle the weapon. I promise to be back before sunset." Kalua stepped out.

Anak licked his sore back as Kalua huddled beside him. The creature knew no bounds. He shone with devotion. Rising early, Nunavut prepared breakfast for the family. She wrapped slices of walrus tongue and kidneys for Kalua. He held her close. "I love you, Nunavut. You are my wife."

Kalua coiled the shreds of ripped coat and hair with sinew strips and pressed it close to Anak's nose. He sniffed and stamped his massive legs, bellowing.

Anak followed the strong scent for miles north. When they found him, Okpatok was asleep beside the sled. The fox leapt up and fled above the hill when the bear loomed in the distance.

Startled, Okpatok raised himself. The huskies barked. His blood turned cold. The brothers glared at each other with hatred.

"You cannot escape. The bear should have killed you when he pulped your hand." Kalua screamed with fury. "You harmed my wife, infested her with the foulness of your body."

"I am already dead. Life without Nunavut has been a slow death for me. Can you understand that? My only friend is a fox." Okpatok fumed, saliva fuelled by madness dripped from his chin.

"My giant will tear you apart. The wolves will feast on your rotten flesh." Kalua pounced on his brother. Towering, Anak snarled and crushed Okpatok's other hand then hammered his skull again and again with his giant paws.

As his life ebbed away, Okpatok turned his eyes and saw the fox. "Nunavut."

The two dogsleds and Okpatok's huskies trailed back. Kalua turned to where the lonely fox waited on the hill. The fox howled, descended and approached Okpatok's body.

* * *

Nunavut developed a chronic cough she could not shake off.

"You'll feel better with the warmer weather," he assured her.

Pups, calves and chicks broke out in rhapsody. Honking geese flew above them in formation as they migrated back for the summer. Nunavut gave birth to Narkees.

Anak licked the girl's face just as he did Tayal's. The boy was seven years old. Spring had arrived and the land was sprinkled with red, blues, pinks, yellows and orange. White hares and stony grey leverets nibbled at wild poppies. Kalua took the children hunting and canoeing.

Instinctively wild and restless, Anak roamed the ice sheets in the north.

Nightmares tormented Kalua, flashes of two stumps floating in the air, the solitary fox approaching, Okpatok's body and Anak crushing his brother's head as he cried Nunavut's name. Drenched in perspiration, Kalua awoke shivering. Nunavut understood, as she soothed him. "My Kalua, your shadow I shall follow wherever you are," she promised.

The years spun, and Tayal and Narkees were inseparable. Nunavut's health deteriorated, coughing blood. Fierce battles gnawed inside her. Memories of Okpatok, Kalua's fading and retreating into the darkness of his mind, Narkees drifting away to cling more and more to Tayal as the years had passed.

Narkees inherited qualities which stunned and frightened Kalua. In death he hated his brother even more for the legacy he'd left behind. The child bore all Okpatok's characteristics—the magnetic, powerful force of life, his persistent energy all lived in Narkees. Kalua regretted he would never be the man his brother was. He swallowed the bitter taste of humiliation. His mother had loved Okpatok. She was inconsolable when he'd left.

Seven-year-old Narkees would stroll for hours by herself. "Exciting what I saw today." The young girl's voice rang with the morning breeze, as she fastened the red ribbon around her braided hair. "A brilliant white fox suckled her four cubs. Across from her, a hare and her two young were chewing willow, completely ignoring the predator," she chuckled. "Suddenly the mother hopped away with the leveret. Quite content, the vixen decided it would be better to feed her offspring than chase the rabbit." Narkees's high cheek bones and contours of her mouth were Okpatok's as she spoke. "From a distance I heard the call of another fox, probably the father."

Narkees was unaware the other fox was Okpatok's companion until he died. "He howled and approached the female. His piercing eyes watched me for a few moments. Then flicking their magnificent bushy tails in the air, they disappeared with their young behind the trees."

Kalua hardly spoke. The ground swayed and slipped beneath him as he held onto the child's shoulder.

"Father, the headaches again..." She kissed his brow.

"Yes, they come so frequently now." Haunted by frightening visions, he sobbed at Nunavut's breasts. He felt strangled at the premonitions that loomed threateningly.

Nunavut was yoked to Okpatok's destiny. She remembered his precise words. "Hating me will only torment you."

Wrapped in fur, the frail Nunavut dozed in the sun. "Where are you going?" she asked as Kalua pulled away from her and stood.

"I'll take the kayak out on the ocean. I'm going to look for Anak," said Kalua and knelt beside her.

"My beloved, I love you, Tayal and Narkees, but I miss Anak. He's been gone all summer—probably found a lady bear."

Narkees hailed from across the water. "Tayal speared an elephant seal near the rocks. We are going to skin it."

"It will take most of the morning to strip the huge beast. Use the three-pronged axes," Kalua barked.

Tayal approached. "I added an extension of stakes to hang the meat. Narkees has nimble fingers. She handles the knife better than I do," he chuckled. His face broke into a lovely smile.

"You asked me long ago, Tayal, what lies beyond. I will touch the timeless, infinite horizon," Kalua murmured.

"One day I shall also reach the boundless horizon." Tayal held Kalua's hands and kissed them.

With quivering lips, Narkees drew close to her father and clasped him. The kayak buffeted the galloping waves as he rowed away. Kalua never returned.

* * *

In early autumn, Anak reappeared. Nunavut uttered a mute cry when she saw the golden hulk leap towards her, as colossal and powerful as she was frail and small. He bent and licked her face with his rough tongue. Narkees and Tayal sprinted towards him. To love a bear with such tender passion lanced the heart. Anak circled for hours sweeping the beach, then back to Nunavut, his beseeching eyes pleading. Where is Kalua?

Nunavut choked with emotion as she burst into tears. She raised her hand and pointed to the ocean. "Kalua went far away. He was not well. The sea will make him stronger. He loved you, Anak."

Anak beat his chest with his paw. He rubbed his wet nose on Nunavut's gaunt cheeks and cried with her.

Tayal had a second kayak he'd built with Kalua years before. "We'll take Anak out daily," said Tayal to Narkees. "He will feel closer to Father and take some consolation from that."

Anak paddled for hours between the kayakers. He loved his domain. Returning home, Narkees fed him chunks of elephant seal. Satisfied, he lay beside her and snored.

Nunavut pined for Kalua. Her coughs became frequent and violent. Sad and lonely, she snuggled against Anak's wide chest. He felt her grief and wrapped his paws around her.

A brutal winter whirled in. At night, the bear slept in his snow hole. Narkees and Tayal were asleep. Nunavut lost all will to live. Kalua was gone and all those years of hating Okpatok gnawed at her bones. Narkess clung to Tayal and no longer needed her.

"Anak," she whimpered, missing the bear's comforting warmth. The wind howled as Nunavut crept out, the blizzard raging around her.

In the morning, Anak found Nunavut not far from the huskies. He pulled her from under the drifted snow. She smiled. The disconsolate creature sheltered her from the icy wind.

* * *

"It is six months since Mother died. I've been thinking lately about our life. What we should do, since we are on our own," said Tayal to his sister. Now twenty years old, he had grown into a handsome young man. "We are the last ones left. The whole village is lost to the smallpox. The elders once told me about the Thule people who roamed great distances to the East. They settled on a remote Island far north. Their history goes back hundreds of years. We could join them. There is a narrow passage leading to the island."

"We are going there?" Narkees asked, her eyes flashing with excitement.

"We must reach our destination before the end of winter to force the dogsled on solid sea ice. In summer that narrow stretch thaws to open water."

The huskies lurched eagerly. They travelled for many days along the coast. Anak fed on whale carcasses and stalked seals. The nights were bitterly cold as the northern lights parachuted across the sky.

Long ago, Okpatok had gazed at the sky and his heart had swelled. Creation, the ineffable, shrouded in mystery, was beyond his comprehension. Narkees was spellbound, like Okpatok. Her voice shivered above the phenomenon. "There is no beginning, no end. This splendor is forever." The beautiful Narkees approached her brother. "I love you, Tayal, and that's forever."

* * *

The two explored the vast wilderness until one day Tayal said anxiously,

"Anak is getting old. I noticed him limping and sometimes, I hear him moaning when he rests. Though he still loves swimming and trying to catch waterfowl."

"Yes, I had hoped it would disappear," Narkees sighed.

"We can't pass the channel. The thaw has begun so it is too risky. We'll do so next winter. The weather is getting warmer. Soon the sun will rotate around the horizon each day. For five to six months light will skirt this lonely land," said Tayal. The rich orange aurora rose. "I prefer six months of light than dark."

"Both are exciting. Curling shadows in the dark or chasing game in broad day light," said Narkees.

The long summer flew away with the flocks of white geese bidding farewell to the approaching winter.

"We can cross the channel now." Tayal looked across at the thick layer of ice covering the channel.

The dogsleds carved the frozen ice at a slow pace as Tayal made sure Anak followed closely behind. In the distance he saw smoke spiraling against the sky. "Look, Narkees! We're there!"

Meeting the Thule was overwhelming. Visitors were rare and unexpected. Their dogs howled a welcome to Tayal's. Wrapped in musk oxen hides and collared lemmings on their heads, the tribe circled round smiling.

"Greetings," the chief hunter hailed and rubbed noses with Tayal and Narkees.

Anak snarled a warning and Tayal soothed him with a kiss on the face, "They are friends." Anak purred in response.

Late into the night, the feast lasted as the tribe danced and chanted. They roasted elfin caribou on the open fire and drank melted snow mixed with willow resin. Ravenous, Anak loved the succulent caribou meat.

"Tonight you will be my guest in our igloo. My wife will welcome you," the chief offered.

The following morning, the Thule helped erect a large igloo for their welcome strangers. The entrance snow blocks were high enough for Anak to crawl inside. Musk oxen and caribou hides insulated the walls, hung with wolf pelts for extra warmth.

With a twinkle in his eyes, Tayal asked his sister, "Don't you wish to marry a Thule one day? They are brave hunters with handsome physique."

"I shall never leave you and Anak. Across the Northern Lights, my destination is carved with yours and the golden light in our life, Anak," she said.

"The villagers no longer fear him. He even rubs his head on the chief," Tayal laughed.

The frozen passage to the isolated island was mantled with waves of snow and ice. Glaciers soared in the distance.

Happy years stretched before them and the Thule and Inuit integrated, their bond cemented in friendship and loyalty. Sitting near the fire one day, Narkees watched Anak.

"I smeared marrow on his back and legs. His muscles are wasting away. He didn't like it and kept sneezing. He is thirty years old now. His sad brown eyes stab my heart." Narkees sobbed. She knew the bitter end was lurking, ready to snatch him. The invisible death choir followed her golden Anak.

Tayal got up and wrapped his arms around Anak's neck. "Life without Anak? I have no wish to live then either." His temples throbbed.

Narkess brushed her flushed cheeks against her brother's. "We must watch his movements and keep by his side all the time. Walking slowly is good for him even if he shuffles. He needs to keep his strength up otherwise his body will die."

Tayal brushed his moist eyes. "Oh, it is freezing tonight. I will cook a special meal for us. Musk oxen tongue, caribou slices and stew spread with seaweed and fat. Anak will share. He is partial to rabbits."

Tayal remembered his mother sitting behind the curtain of seal skins. He was a young boy then but Okpatok's severed hand was vivid in his mind. Nunavut's eyes were sealed with sadness. Tayal did not understand what had happened that horrific day. Hidden secrets were never revealed. Now, years later, Tayal recognized who Narkees's father was. He lovingly placed a soft, warm lemming pelt on his sister's back.

"We are going hunting musk oxen below the towering cliffs, early tomorrow with the villagers. The headman told me the beasts feed on Arctic willows, lichen and sedges. Wolves attack them in packs. Life and death cloak this brutal yet inspiring land," Tayal said.

"Ravenous wolves also prey on elfin caribou. They are much smaller and paw sprigs from under the snow, fast runners." Highly strung, Narkees was nervous.

The winter sleeved the white gallery as the hunt started. The villagers veered to the left where the oxen herded.

"We'll go the right," said Tayal. "There's more small game we can stalk out there."

Within half an hour they stopped. Tayal spotted two elfin caribou near the willow. He sprinted and speared one. Limping, Anak approached the dogsled and rested. The weather changed. Anak stood, lifted his head and sniffed then bellowed. The snow started to fall. "Anak is warning us of a blizzard approaching. We can't take the dogsleds. The poor soul won't be able to keep pace. The dogs will scent the way back to the village. It's coming over black. Hold firmly onto Anak," Tayal shouted.

He raised the long leather whip and slashed it high in the air, shouting at the huskies. The wind shrieked, cutting through the sheets of icy snow. Tayal's eyes stung and he whipped once more. Confused, the animals pulled the sled until they disappeared from sight.

Anak's nose sniffed again. His mind whirled and he panicked. The hero thought of Tayal and Narkees. He must find shelter and protect them. His cry echoed above the fierce elements. Blindly, the three struggled against the storm. Limping badly, Anak dragged his aching body as Narkees and Tayal gripped his sides.

Within a short distance a jutting rock loomed, massive against the blinding landscape. They took refuge in the cave below. Scattered inside where bones and hides of the animals that had sought shelter there before them.

Outside, the blizzard raged and the dogs ploughed blindly against the wind. They did not see the crevasse coming up. Unable to stop, they slipped over the edge, yelping with fear, scrambling for footage.

The sled rocked and swayed behind them as the walls caved and closed in on them. Dogs and sled plunged into the deep crevasse and were swallowed by the dark.

In the cave, Anak slumped against the cold stone. His breathing was shallow as he gasped for air and he appeared to be in pain. Narkees massaged his chest with gentle strokes. His eyes opened and shut as Narkees and Tayal nestled against him. He wrapped his paws around them, purring. He tried to keep them warm but his own strength was fading fast, unable to maintain his own body heat. He licked their faces.

Tayal whispered in his ear, "Anak, my Anak, in life and death, we are not separated. From the crib, I have loved you all my life." He kissed the bear's eyes. "Oh, Anak, take me with you. Let me ride on your back again like I did when I was a boy. Remember?"

The weak bear purred. Tayal's tears fell on his neck. "Side by side we will keep you warm. "Farewell," he sobbed.

Two hours later, Narkees cried, "Anak's eyes are closed. He's not breathing." Anak's paw rested in her shaking hand. Icicles formed below his nostrils.

For three days the blizzard swept the savage land. Tayal and Narkees fell asleep huddled together close to Anak, their hero, and froze to death as the Northern Lights played across the sky.

2 BEN AND THE BUSHRANGERS

A New Life, a New Hell

Australia 1846

When the Irish famine struck, Sebastian O'Malley, his wife Donette and six-year-old son Ben, sailed to New South Wales, Australia where the government granted small plots of land to new settlers. With hope in their hearts for a new life, the sponsored migrants embarked on their hazardous journey through the untamed outback to the remote Blacktown.

At the trading post, they were supplied with provisions—barrels of fresh water, casks of salted meat, bags of grain, dried fruit, biscuits and a few livestock. Two young oxen were hitched to wagon with a cart attached to the rear by thick ropes. A wooden frame supported a canvas awning that would protect them from the weather as they travelled. Mother and son slept at the back of the wagon on bales of straw while Sebastian curled up in blankets on the riding seat up front.

On their travels one evening, Sebastian unloaded the goats from the cage on the cart and tied them to the wagon's wheels on a length of rope so they could wander. Soon they'd have a kid to add to their livestock as one of the nannies was pregnant. Sebastian loved his goats.

He kissed a billy on its soft nose. "Soon we'll be home," he whispered into a floppy ear. He left the four goats to graze in the scrub and went to feed and water the hens and roosters in the ventilated crate.

Donette cooked over the open fire. She scooped ladles of thick stew into her son's bowl. "Come, Ben, eat with me on the wagon. There are too many bull ants out here."

"And poisonous snakes," said Ben.

"Yes, those too." She ruffled his hair and held his bowl as he scrambled up onto the wagon.

"The oxen will need to rest more often. It's getting warmer and they are thirsty." Sebastian sighed. "I'll have to fill their water buckets more often."

"We need to watch our water supply as it warms up. The oxen munch on the bushes and leaves of trees, so they are getting some fluids from the sap," replied Donette.

Sebastian wiped his sweaty brow and gazed up at the sky. "There are dark clouds gathering. Perhaps it will rain. With some luck we can capture some of it in the water barrels for boiling. Tomorrow we will reach our destination at the foot of the Blue Mountains."

The next day, Sebastian pulled up on the outskirts of Kurrajong, and jumped off the wagon. Above the canopy of trees, the forest hummed with life. The call of a solitary hawk shivered on leaves heavy with dew. Sebastian looked around, intoxicated by the beauty of his surroundings. Against the tree trunks, brilliantly colored orchids twisted and weaved towards the sunlight in contrast to the bare outback they'd travelled across to reach this oasis.

"Behold the splendor of creation, Donette. We are home." He raised his gloved palms to the sky.

Donette held Ben's little hand and stood beside her man. "To new beginnings and a world without boundaries..." She leaned her head on his shoulder.

* * *

It took almost three months for the settlers to clear the plot. Sebastian chopped down gum trees and sawed logs, only enough to build the cabin. The family lived in a tent until it was completed, their livestock roaming free to graze while the fowls roosted high in the trees at night.

Donette and Ben gathered dandelions and herbs to make remedies for their ailments. Medical help was far away and they needed to be prepared for emergencies.

After a month, the log cabin and porch were complete. Summer soared in with high temperatures, sleepless nights and mosquitoes in spite of the nets Donette had fashioned for above their beds.

They grew vegetables, fruit trees, raised chickens, eggs, goats and extracted wild honey from the hives in the trees. Once a year, a salesman travelled in his wagon packed with provisions to barter, and they exchanged goats' meat preserved with herbs and cheese for goods they required.

Ben could still hear his mother's voice as if it were yesterday.

"Leaving one hell across the seas and entering another hotter one with dirty, hoppy kangaroos and dangerous bugs and snakes," she complained, tired from the heat and hard labour.

His father chuckled, ever patient with his mother because he was a man of vision who could see beyond the trials of their existence.

"This haven is ours. A streams runs alongside it for water, the yabbies in it provide food and the trees give us shade. We have livestock and food, oxen to pull our wagon and a solid cabin for a home. Why don't you cook us up a goat stew and stop chattering like the parrots do, darling?"

"I know, Sebastian, but as grateful as I am for this new life, sometimes I miss our life in Ireland. The heat gives me headaches and the constant physicality of the work makes my back ache." Donette suffered frequent attacks of migraine, so severe they laid her out for days. "Bloody savage land with its hot sand and creepies."

"I do understand, my dear. I will do everything I can to ease your plight. What is it you need?"

Frustrated with the lack of facilities, she begged Sebastian, "Please, build a dunny. It's easy for you men to urinate on the bushes, but I can't just squat anywhere. The sting of the spinifex is vicious."

"You are quite right, darling. How very selfish of me. I promise to start on it first thing next week."

* * *

Sebastian and his son sat in the shade below a magnificent Bluegum tree. The nanny goat beside them bellowed. After a prolonged birthing process, the billy kid was finally expelled.

"He is beautiful," Ben murmured.

"So is his mother." Sebastian smiled and stretched his stiff legs.

The land was harsh. Predatory dingoes stalked the hens and suckling kids, waiting for an opportunity to strike. Nature had its own protection. The loyal and protective billy goats herded the livestock, on the alert for danger with strained ears. When the dingoes closed in, they leapt like galloping horses, darting faster than the dogs. One male hoisted the retreating dingo with his sharp horns and flung him away. The other billy goats pursued the second dingo, and it disappeared into the grass with a despairing howl.

One afternoon, Sebastian approached Donette where she was hanging out the washing. "I saw a pack of dingoes prowling around. I must finish erecting the chicken coop so I can lock them up at night."

"Yes. Get Ben to help you. It will be good for him to learn."

While Donette spent hours tending the vegetable garden, her gum boots the only protection against bugs and nasty spiders, Sebastian and Ben built the chicken coop to protect their stock against the predators of the bush.

* * *

Unusual Friendships

August 1855

When Ben was fifteen years of age, an unexpected twist of fate struck one night during a blustery storm.

Sebastian heard the snorting of the horses. "There's someone outside," he said. "I'll go take a look. You stay inside and be as quiet as you can."

"Who would travel in this foul weather?" Donette whispered.

"I'll go with you, Dad."

His father took the shotgun off the rusty hook. They hid behind the fowl shed, waiting.

The bush rangers' faces were covered except their eyes.

"We better walk the horses, can't see a damn thing. I hear bleating goats," said one nervously.

"And cackling chickens," the second fellow muttered.

Sebastian cocked his gun. Father and son jumped out from behind the barn, confronting the alarmed men.

"Don't move! What are you doing here?" Sebastian demanded. "Remove your masks.

"We got lost, disoriented," said the older man, removing his mask and telling his companion to do the same. "We've drifted for days with hardly any shade except spinifex, dry waterholes, and rising heat. Our food became scarce." He rubbed his bleary eyes. "Temperatures dropped at night. The storm hit before dawn, driving us to move and the horses followed the scent to your place. The horses need rest, water and fodder. We'll be most grateful for your hospitality, and gladly pay you for lodgings."

Sebastian's eyes shifted from the burly man to the trembling young one. His heart pounded like a drum, a cold sweat on his forehead as he wondered if he could trust these men. Something in the stranger's voice, his suppressed plea for help and the expression on his face changed Sebastian's mind. He lowered his gun.

"We don't have any money at all, and no horses," said Sebastian emphatically. "You can stay here for a few days; sort out where you're heading to." He glanced with amusement at the strapping fellow. "Tie the horses in the shelter of the tree."

Ben opened the front door. The gush of swirling wind tumbled the four inside.

"Darling, we have visitors, some travelers," announced Sebastian.

"How do you do, madam? I am Thomas, and this is my friend Patrick."

Donette did not move, bewildered as she gaped at the lanky man with impeccable manners.

Sebastian winked at his wife. "Let's have your favourite dish and listen to our guests' exciting adventures. They can sleep in the barn. The heavy door will protect them against the wind."

"Guests are rare in these parts. I will make more stew." Donette smiled and started cooking.

"What are your plans," asked Sebastian.

"We are always on the move, accepting work on farms or in towns along the way. Most of all we like working with horses. From here, we'll steer north," said Thomas.

"Yes, horses are our passion—magnificent creatures," remarked twenty-one-year-old Patrick.

Sebastian tapped Patrick on the shoulder. "You must be hungry. Have you ever tasted goat stew?"

"Never."

The room blurred with warmth and laughter. Later that night, all retired.

The rooster crowed at dawn. Ben opened the chicken coop. A billy goat followed Patrick and rammed his horns on his bottom.

"This is so funny, ridiculous, and beautiful." Patrick doubled up laughing, and held his sides. "I could spend the rest of my life here."

"I wouldn't want to live anywhere else," said Ben.

"Don't you feel lonely?"

"Look at my friends." He waved a hand at the animals surrounding them. "They speak to me all day long, even the oxen. Listen to the birds chatter. I understand animal language, their behavior. I feel their moods. My special, dearest gift is that billy goats live for many years. This is where I belong. Come, we'll check the honey." Ben beckoned to Patrick to follow him.

The bees droned in the hives. Covering their faces with nets and their hands with gloves, they quickly scraped the honey off the comb and filled a large jar. The bees buzzed angrily around them. The persistent billy rubbed his head against Patrick's side.

Ben chuckled. "He likes you. Animals sense when they are loved. Let's go inside."

"It must be nice to have a home. Some things can never be changed." Patrick sighed.

Baffled by his new friend's sadness, Ben decided not to question him further. They entered the cabin in silence. Smoke belched from the chimney spirals. Donette baked damper in the wood stove.

"This is absolutely delicious." Thomas glanced at Donette during breakfast, licking his fingers, dripping with honey. "Thank you."

Sebastian studied the tall, educated stranger. Who were they running from? Who did they pursue, he wondered.

Two weeks later, while having their evening meal, Sebastian impulsively paced to the wide sideboard and brought out a drawing. Eager, he moved his plate aside and spread it out on the table. "We've been planning to build a shed for ages. Perhaps now is the time. I do hope you'll be able to assist us. The timber shack is behind the cart. It should only take us a few days with muscles and brains." Sebastian looked at Thomas and Patrick.

Thomas thumped his knuckles on the table, his excitement charming. "Of course we'll help. Your kindness, your heart will pulse wherever we go. We are in your debt for far more than to help to build a barn."

A hush fell in the kitchen. Tears of appreciation flowed on Donette's flushed cheeks. Speechless at the generosity of their visitors, Ben dug into his favourite damper.

Excited, Sebastian said, "My wife has prepared the storeroom at the back of the cabin for you to sleep in. It will be more comfortable than the barn. We will start on the shed next week."

Black cockatoos frolicked beside the stream and two kookaburras perched on the magnificent Bluegum, laughing as the men and boy worked under the hot sun. By midday, six posts were propped deep in the ground. Together Ben and Patrick carried one beam at a time from the pile to Sebastian and Thomas.

"We need one more piece. Have a rest and continue later," said Sebastian.

Ben sat in front of the timbers and waited for Patrick to finish his business behind the tree.

Donette appeared on the porch holding a large teapot. "Lunch time, Muscles and Brains," she called, laughing.

Disaster struck quickly, only seconds in time, and no-one had time to react to prevent it. Distracted by a shuffling behind him, Ben glanced back curiously at the goats. A billy goat chased a nanny on heat. They hurtled to the top of the stack of timber, hooves drumming faster and faster. The logs rolled beneath them as they skipped to the right. The wave of timbers bowled down like an avalanche.

Panic stricken, Ben flung himself sideways but his leg was crushed beneath two posts. He screamed. Donette dropped the teapot and ran towards her trapped son. The men lifted the heavy timbers. Aghast, they held their breath. Below the knee, flesh, bones and muscle were a mangled pulp.

"A tourniquet immediately," Thomas cried out to Sebastian. "I want a tough cord and a thick peg. Donette, get me a long knife. Hurry!"

"Long knife?" she stammered, pale and shaking.

"Every second we wait, Ben is losing too much blood. He won't survive if I don't amputate the squashed leg. Please Donette, trust me. Have you got rum, laudanum? Hurry, think of Ben's life."

Swift as an eagle, Sebastian returned with the makeshift tourniquet. They cut through Ben's trouser legs. Thomas' face was ashen. Sebastian's ears and temples ached. They strapped the twine around his leg above the angry wound that oozed blood, and clamped the peg, twisting it tight several times to make two large knots.

Donette lifted Ben's head and trickled the laudanum from the small vile into his mouth. A few minutes later, Sebastian gave him a dram of rum. The sharp knife came down below the knee. Ben's shrieks of pain harrowed the soul. The men carried him indoors on a hammock where Donette made him as comfortable as she could.

Animals possess an acute sense of love and sorrow. The silence was profound. Goats', fowls' and birds' repertoires ceased. Through the night, the four lay on the floor beside Ben's bed. The bleeding stopped at last. Each took turns to watch his progress and administered laudanum to ease his pain.

Donette sponged Ben's feverish face and dabbed water on his lips. "The wound looks angry. We should cover it with a poultice to avoid infection."

She ground garlic, onions, vinegar and plantain, to a paste and wrapped it in muslin before placing it on the stump. Every two hours, she redressed the wound with a fresh poultice.

For two days, Ben was delirious with pain and infection. Exhausted, Sebastian lay beside him, resting his head on the bed. The cock crowed and Ben opened his eyes. He stroked Sebastian's hair. Donette, Thomas and Patrick jumped.

Sebastian wept. "Bloody goats, bloody damn goats."

Ben smiled. "It's not their fault. They were playing. You still love them."

Everyone cried and laughed. Sebastian rushed outside and brought a small honeycomb from the hive. Gently he funneled a few drops on Ben's tongue.

"This will give you strength," he muttered.

It took weeks for the stump to heal. Patrick built Ben a crude wheel chair. They whirled and zigzagged, laughing.

"You are ready for a wooden leg. It will be padded on top." Patrick chuckled.

The exciting day arrived and all gawked with suspense as Ben tested it out. He felt the leg slipping on the ground beneath him, and held his shaking hand on his father's back. He nearly tripped over, and Thomas and Patrick sprinted towards him.

"I'll try once more." Ben waved them off, not wanting them to help. He knew he had to do this on his own.

He achieved ten steps that morning, and every day his walking progressed a little more.

Four months had passed since the storm. Resting on the porch one afternoon, Thomas seemed in a melancholy mood. He never spoke of his sealed secrets, and remained an enigma to his hosts.

Sebastian wished he could unlock the past of the two silent men and help them heal the wounds in their hearts.

"You have pain in your heart, Thomas," Sebastian murmured. "What are you running away from?"

"It's a long story." Thomas' eyes were sad.

"We have time. You have done a lot for Ben and now, perhaps I can help you?"

Thomas settled in his chair and stared out into the bush as he told his story, his voice flooding through the humble home.

□ * * *

A Tragedy of His Own

August 1846

Forked lightning struck the dry bush. The fire spread ferociously. On the porch of their home, the McGill family was trapped as belching flames closed in on them.

Across the thorny field, Thomas was repairing the fence around his house. Horrified, he watched the leaping fire engulf the neighbors' property. Immediately, he emptied the sack of tools beside the trough, soaked it and wrapped himself in it, sweeping blindly through the suffocating heat. He grabbed hold of twelve year old Patrick as he tried to outrun the flames. It was too late for the boy's parents, they were already alight. The wind changed. The scorching inferno raged north of the farm.

The following morning, dark clouds gathered. The acrid smoke drifted to the hills. The stunned youth found his parents' charred bodies. Inconsolable in his grief, he sat silent for a long time before Thomas helped him bury them.

The Irishman and his wife took Patrick under their wing. Both were keen readers, the shelves in their home piled high with books. Since there was no school in the remote outback, Mrs Morgan tutored Patrick on various subjects. History and explorers of the seas fascinated him.

Thomas rode with him in the bush and trained the eager Patrick to rustle horses. When Patrick turned seventeen, Thomas bought him a gun. "You might need it one day." The youth loved the wild life.

On occasion, police on horseback patrolled the isolated farms, hunting down the marauding bush rangers who stole horses, food and money from the settlers' homes.

As a young man in Ireland, Thomas had despised aristocracy. The unjust social laws made his blood surge with fury and vengeance. They crushed the poor and stripped them of their dignity. In Australia, he disliked the authorities even more. Corruption was rife in government and the police on horseback were no better. Times were hard and many of the captured outlaws were imprisoned under appalling conditions.

Thomas would never let his family go hungry, and the hard times brought with them desperation. An excellent horseman, he turned to rustling to put food on the table. Thomas was keen to avoid being caught.

"We'll take the horses in the stable and sell them in the markets beyond the mountains. It's too risky here. We have to avoid the police."

Sadly, Thomas had left it too late and one day in late August, the police came searching for missing stock.

Mrs Morgan was hanging the washing; her infant son in the cane bassinet beside her. She turned around, hearing the noise of trotting hooves. Three men rode towards her. Swiftly, she ran to the house and returned with a gun. They wouldn't intimidate her this time as they had in the past. Her hungry baby howled as she loaded the gun.

"Where is Mister Morgan, madam? Out fossicking again?" Sergeant Fitzroy mocked.

"He is watching you and your scum," she spat at him.

The sergeant's eyes blazed with fury. They approached.

She pressed the trigger and riddled the policeman on his right. He reeled off the horse, clutching his stomach, screaming.

Desperate, Mrs Morgan cocked her gun again, trembling and unsteady on her legs. She wasn't fast enough. Fitzroy's lead ball hit her in the chest. The wind billowed the white sheets on the line and she fell grasping them.

Fitzroy was nervous. On the summit of the hill, Thomas and Patrick came into view, stampeding down.

"Let's get out of here," he stormed.

The second policeman rammed his spur against his horse's rump; the feisty animal reared up before crashing down and trampling the infant's crib. The two riders escaped in the thick scrub.

Thomas rushed to his wife's side. She was barely alive.

"Thomas."

Her voice was almost inaudible. He pressed his ear near her lips.

"The baby…"

He cradled his son upon her breast. She closed her eyes. Weeping, Thomas covered them both with the bloodied sheets. He laid them to rest below the Bluegum she'd loved.

He unhinged the heavy gate where the flock of sheep were penned and swung it wide open to let them go. Slowly he paced back to the adjoining yard and entered the stables. Thomas nuzzled the horses and stroked their manes.

"Go, you are free now. Gallop with the wind."

The cackling chickens were preening themselves in the coop. He took off the rattly, loose door and flung it away. "You are free too."

Above the Bluegum, the kookaburra called. Thomas wiped his eyes with the back of his hand. Both men went to the rear of the house and untethered their two horses. "I'll get the killer," he vowed as they rode away.

* * *

Revenge and Regrets

August 1855

"So you see, my friend, love knows no bounds, winds have no bounds. The time has come for us to continue our journey. We leave tomorrow."

"I'll pack goat's meat, cheese, damper and honey." Donette wiped her eyes with the apron.

Pleading, Ben turned to Patrick. "Won't you consider staying with us? This will be your home?"

"I shall never leave Thomas. Perhaps someday, we will return."

The sun peered between the clouds as the two men left. The sudden emptiness of their home and the void left by their guests struck the family with unbearable sorrow.

Ben spent hours near the stream, where his loveable billy goat followed him. The goat rubbed its head on Ben's wooden leg as if pleading forgiveness. Ben soothed the long velvety ears with his hand.

"You are forgiven." Ben knew animals felt deep sorrow. His tears trickled on the goat's soft nose.

* * *

The dingoes' howls echoed as evening shadows cloaked the land. A year had passed since Thomas and Patrick left. The salesman arrived with an assortment of provisions, gazette and latest newspapers. Sebastian read one dated several weeks earlier.

Bushrangers Thomas Morgan and Patrick McGill ambushed Detective Fitzroy in a remote area in the Blue Mountains. Morgan and McGill waited in thick undergrowth until Fitzroy dismounted, unaware of the imminent danger. Devoured by revenge for the shooting death of his wife, Morgan shot him in the head.

The three constables with him surrounded Morgan. McGill jumped out of the bush, shielding Morgan and fired at police. McGill was mortally wounded under fire. Morgan was arrested.

As he awaited the gallows, Morgan uttered the words: 'your heart will pulse wherever we go'.

Sebastian's throat swelled with grief. He wanted to reach out and walk with Thomas to the gallows and say, "Don't look at the noose, follow the light," but he was too late.

Years of hard work took their toll on Donette. She went to bed early one night in winter and did not wake. Sebastian pined for her. Daily he sat beneath the parasol of shady giants and spoke to his wife.

An eagle soared above and Sebastian waved. "Soon I will fly on your wings."

* * *

Twilight Years

Blue Mountains, New South Wales, 1905

The copper kettle gurgled and spurted steam from its spout. The wind moaned through the trees, the cat purred beside the wood stove, and the dog scratched his fleas. In the distance a cock crowed with the rising sun.

Ben's remote, dilapidated bush cabin stood stubborn as it faced the seasons, year in and year out. Rats scurried between the rafters in the roof.

Donette's dunny was down the path, abandoned since her death. There was still no running water, only a large rainwater tank. Ben hardly ever washed anyway, and if anyone were to ask him, he would claim the layer of dirt kept colds away. His bushy beard had turned grey.

The smoke belched from the chimney in loops and spirals with the shifting, moody wind as he baked damper in the wood stove. The tall trees towered over his roof like a protective parasol. Ben stoked the charred woodchips and they glowed with heat. He peeped through the smudgy, greasy window, watching the dark clouds scud across the ominously greying sky. It was time to milk the nanny goats. Ben was an expert at making goat's cheese which he preserved in large wooden casks filled with brine, a recipe he'd learned from his mother. Opening the battered and creaky cabin door, Ben gazed up at the magnificent giant eucalyptus and listened to the screeching sounds of galahs, parrots and kookaburras. The herd of goats shaved the wild flowers and weeds, and peeled the bark and leaves of their favourite bushes. Seeing Ben step out the cabin, they scampered towards him with affection butting their heads and swinging their floppy ears. He stumbled and could only keep hold of the empty pail by jamming his wooden leg into the soft ground, and leaning on it.

Now an old man, Ben had difficulty sitting on the stool with his wooden leg. At last, he managed to flop down and milked the goat gently, directing squirts of warm milk into the solid bucket. His task complete, he panted and shuffled up the wooden steps, went indoors and emptied the milk into cans.

From dawn to dusk, the fowls roamed around but at night he locked them in the leaning shed.

There were two wicker chairs on the porch. Baggy, the old tortoiseshell cat always sat on the right grooming until she dozed off to sleep. Before noon the following day, Ben was surprised to see a brown egg on the wicker chair. His tired, wrinkled face etched with the silent stamp of hardship, cracked with a wide smile. He took the egg inside the kitchen.

The next morning when one of the fowls tried to get into the fenced garden, Ben was intrigued. She turned around and around in desperate circles, pushing her head in every conceivable hole, frantic as she up and down.

Ben opened the front gate. Ignoring him, the hen rushed across the lawn with a flutter of wings, glared at the moggy for a moment, then hopped on the second chair. The cat twitched her ears, looked at the silly hen, yawned and curled back to sleep.

Once the arduous performance of egg laying was over, the hen burst into triumphant clucking with feathers flying. Through the gate she went and joined the others. From then on Ben left the gate open.

At midnight, a weary Ben heard a terrible commotion outside. He quickly rose from the straw bed and strapped on his wooden leg. At times it was quite an ordeal, especially during the extreme heat of summer. The wood chafed and blistered the stump of his leg. He rummaged around for his pants. His shotgun hung nearby on a rusty hook.

"That bastard," he mumbled. The dingo often prowled at night. "Damn it," he cursed and fumbled awkwardly in the dark to get his oil lantern. He tripped over Bruce who yelped, opened the wood stove, poked a small stick inside and lit the wick of the lamp. He turned around once more, trying to avoid Bruce, instead accidentally kicking Baggy who let out a startled yowl.

Ben bashed the door open with his wooden leg as hard as possible, staggered outside and was swallowed in the blackness of the night.

He reached the fowl shed more by feel than by sight, and raised the lamp. There was no sign of the cunning dingo. Carefully, he lifted the flimsy shed door. As the hens flew out, he heard hissing. It was not the dingo. Somewhere in there was a snake. Cautious, he poked the butt of his shotgun behind the bales of straw and listened. The crickets clicked away. He saw a tiny movement in the dark.

A Tiger snake slithered out and confronted Ben.

"I'll get you, you bastard."

Snake and man looked at each other for a few seconds. Ben gave it an almighty kick with his right leg and missed. The snake inflated its neck and struck, sinking the poisonous venom into Ben's wooden leg.

A self-satisfying smile lit his craggy face. "Silly bugger," he mumbled.

He cocked his shotgun, took aim and blew its head off. Benn wiped his pants and sat under the tall Bluegum tree. He stayed there all night guarding the scattered chickens that roosted in the low branches.

At dawn, the happy fowls pecked grubs and cackled. Ben flung the snake on an anthill. Within minutes the bush ants emerged, attacking with ferocity. Tired, Ben went indoors, slumped on his rocking chair, unstrapped the wooden leg and fell asleep.

Hours later, a startled Ben woke drenched with perspiration. Painful twinges shot across the stump and muscles of his thighs. It had happened a lot through the years. He rubbed camphor oil bought from nomadic Chinese travelling on their camels in search of gold. He tried to rest his head on the straw pillow, but he was restless. He stood, strapped on his wooden leg, sipped some milk, had a slice of cheese and shuffled to the porch.

His pet cockatoo knocked its beak on the old man's shoulder. The hot wind whistled. He looked across at the dilapidated shed never completed, overrun with weeds, a harbor for rats and snakes, and remembered.

In the evening, he sat near the blazing log fire and smoked his pipe. Bruce, his loyal scruffy dog lay beside him asleep, twitching his left foot spasmodically. This was the world he loved.

3 BEYOND ALL BOUNDARIES

Sarah Jordan was bored…and drunk. She sprawled naked on the bed with a bottle of whisky beside her. She took a few more swigs and placed the bottle on the small cabinet. The ceiling fan whirred round, stirring puffs of somewhat cooler air to relieve the oppressive midday heat. Her long, ash-blonde hair was tied up with a wide blue ribbon. The pony tail suited her wild character and slim figure, burnished with a golden tan—skin firm and supple—and long shapely legs, strong from years of riding her magnificent Arabian horses.

She hiccupped, rose and stumbled to the window. She looked across her homestead. Three thousand acres of land and bush rolled far beyond the hills. The sun was at its zenith. Everything was quiet. Cattle flicked their tails at pestering flies and dozed lazily in the shade of the trees. Two warthog wallowed and rolled with their young in the mud, boring their curved tusks into the ground, coating their grey-brown, hairless hides. From the garden, the raucous cry of peacocks pierced the air.

Sarah rubbed her eyes. Down the dusty road a car approached. Everything seemed blurred and hazy, but vaguely she remembered.

Lawrence had left at dawn with his overseer and the stockmen to take cattle to the market. He said he'd be back later that afternoon.

Her body was saturated with perspiration as she stood near the window for a few moments and watched the Landover come to a stop near the front gate.

Police Commissioner Montcliffe stepped out and walked up the cool path.

Sarah staggered towards the wardrobe and clumsily rummaged through her clothes.

"Sarah, are you there?" called out Montcliffe.

She emerged through the bamboo curtain, still hiccupping, her eyes bloodshot. The polka dot dress buttoned only half way, exposing part of her bare breasts.

"What on earth are you doing here at this hour?" she snapped.

"Thought I might drop in and see if all's well, there was quite a lot of trouble in Nanyuki and Navasha. The locals are brewing up something. Can't quite put my finger on it. You, Sarah?" He smirked. "On the bottle again. I suppose Lawrence went to market today?"

"Yes he did, with Jedidiah. You know damn well he goes every Thursday."

"Tut, tut, tut, Sarah. You're drunk."

"So I am. So what? And you, Montcliffe, are rotten! Whoring with every woman in the territory."

He laughed. "Look who's talking—the elite Madam. It's written all over your face. Don't think I don't know about the farmers who have been with you. The Chief Justice, the Game Warden ... I can name more," he said as he approached. "Yes, you've been around, you little bitch."

"Oh no you don't! Never ... never a slimy bastard like you!" Sarah cursed as she ran across the room.

He leapt at her like and animal on heat, grabbing the hem of her dress. It ripped in his hands. Savagely he pulled at her hair, yanking her head back.

Desperate, fearful of what was to come, Sarah kneed him hard in the groin. He staggered back and doubled over in agony, momentarily stunned. "You bitch." he spat.

Sarah knew it wouldn't take him long to recover. Desperate to escape, she ran to the kitchen and grabbed a carving knife from the drawer.

Montcliffe appeared in the doorway moments later. "I'll get you," he shouted, his eyes blazing like daggers.

He raced forward, chasing her as she dodged away using the kitchen table as a barrier between them. With an enraged cry, he pounced, pinning her against the wall. Terrified now, she thrust the knife at him. His hands squeezing her throat made her weak and dizzy, his foul breathe on her neck. The knife slipped from her nerveless fingers as he thrust his pelvis against her, panting and groaning.

"Yes, it's my turn now. Who's here to save you? Who's here to witness you say no? It's my word against yours—a man of the law against a...whore!" He spat the words at her.

He pulled at the blue ribbon on her dress. She struggled against his seeking hands, desperate to free herself from his grip.

"You knew Lawrence wasn't here, that's why you came."

Frantic, she shoved him away and ran across the room. It was pointless calling for the houseboys. They were all in their *kibanda*, safe in their little round mud houses. Even her fat housekeeper Mimi, her only hope strength-wise, was fast asleep and snoring.

Sarah's mind raced. The gun, where was the gun? There was one in the shed, another in the hall. If only Jedidiah was here. In all her thirty years, she'd never felt so helpless. She might as well go down fighting.

"You stink, you vermin! Call yourself a policeman? A man of the law? You're no better than a criminal!" She struggled to free herself from his grip.

Fuming, Montcliffe pushed her onto the floor, pinning her down with his cumbersome body. Spread-eagled, she squirmed beneath him until she realized it only excited him more. She lay limp as he drove into her and wished it was over. Minutes later, it was over and he stood to button his khaki shorts.

In the haste of his bestial act, Montcliffe did not notice he'd dropped his wallet from the back pocket of his khakis, but Sarah did. With his attention on tidying himself, she concealed it under her thigh.

"You'll pay for this, if it takes me the rest of my life. Remember my words!"

"Don't bother to tell Lawrence, he couldn't care less. Swallow your pride, Sarah ... Oh! You are a wild one!" He stepped over her and walked out.

Nauseated, she struggled to her feet, ran to the bathroom, heaved and vomited. She sat a moment on the cool floor. The wallet! Where could she hide it? She heaved herself up off the floor and staggered back into the kitchen where she retrieved the wallet. Picking it up, she walked to the window. Montcliffe's car was gone. What if he came back? Sooner or later, he'd know it was missing, guess where he'd left it. Panic gripped her.

The stables! Yes, the perfect hiding place! She raced out the front door and across the yard, making sure no-one was around to see her heading for the tack room. Inside, she lifted the oat box off a large crate and placed it on the floor.

She pushed up the lid of the crate and hid the wallet in its depths, under the old horse blankets. No-one used them anymore, the wallet would never be found. She closed the lid with a thump and placed the oat box back on top.

Weary, dirty and smelling of the vile policeman's scent, she headed back to the house. In the bathroom, she stripped and stepped into the shower under the warm, soothing flow of the water. She scrubbed her skin vigorously, ridding herself of the humiliation and degradation forced upon her by the vile Montcliffe.

As the water washed away the dirt, a great ache overcame her. She longed for the comfort of Mimi, her housekeeper and only true friend. The only person she could trust and confide in.

Sarah hardly associated with the other farmers and their wives. In their eyes she was a parasite who bonded with the Africans. She distanced herself from their virulent gossip and chatter about her drinking, the rumors of her husband's lack of interest in her by retreating into the cocoon of her land, surrounded by Mimi and her loyal friends.

Stepping out of the shower, she dried off and snuggled into the warmth and comfort of her robe. With a sigh, she walked out on the verandah and sat in her favourite rocking chair. An ache, a terrible loneliness gripped her. Tears trickled down her cheeks. She watched distractedly as brilliant blue and green bulbuls preened themselves on the hibiscus bushes. Two flame trees, bursting in bloom, were dotted with a flock of noisy chirping red-headed love birds.

Sarah looked across her land. She loved every acre of it. She and Lawrence bought the barren land ten years ago when they'd first arrived in Kenya from England. Now they grew sisal, coffee, wheat and maize on their lush and fertile farm.

They bred Devon cattle for beef and their pedigree Guernsey dairy herd won several awards for the best milk yield and butter fat. At the peak of lactation, the cows produced eight to ten gallons of milk a day. They also had several of the finest Jersey bulls and Charolaise.

The goats and sheep roamed freely around the *shambas*; the small fields allotted to the staff to grow produce for their own consumption. Once a month a few bullocks were slaughtered, which supplied everyone with meat. Sarah knew she was loved by her workers, most of whom were Kukuyus, or from the Luo tribes. She cared for their welfare and always discussed any problems with Jedidiah, the wise head stockman.

Above all, Sarah loved her horses. Her two black stallions, five bay geldings, four sorrel mares and two colts gave her great pleasure. At dawn, she would walk with Jedidiah down to the corral near the big Baobab tree to groom her animals. Then they would mount the mares and ride beyond the hills.

The natives feared Lawrence, for he was a strict disciplinarian—often violent, sullen and bad-tempered. His life was focused on his work on the land, and with each year he withdrew more and more from Sarah. Theirs was a war of few words. She longed desperately for a child. She sought out lovers to overcome the yearning, the need that raged with such force inside her.

Sarah feared growing old alone. She feared death and above all, loneliness. Depression haunted her soul. She hungered for something, anything to soothe the savage assault of loneliness on her heart.

Exhausted, Sarah fell asleep on her rocking chair. Down the dark tunnel she spun, dreams clawing at her mind. Montcliffe's wallet teased her from the brink of her tortured dreams. What secrets lay in that pouch? She ripped it open but could see nothing as noises pierced the valley and the hounds of hell pursued her.

Sarah awoke to the noisy clatter of the trucks approaching the house. She stood, rubbed the restless sleep from her eyes and walked across the verandah.

Peering over the wall, Sarah saw Mimi approaching, her massive hips swaying as she moved.

"*Bibie*, you want *chakula* now or wait for *Bwana* come?" she asked from the garden below the verandah wall.

"No Mimi, *itakuwa na chakula* later, just bring me a cold drink. I will wait for *Bwana* Lawrence to eat."

Sarah smiled, watching the fat, lovable, loyal woman mumbling and grumbling as she disappeared behind the house to the kitchen. She loved Mimi who had been with her ever since they bought the farm. Often in the evenings, Sarah strolled amongst the kibanda and sat with Mimi, cross-legged on the ground, discussing meals and other domestic issues. When Mimi laughed, her whole body wobbled.

As soon as the truck stopped in the driveway, the head stockman, Jedidiah hopped out. Lawrence rummaged through his papers for a few minutes before emerging the vehicle, swearing. Sarah felt the anger projecting off him in waves. She shuddered. It was going to be a miserable evening.

"Hello, Sarah. The steers brought a lousy price." He walked up the stairs to the house. "Should have kept the bastards a bit longer. What a bloody day," he muttered as he as sat on the chair and loosened his boot laces.

Sarah ignored him and approached Jedidiah, who was preparing to take his leave. Immediately he looked at the lacerations on her arms and his eyes filled with sadness. He shook his head but didn't ask the questions she saw in his eyes and the rigid way he held his body, as if poised for a fight.

"I must go now, *Bibie*. I will see you in the morning near the Baobab tree."

Jedidiah was a Kikuyu; tall, lean and willowy. Lithe and supple like a panther, his magnificent body rippled with taut muscles built through hard, physical labour. The material of his breeches clung tightly to the contours of his loins, exposing a man of strength and vigor. Satiny dark skin glistened in the heat, the same rich shade of freshly roasted coffee as her stallion's coat.

Not only did he cut a fine figure of a man, he was also extremely intelligent. In his presence, Sarah felt safe and wanted, comfortable enough to share daily discussions on the welfare of the farm. To her he was the lighthouse, her anchor as she reached for the unreachable.

She watched as he shifted under her gaze. Even his gait fascinated her, a man who walked on air, who held the grace of an impala with every step he took, exuding an aura of power.

He turned and, with a nod, walked away. Sarah watched him until he disappeared over the hill, wiping the tears from her cheeks, knowing he'd understood what had happened to her.

On the verandah, Lawrence's boots hit the floor with a bang. He flung dirty clothes on top of them. Slamming in through the front door, he crossed the hall to the shower, shouting to Mimi at the top of his voice "Mimi, *chakula, chakula, haraka*—hurry!"

* * *

For a short while they sat out on the verandah having their meal in silence. Lawrence smoked his pipe. Having ignored Sarah most of the evening, he suddenly broke the silence.

"This country is becoming dangerous, crawling with *Mau Mau*. I heard at the market that Alister was butchered and his house burnt to the ground."

"The farmer," Sarah, said, shock ringing in her voice, "I remember him."

"Yes. I sometimes wonder what to do. What if we sold the property? Would you consider a move to Canada? A beautiful wilderness with no savages." He tapped his pipe in the ashtray.

"Are you serious?" Surprise echoed in her question.

He'd never considered her opinion important before. Lawrence always executed all plans and projects on the farm based on his own decisions. His words were final.

"I love this place. I'll never leave! After all, this country belongs to them. You made your fortune out of these people you call savages. If we treated them like humans instead of slaves, we wouldn't feat them," she blurted out.

"So now you meddle in politics?" Lawrence was livid. "How dare you accuse me of slavery? I make sure every single person on this farm is well provided for. They get food, shelter, doctors, and transport to the local school!" Lawrence pushed out of his chair, threw his pipe on the table and left the room mumbling, "Had a long day ... I'm beat ... I'm off to bed."

Sarah drew a deep long breath, leaned against the balustrade and looked up at the sky. Tonight it was dotted with a myriad of stars. The full moon beamed down across the vast land of shadows. The night throbbed with life. She listened to the incessant orchestration of cicadas and hooting owls. Sarah's restless, impulsive nature awoke in her and without hesitation she walked towards the compound. Silhouetted against the tree, Jedidiah's waiting form excited her. Mimi stood outside her hut and watched them in amusement.

"Would you mind riding for a while with me tonight," she asked Jedidiah. "We could check the north boundaries; see if everything is in order. We haven't been there for over a week. It's a full moon; we should be able to see the fence."

"Yes, *Bibie*, it's a lovely evening. I'll get the gun."

They walked towards the big shed, not far from the house. "Tomorrow we will check the heifers. Number sixteen is due to calf any day," said Jedidiah.

"Yes, we could start at dawn."

They entered the tack room and Jedidiah brought out the bridles and saddles whilst Sarah fetched a bucket. With a dipper, she scooped oats from the large box to feed the horses.

After a moment, she slipped outside to look around and went back inside. "Quickly, there's no one in sight. I need to show you something, something most urgent and dangerous for both of us. Help me lift the lid of the chest."

She held the torch and pulled out the wallet from under the blankets. Quickly, Sarah opened it. Inside was a small map showing the route between two villages and a photograph of African rebels. She turned it over and read the back.

"Six most wanted *Mau Mau*. Attack Friday June 10. That's five days from today," said Sarah, trembling with fear.

She bent down again and grabbed a battered, leather satchel from under the straw bales. She opened it to reveal a wad of pound notes.

"I've been saving this for years." Her eyes sparkled with excitement. "This is for a good cause, the best decision I've made in my life. Take the wallet and the money. Give these to your friends. Let them buy arms, lay in ambush against the police."

Jedidiah clutched Sarah's hand and rubbed his face against her palm, kissing it dead centre. "Thank you," he whispered, the gratitude in his voice came from the heart. Sarah knew his cause to free his people meant everything to him. He raised his head, dark eyes pools of sad longing. "You are the dawn and dusk of my life. You belong in the realm of goodness for my people." He ran his fingers over the blue marks and deep scratches on her arms. "He hurt you?"

She buried her face against his chest and told him of Montcliffe's attack. "I won't come to the compound tomorrow night, in case you decide to take action."

"I understand, Sarah." Jedidiah strapped the satchel on his back. "I will have my revenge for you."

"To freedom," said Sarah.

She mounted her sorrel mare and rode out with him. There were a few scattered *kibanda* inside the *boma*—a thick thorn bush fence protecting the cattle against the large prowling cats that roamed at night. For a while they rode in silence, surveying the northern part of the *boma* for gaps, until finally they galloped across the open country.

"Come on, Jedidiah, let's race to the sisal fields." she shouted, the wild thrill of adventure soaring in her chest.

Jedidiah shouted back, "I am ready."

Sarah jabbed the mare's flank and the horses' hooves thundered into the African night.

Triumphant, she reached the fields a few seconds before him. Her mare foamed at the mouth. Jedidiah's features conceded his defeat as he nobly dismounted and walked towards her.

"Take me down, Jedidiah. I'm so happy." Lifting her right leg to a side-saddle position, she leaned towards him. He caught her with his strong arms, sliding her slowly down his muscular body.

Excitement shot through Sarah's body, flooding her abdomen, heat flowing to her thighs, curling through the dark corridors of her womb and streaming up to her breasts. Jedidiah towered over her.

"I never want this to end. You and I riding without fear, always together," he said, releasing her from his hold. "I have grown to love this place," he said, pressing her closer as he stroked her soft hair. "Always together." His lips touched her ear, traced the path of her neck.

Jedidiah's hushed tone intoxicated her senses. "Always together," she repeated, feeling his erection against her.

"I will never leave you, *mpendwa*. Our blood is one."

"Our paradise," Sarah's voice drifted across the wild land. "No one can ever take it away from us. Yes, darling, let time stand still, stop the clocks from ticking." Sarah laughed excitedly.

They tethered the horses to a large stump. Holding hands, they descended the slope and into the field where they were swallowed by the gigantic, twenty-foot sea of sisal, whistling and rustling in the evening breeze.

"Oh, it's so beautiful out here. My special hiding place." She puckered her nose, sniffing the scent of the cool giant stalks.

"How many acres of sisal do we grow?" she asked.

"Over one hundred," he replied

She knelt and touched the warm earth, then lay down, her body hot as she looked at him.

"Take me, *yangu mpenzi*," she whispered. "My love, my passion."

Gently, he knelt over her and lifted her dress, exposing her firm, golden legs. He brushed his face against her warm thighs.

"Sarah, *moyo wangu*," he murmured. "My heart belongs to you."

"You are gentle...so gentle." She clung to him. Sarah traced her fingers across his broad, sinewy shoulders and slipped her hand lower to his loins. She marveled at his size, his blood throbbing for her.

"For years I have hungered for you. What are we doing? This is madness. *Kimkumku!* The consequences! What if they find out?"

"No one will, Jedidiah. We ride every morning as we have done for years. Nothing has changed. In the evening, we will meet here. Kiss me, Jedidiah, kiss me now. I want to remember tonight as long as I live. I am yours alone. Don't think about tomorrow, we have no tomorrow—never had—not you and I—"

His mouth sought her trembling lips and she clung to him, kissing him back with wild abandonment.

She moaned against the heat of his kiss, reveled in the hard, calloused hands that drew her body closer until she could think no more.

* * *

The following day after Lawrence left, Sarah and Jedidiah rode to the Baobab tree to tend the heifers.

"Thank you for yesterday," she said before tapping her mare's hindquarter with her heels. The horse bolted, and Sarah's golden hair blew in the wind.

"Over here." Jedidiah pointed, "On the far right, lying down, is number sixteen. I think she is calving."

They dismounted and crouched near the heifer, who bellowed constantly. Jedidiah lifted her tail and they noticed how swollen the opening was. "She is in great pain, has been in labour for quite some time. It would be wise if we stay here until she calved."

"You make a good vet."

"It takes years of experience to know all about cattle." Jedidiah rubbed his hand over the cow's rump. "She is rolling her eyes too much." With each strong, muscular contraction of the uterus, the cervix gradually dilated. He inserted his hand in and felt for the calf's buttocks.

"It's a breach birth. I'll try to turn her to bring the hind legs forward and slide the calf out."

Jedidiah was drenched with perspiration. Sarah wiped his forehead. It took almost an hour before he succeeded in pulling out the large calf. Within minutes, the unstable newborn stumbled, fell, rose again, then stood and sought for her mother's teats.

* * *

Over the following months, Sarah radiated with happiness. It was her eyes—those soft pale pools of blue—that betrayed her. Lawrence had suspected for quite some time by the way she gazed at Jedidiah that something lay between them. That same look had once been for him, her husband, a long time ago. How well he remembered.

What happened to us, Sarah? he thought. He knew deep in his heart, he had lost her forever.

Lawrence paused on the veranda as Sarah walked by, on her way to the stables. He'd watched his wife closely these last months. He saw her mount and ride away with his lead stockman, he knew what he had to do. The wind had increased, and they did not hear Montcliffe and Lawrence creeping up on them until their rifles pointed at the two entwined bodies.

"You bloody filthy ...*mtu mweusi*! All those years and you betray me... like this? I'll show you."

Jedidiah's eyes widened with fear. Sleek as a panther, he sprang up, his hand on Sarah's as he helped her to her feet.

"I'll make sure no one touches you ever again, Sarah!" Lawrence screamed.

Montcliffe laughed cruelly. "So now you turn to blacks! White men are not good enough for you?"

"At least he is a gentleman! More than you'll ever be, Montcliffe." She turned to Lawrence, "You want a divorce? Fine with me, but I will not leave this land ... I'll fight you. You can never take away the happiness he gave me."

The veins twitched on Lawrence's temple. He bit his lip and, without saying a word, took out his stiletto and approached her. Jedidiah pounced.

They fought savagely. Jedidiah lashed out with fury, twisting Lawrence's wrist. The knife fell to the ground. Eyes of a lynx, Jedidiah bent over and snatched the stiletto. Lawrence was just behind him. Swift as an arrow, Jedidiah swung and razed the sharp blade across Lawrence's ear, severing the lobe. It dangled against his neck as he screamed. Jedidiah charged and pinned his enemy down, pressing his hands against Lawrence's jugular vein, slowly suffocating him.

Montcliffe realized the peril and sprinted towards them. Cocked the gun and put the muzzle to Jedidiah's head. "I'll blow your brains out, bastard. Let him go! Drop the knife!"

The cold steel pressed into Jedidiah's neck. Sarah was paralyzed with fear as the situation grew volatile. She stared at the three men: the cruel, selfish husband she detested, Montcliffe who hid his detestable rape crime behind a badge, and the warrior Jedidiah, her man, her lighthouse. As an ominous premonition welled inside her, she broke in a sweat, shivering.

It's all my fault, this nightmare.

Jedidiah looked at her. How could he not see the sorrow, the forlorn hope and despair in her face?

Lawrence took off his shirt and looped it around his head to stop the bleeding. "I'll get the rope." Lawrence spat blood on the ground and wiped a sleeve across his mouth. Rope in hand, he forged a noose and placed it around Jedidiah's neck. With the remaining rope, he tied both Jedidiah's hands. "Now we will wait for dawn."

Montcliffe kicked Jedidiah repeatedly, his heavy boots striking him in the kidneys. The stockman slumped onto the warm earth, wracked with pain. A few feet away, Sarah swooned.

"My people will find out," Jedidiah yelled.

"You will disappear from the face of the earth," Lawrence said, his face a mask of hatred and fury. "I've got the law on my side...haven't I?" He looked at Montcliffe. "Who will ever doubt a white man's word?" Lawrence clenched his teeth.

"Your days are numbered, Montcliffe," Sarah hissed.

"What do you mean by that?" Montcliffe fumed as he approached her.

Sarah said nothing. Instead she spat at his feet and waited for realization to dawn. She didn't wait long.

"My wallet..."

He thought of the last time he'd seen it. He was never certain where he'd lost it, whether it was in her house or somewhere else. Doubt clouded his mind. On Friday June 10 the police did not attack the two villages. Now he suspected she had alerted the *Mau Mau*. The six rebels had escaped to take shelter far beyond their territory.

Sarah cried out at the top of her voice. "Both of you are doomed to Hell!"

Lawrence's eyes glowed like a madman's. "Grab her hands," he shouted to Montcliffe, bucking her beneath him.

She struggled furiously, thrusting her legs in the air like a trapped animal.

"Bitch!" Lawrence ripped a deep gash into the flesh of Sarah's right cheek with the stiletto. "No one ever betrays me!"

She doubled up in pain as Lawrence thrust her aside. Both men rose and walked away.

Desolate and gnawed by grief, Jedidiah watched Sarah drag herself over to kneel beside him. Blood oozed from the slash on her cheek and onto her white blouse.

Whimpering, she told him, "I am with child...our child." She wiped his tears with her lips.

"Our child will grow in freedom. Ride with the wind, Sarah, like we have done for years. What have I done to you? Forgive me..."

"You gave me rare happiness, a most precious gift." She kissed his feverish brow.

"We are one. I shall never leave you." He bent his head and brushed his face against her soft belly. "It will soon be light. Race with me down the valley and up the hill to the end," he whispered.

Sarah rested her head on his chest. "I will get revenge, Jedidiah. I promise. I will kill Lawrence," she murmured.

Dawn broke with clouds scudding across the sky.

They laid Jedidiah on a gnarled stump. Lawrence prodded the corky bark with a long stick and safari ants swarmed out.

Sarah heard Jedidiah's screams, heard him calling her name. She lay back on the damp earth, both hands on her belly, feeling life in the dark corridors of her womb.

Jedidiah's mind burned. He longed for Sarah. In the throes of death, he imagined Sarah riding her sorrel mare. He galloped behind her as the red horizon loomed behind the sea of sisal. Her lithe form grew hazy, her laughter silent until, finally, she vanished into darkness.

The ants crawled in his ears, nostrils, mouth, attacking his eyes. Within minutes, they'd gouged out his eyeballs, revealing two sockets which they tunneled into, their long, jaw-like pincers tearing and clawing. They stripped his skin and bore into his flesh.

Sarah prayed as she hadn't done in years as his screams of pain subsided and silence filled the air.

Montcliffe and Lawrence flung Jedidiah's body into a deep recess behind the stump and covered it with stones. A kite hawk hovered over the bush for a long time, uttering a plaintive cry. Distracted, Sarah only noticed the two men leaving when the engine fired up and they drove away from her, leaving her to the mercy of the wild.

The horses. They were still tethered not far from the sisal field. She hurried as fast as she could. Reaching the field, she mounted her mare and took the reins of the second one to gallop home.

* * *

Sarah snuggled her wrecked and tired body into the warmth of Mimi's motherly arms. Mimi wailed and beat her breast at the tragedy.

"Mimi, organize three men to ride with me now. It's urgent. Let them get the horses from the stable. We must cover Jedidiah with stones before the vultures pick at him. Quickly, darling Mimi. I will rest later." Sarah's blood pumped through her veins with desperation.

Soon, they lay stones on the grave until it covered Jedidiah in a protective dome. Sarah knelt, sobbing quietly.

A few days later, she planted a Jacaranda sapling near the grave of her warrior.

Lawrence disappeared for three weeks. One evening, she heard him enter the house, slamming the door. The following morning, he bawled orders to the men. She watched him from the verandah, his ear bandaged.

The gash in her face had healed slowly but the scar remained. Lawrence kept to himself in the large house. There were no secrets, no gossip. News spread quickly on the homestead. For years, the natives were aware that Lawrence was a violent man who often threatened Sarah. Unable to fight back, they despised him. Montcliffe was their arch enemy.

Sarah entered her third month of pregnancy. She sat for hours in her rocking chair—planning, scheming, burning with revenge—until one day, she walked to the shambas and sought out Mimi. "*Wewe, kuja hapa,*" she called out to one of the men, waving him over. "*Ambapo ni* Mimi?"

"*Zaidi ya hapo, bibie.*" He pointed across to where Mimi picked yams and the banana-like plantain. She often cooked these for Sarah, sliced and dipped in red pepper, then fried in palm oil.

"*Bibie,*" Mimi greeted and smiled as she approached.

"*Hujambo,* Mimi. Could you please come up to the house with me? *Bwana* is not home now."

"*Ndiyo, bibie.*" Mimi nodded. "I am ready." She followed Sarah to the house.

"We need someone we can trust." Sarah said as she sat at the kitchen table.

Mimi began to brew coffee for her mistress. "*Ndiyo, bibie.* That Makuba, the gardener, I trust him. He is a loyal one, and he doesn't like the *Bwana*. He says the *Bwana* hit him all the time. He can also catch the *nyoka* like the bird catches the worm."

"I trust him with my life. *Bwana* Lawrence keeps his gun in the Landrover, and the bullets and cartridges are in the glove box. I checked this morning before he left. He only loads the magazine when he goes down to inspect the *boma* for any breaches."

Much later that night, Makuba carried two black mambas in a sack and carefully placed them in the glove compartment.

* * *

Early the next morning, Lawrence drove to the hills. The chill crept through his thick jacket and into his bones. He rubbed his cold hands together as he looked across the vast land. Five ostriches preened near the thorny acacias. He turned his head towards the boma and noticed a narrow gap. *Bloody lionesses have been at the cattle again. Savage land! Danger lurks wherever you turn.*

He bent down to pick up his rifle and his face was close to the glove box as he opened it. He rummaged for the cartridges. A searing hot pain speared his wrist as the snake struck. Instantly he saw the second black mamba writhe towards him as it struck him in the face. He watched, frozen as they slithered away under the seat.

"God damn it!" Lawrence knew how fatal the venom of the black mamba was. He would never get to hospital in time. Instinctively, he took out his pocket knife and made an incision around the two fang marks. Blood oozed and within minutes, a cold shiver seized his body accompanied by nausea.

"Sarah." How could he have been so careless? He would never have thought she was capable of plotting his death so cunningly. He remembered Jedidiah calling her name as the safari ants bore into his flesh, the deep wound on her cheek, Sarah's venomous eyes boring into him, filled with hatred.

A long, long time ago, he'd loved Sarah. Oh how he'd loved her. Now he was filled with hatred— no, not hate…if only…

The drumming in his ears began a painful throb that reverberated through his body. He covered them with his hands. He did not wish to die. He opened the door and slumped on the ground. *Death, it is here. Sarah!*

The base of his tongue numbed and breathing became difficult as paralysis spread—over his chin, across his lips and down his throat. All sensation in his toes and fingers ceased. Eyes wide open and blank, the irises floated in white pools and the great white boss died a slow death.

* * *

"*Bibie!*" The house boy ran towards Sarah, his shout filled with hysteria. "*Bwana* Lawrence...he dead! The *nyoka*...the black mamba...he bite the master in the face...the hand..."

Sarah remained sitting on her rocking chair and smiled.

There was no inquest. The doctor recorded that death was due to respiratory failure induced by the toxin from the mamba. Within hours of the death certificate being issued, Montcliffe was speeding up the dusty road to her house.

"My sixth sense never betrays me. I know you caused his death. I will find out and take you to the gallows, Sarah, and those who helped you," he gloated.

Sarah stood and faced him, deadly calm. "I forbid you to ever set foot on my property in future. I never want to see your disgusting face again. Do you understand me, Montcliffe? Get off my land. I have loyal friends around me and close my doors on slime like you. You can't touch me anymore. I can fight as well as you."

Montcliffe turned and swished his baton around. "We should have finished you off as well." He laughed so hard he almost choked on his own sarcasm.

* * *

Sarah gave birth to a healthy boy. She watched the tiny lips suck the warmth of her bosom, ran a hand over the soft brown skin of his cheek and cupped his little head.

"Thank you, Jedidiah." Her tears trickled onto the baby's tight, dark curls. She was moved by this new life. She named him Jeremiah.

The natives were jubilant when Sarah had given birth to an African child. Her son brought joy and pride to their nation. The white community received it with shock and revulsion.

For a week they celebrated, tribes coming from the surrounding villages to join them. Sarah invited the Kikuyu chiefs from Niri-Nanyuki and Navasha. Mimi mumbled and grumbled, busy cooking and preparing a feast of delicious African dishes—they chanted African songs, and danced to the rhythm of the drums well into the early hours of the morning. Not a single white man or woman was present.

Jeremiah's childhood years were crowned with Sarah and Mimi's love. He inherited his father's qualities—wise, astute and insightful. Sarah entertained him with stories of his father, ensuring he knew what a good man his father was, rather than the demon the white world had painted him. On his seventeenth birthday, Sarah bequeathed him the farm and ran it until he graduated seven years later. Having completed his education, and awarded a Law degree with honors, he returned home to take the responsibility of managing the homestead.

Montcliffe never gave up. For years he hounded her, constantly bribed and interrogated the natives for clues regarding Lawrence's death, desperate to expose her, without success. Her words from long ago stabbed at his core. *Your days are numbered.* She was a threat to his life. The rebels watched his movements. He was haunted day and night as he felt time running out. He planned to retire in England.

She was respected by the Africans, and their love for her was unswerving, manifesting the kind of loyalty which leads men to give their lives. The *Mau*

Mau were freedom fighters, liberators who rebelled against the British Colonials. The white man possessed their land, yoked, trampled and segregated the Africans under their rule—an abomination.

Sarah rode with Jeremiah alongside the proud revolutionaries, a symbol of freedom crowning their heads.

Montcliffe was on the trail of the escapees in the forests, bush and villages. He suspected many were harbored on her land and provided with food and shelter. Try as he might, Sarah made sure he had no proof.

* * *

"*Bibie!*" Makuba ran up the stairs. "*Gari ni kuja na polisi.*" He pointed down the road, where through the dust; Montcliffe's police car sped towards them, lights flashing.

"*Asante*, Makuba." She patted him on the shoulder. "Keep working, I'll deal with them."

Sarah wore a red blouse and blue skirt as she stepped out onto the balcony to meet her nemesis. Montcliffe was stooped now, bald with a huge paunch that hung over his long khaki shorts shadowing his knobbly knees.

"You still look damn attractive, Sarah," He had the gall to say.

She laughed, "And you, Montcliffe? You can't get off my back, can you? I loved Jedidiah. I loved the son he gave me...and you are full of venom!" She touched the scar on her cheek, faded now but still visible. To this day, she could still hear Jedidiah's screams as he died at this man's hands. Hatred seethed, boiled, gnawed deep inside her. "You are a repulsive and loathsome creature. You will never break me or my people."

"I am going to tear your place apart until I find those bloody rebels. I know damn well they hide here and when I catch them, they'll hang."

"Go on, Montcliffe, you can't prove a thing, you never could. For years you've been chasing me, but I'll get you in the end. I love Africa. I love the Africans and will protect them with the last breath in my body."

Montcliffe's face darkened. "I'll comb your place with my best trackers. I wouldn't be surprised if some of your black bastards are *Mau Mau*."

He coughed violently, almost choking as he spat phlegm at her feet.

"You arrogant pig, you think you know everything when you know nothing at all. You are a rapist, a murderer, a pillaging policeman and a pariah, hated by everyone on my property—most of all by me. The noose is getting tighter around your neck, you paunchy bastard." Her voice held enough chill to make him shiver.

Casually, Sarah leaned on the balustrade and watched Jeremiah riding his gelding. He approached rapidly having seen the police arrive. She couldn't help but feel a quiver of relief when her son took his place beside her and held her tenderly. She trembled and whispered, "Tell him to go. He makes me sick."

"Sit down, Mother. Please." He spoke so eloquently, even Montcliffe appeared astonished. "May I remind you that you are trespassing on our land and offending my mother? As for searching the property, unless you have a warrant, please leave at once. Do not come back."

Montcliffe stamped his feet, slammed the car door and sped away down the road.

* * *

During the months that followed, many *Mau Mau* guerrillas were caught, imprisoned and shot for subversive activities. Jeremiah met secretly with the rebels, providing them with food.

For weeks Montcliffe and his men were on the hunt for them. Makuba went south to meet with another gang and was caught, tortured under extreme interrogation by Montcliffe. Defiant, he did not flinch as the whip lacerated his already raw back. Eventually, he was hanged.

"Get him, Jeremiah. We must avenge your father's death and Makuba's…and my own personal grievance." Sarah's eyes misted with tears she refused to let fall.

* * *

The tall jacaranda tree was in full bloom, covered with clusters of blue-bell blossoms. Montcliffe and his band of trackers approached the escarpment. Jeremiah waited in hiding in the vast sisal fields with twenty *Mau Mau.* They waited for Montcliffe and his men to reach the cliff's edge then charged, slashing with their pangas. Within minutes, the policemen were dead and their bodies flung over the thousand foot precipice. They manacled Montcliffe and laid him across a twisted trunk, not far from where Jedidiah was buried.

"Remember my words, Montcliffe, from many years ago. Do you remember?" Sarah drove her panga into the cork-like surface of the trunk. Safari ants emerged, crawling over him, covering his battle-tortured body.

"Damn you, Sarah. Damn you." His screams echoed across the valley.

He did not scream for long. The ants filled his throat. She slashed the panga across his thighs and watched the safari ants dip under his khaki shorts. He flung his head from left to right in agony as the vermin punctured his testicles and feasted on the flesh. Montcliffe would never rape again. Sarah had her revenge.

Much later, Sarah sat on her rocking chair, gazing at the studded sky.

"It is a beautiful evening, Mother."

"Yes, darling, it is beautiful."

4 CRY BELOVED CRY

Doctor Sudharkar Rao entered the hospital with quick strides, immaculately dressed in a white cotton suit, lemon cravat, white shoes and a straw hat.

"Good morning, Doctor," the nurses greet him.

His face lit with a charming smile, showing a set of even white teeth.

"Good morning," he greeted with nod.

Tall with silver-grey hair, dark eyes and heavy eyebrows, there was a dignity about him. An Edwardian beard hid sensuous lips and prominent jawline. His muscular neck, broad shoulders and confident carriage showed he was a man of great intellect. But it was his striking personality that drew patients and staff alike to respect him.

He entered the spacious consulting room, took off his hat and jacket, and hung them on the coat rack. Hooking his white coat off the hanger, he put it on as he wandered over to the window. The mountains beyond were capped with snow. He gazed at them pensively. He loved this part of India. A great longing overcame him for a time long ago when the laughter of youth had escaped his lips, running down the hill with the children tugging at his shirt, the young woman picking wild flowers and berries, and chasing rainbows he'd never caught. He sighed.

Twenty five years have passed since I became a physician. In India, social class prevailed and he didn't want to fit the requirements. He felt like a solitary wolf away from the pack. Although both families were wealthy, his marriage was a failure.

He craved for the greatest gift—to be loved, to share his life's passions, pains and work. Instead, his wife was as cold as marble, cocooned in the false, opulent world of *coterie* gatherings and entertainment, *pattes de velours.*

Lonely flashes of a woman in bright colours were always there, hidden behind the nebulous curtains. Fate had betrayed him. Long ago, he was not true to himself nor humble. Past illusions engulfed his mind, thrust upon him in brilliant shapes.

He was young, dedicated and full of enthusiasm. Back then he was assigned to the Leprosy Mission north of Darjeeling and the villages surrounding it. For five years, he treated the villagers when the disease was most prevalent.

After leaving the leper colony, he was reassigned to Europe. Experienced in the field of leprosy and with his profound knowledge of the disease, it wasn't long before he travelled to Africa to heal the sick. But the call of his beloved India was too strong and he returned as soon as he could to specialize in the research of the disease.

India was a magnetic force in his life. The colours, the smells and appetizing dishes, the rhythm of life and death in perpetual motion, the music and dialects and customs that drew him in as life bustled with feverish spirit.

Doctor Rao gazed at the majestic mountains. His breath caught in his throat as tiredness seeped through his muscles. Memories, vague faces, all fused and blurred. A small village sprawled across the land with shacks and winding lanes. Beyond it lay rice fields, whispering trees, a young woman, and a cave. She floated in and out of his mind, yet her eyes stabbed at his memory, deep green eyes that pierced his soul. The fragrant scent of her frangipani crown teased him, the image so real he could almost touch her. The image faded, replaced by queues of lepers, glassy eyes that stared at him, pleading for final release, and the merciful Buddhist monks praying for their souls.

The sharp knock at the door drew him from his thoughts.

"Come in, please."

His colleague, Doctor Gupta, entered the room. "Hope I'm not disturbing you?"

"No, not at all." Dr Rao smiled warmly.

"I have a rather unique case I would like you to examine. A woman has been brought in from the hills with septic ulcers all over her body." Doctor Gupta looked over the glasses perched on the tip of his nose. "I haven't seen anything like this in years. She is fading rapidly. Two monks brought her here in a hammock. The sores on her foot crawl with maggots."

"Where is the patient now?" asked Doctor Rao.

"I've placed her in the Isolation ward. Absolutely imperative," he sighed. "How does one cling to life in such a mess? You must see her for yourself." Doctor Gupta held open the office door and waved Doctor Rao through. In solemn silence, they walked the short distance to Isolation.

They entered the ward and Doctor Rao saw a frail woman huddled in a bed in the far corner. They approached. He was struck motionless and silent as he stared at the heartbreaking sight before him. Anger warred with helplessness in his soul, for the poor woman was beyond all help.

Like a corpse, a foul stench exuded from her putrid body. Doctor Rao was about to put on a mask when her right eye opened to peer at him. A chill ran down his spine. He tucked the mask into the pocket of his white coat. Pity was his other failing in life.

Death lurked in the corner as her gaze raked his face.

"We must get rid of the maggots immediately. Sponge her body with antiseptic and rub on some soothing lotion. And put her on a drip, she is dehydrated and starved."

Desperate and tormented by the sight of a wasted life, Doctor Rao struggled to focus.

"What we have here is a classic case..." he paused, weighing every word, "...of Syphilitic Lepromatous leprosy in the final stage."

"I gave her an injection to ease the pain and bring down the fever," said Doctor Gupta. "Quite honestly, it will be a miracle if she survives until tomorrow."

Her swollen, puckered face was disfigured with prominent nodules. The unforgiving disease had eaten away at her septum until the bridge of her nose collapsed. Doctor Rao could only imagine the suffering she'd endured. Abscesses seeped on her neck. Nerve paralysis had frozen open her mouth, exposing her teeth. The fetid discharge that gathered there emitted an odor anticipating death.

"There is something so bizarre here," Doctor Rao whispered, putting on his rubber gloves. "Notice her left eye, atrophy of the lower eyelid and the paralysis. She is unable to close the eye—so typical of the disease— and it has a glassy look. She probably hasn't had a decent sleep in months." He paused and cleared his throat. "The cornea is very inflamed, ulcerated and opaque. Yet if you look at the right eye, it is absolutely clear. Amazing, a healthy eye...even the lashes are still there."

He bent over and gently touched her forehead. "The other eyebrow is swollen with loss of hair and, as you can see, large bald patches on the scalp."

He felt her gaze upon him. It disturbed him. He wasn't quite sure why. That green eye, beseeching, imploring, followed him as he paced to the medicine cabinet on the other side of the room. He returned to her side and took out a piece of lint from a large sterilized jar. Lightly, he dabbed emollient ointment on her seeping ulcers.

He took out another piece of lint and wiped her damp face.

"She has difficulty breathing."

"Yes," said Doctor Gupta, "I examined her before and there are tubercles all over her tongue, even down the larynx. Worst of all is the contraction of the glottis. No wonder the poor woman can't breathe well. If we performed an immediate laryngotomy she would never survive. There is too much poison in her system. Sadly, she is too far gone."

"Where have you been all this years? Why did you not come sooner? You could have gone to the leper mission. Why did you let the disease waste you so? If only I was there to help..." Rao's lips trembled, beads of perspiration formed in the groove of his nose.

"Nothing will help her now... nothing. She is trying to tell me something. There is pleading in her eye. What hidden secrets are veiled in darkness? I can't reach her," he said to Doctor Gupta.

Frustrated, he turned toward the medicine chest again. Bottles of Chaulmoogra oil, dapsone and sulphetrone lined the shelves.

"All will be useless at this advanced stage," he murmured.

"I am running late," Doctor Gupta said. "I must go on my rounds now before we go to theatre for afternoon surgeries. We must do what we can. Brew sassafras," he said to the two nurses attending the patient. "Add sweet coconut juice, drain the fluid onto poultices and cover the inflamed lesions. This should help her sleep and relieve the pain somewhat."

* * *

82

Jyotafna followed Doctor Rao's movements as he approached the window, silhouetted against the bright sunrays that streamed into the room. In the distance she heard the cry of a hawk as it flew beyond the horizon.

Thank God he doesn't recognize me.

He hadn't changed much…a few wrinkles, grey hair. He was still the same beloved Rao she knew, had loved so long ago. She wanted to call out his name, to scream and beg for his help, but the constricted muscles in her throat had rendered her mute. Tears trickled from her right eye onto her sunken cheeks. She tried to wipe them with her ravaged hand, now a misshapen lump with clawed fingers.

His magnetism was still as powerful as he paced back towards her. She wanted to touch his handsome face, to flex a healthy body against him as she had when they were young. So near, yet so untouchable. She felt his fingers on her cheek as he brushed her tears away.

"Tears of hope," he said, smiling.

* * *

Doctor Rao felt the weight of her gaze on his face.

"I know you can hear me and understand. I wish you could speak." He watched as her healthy eye blinked, the lashes fanning her cheek. Rao shivered, unsure why the green gaze teased at his memories. "Who are you? Where do you come from? What story hides behind your eyes—a fairytale, perhaps?"

She blinked again and a memory battered his mind again. "You remind me of someone. Tell me, do you like mangoes and paw paws?"

She stared out the window, her lips twitched with the effort to speak, her face contorted with the pain the movement caused. ""No, don't try to talk.

We'll solve the riddle together later. Why did you let yourself go like this?"
Putting on his gloves, he gently examined the inflamed lymphatic glands in her neck. Beads of perspiration accumulated on his forehead. Helplessness weighed heavily on his shoulders as her doleful expression tore at his heart. He had treated hundreds of leprosy patients but none touched him like this unknown woman did.

"I would so much like to help you. I must go now but I will be back later this evening."

His eyes sparkled as he smiled charmingly at her.

* * *

As the door closed at his back, Jyotafna fanned the embers of her memories and raked up the past. She ached with longing and remembered the first time she'd seen him in the markets, a young practitioner. She'd stood near her fruit stall when he'd approached. The scent of Frangipani surrounded her from the garland plaited into her long hair.

"I'll have two paw paws and two mangoes, please. Nectar of the Gods."
He'd chuckled, his eyes riveted on her high cheek bones shadowed with ochre. He'd come to the market every Saturday after that without fail.

One day, she'd said to him, "I am closing the stall early today. Mother is not well and I must prepare her meal. Would you like to come with me?" She's smiled up at him happily.

"Yes, of course!"

She'd lived with her ailing mother in the village. Their dilapidated shack was crammed but tidy. The rats infested the alleyways and poverty stamped its ugly mark on the open sewers, but it didn't seem to faze Rao.

They'd entered the hovel where an oil lamp glowed on the tin walls. Her mother lay on a small bed in the corner, her cough rasping in her chest.

"I'll give her warm vegetable soup. She'll sleep. We can climb up the hill as I often do. Not far is the Buddhist monastery. I go there when I can to study, read and write."

And so their affair began. The villagers assembled once a week at the clinic for examination and treatment. In the small white-washed room, he examined her for any symptoms of leprosy. They met in the hills, their hiding place a hidden cave where he kissed her. His fingers caressed her youthful face, neck and firm breasts, slowly travelling to her soft abdomen and down her thighs. She whimpered with pleasure. She loved him deeply, totally enraptured.

For five years, they were lovers. For five years she was blissfully happy, giving herself with an exhaustible passion. *Darling Rao, to be yours, to be your woman, extracted from the fire of creation – that I desire.* Jyotafna shivered as she remembered the words she often whispered to him.

"I have to travel to Europe soon for further studies to help your people. Will you wait in the hills for me until I return? Then we will fly like butterflies between the flowers and catch the sunset when the day is done," he'd promised.

How she'd missed him when he left for Europe...all those empty years, more so when her mother died from pneumonia six months after he'd left.

She never married. He said he would be back one day, so she waited. He never returned, and why should he? Who was she but a peasant's daughter, and he the rich young doctor from the wealthiest, most distinguished family in Darjeeling. So from man to man she crawled, desperate to forget the man she loved. She crawled deeper and deeper into the quagmire.

Three years after he left, the first signs of syphilis erupted, followed months later by leprosy, bringing death to her door.

Jyotafna disregarded the pale patches for months. Occasionally she applied vegetable extracts and balms from the local herbalists and medicine men. At times these helped to stimulate re-pigmentation of the light-colored skin patches, but the disease progressed and gnawed at her nerves and bones. She became an outcast.

Lepers were an abomination, a curse. She was mocked, avoided and children threw garbage at her. She collected the scraps and shuffled up the hill to the cave where she took refuge. A mangy, stray dog followed her, keeping her company in her exile.

The only kindness came from the Buddhist monks, who would pass by to bring her rice and fruit. Occasionally, the dog would bring home a dead chicken he'd snatched from the market and they'd share it together, outcasts shunned by the world.

The haven lit with the warmth of a fire, Jyotafna yearned for her beloved until she no longer felt pain or hunger. The dog howled a forlorn call, scratched his fleas and fell beside her.

* * *

While Jyotafna lay immersed in memories on the other side of town, the eminent and most respectable Rao family entertained lavishly in grandeur and splendor. Their guests, the Maharaja and Maharani, Professor Ranji Rama and Darjeeling's cream of society indulged in feasting, drinking, gossip and dancing. Doctor Rao's wife, ever the efficient hostess, was exquisitely dressed in chintz, bedecked with gold around her neck under her double chin. His two sons, both respected merchants, mingled with the crowd.

He could hear his wife's feigned laughter echo across the mansion. It irritated him more than ever so he stepped outside onto the verandah for a breath of fresh air.

How futile everything in his life seemed. His dull, frigid and vain wife, all those puppets inside their home. He thought of the woman in the throes of death. Embalmed memories awakened and reached the forefront of his mind. The market, the cave, colours and butterflies, paw paws and mangoes! Desolate, she'd stood on the hill as he'd left, her plaited hair blowing in the wind. He'd been empty and aching for her as duty had called from across the ocean.

Jyotafna! No, it couldn't be.

Shattered and torn, he ran across the garden towards his car and sped to the hospital.

Through the corridors he rushed into the dimly lit room. Her gaze fixed on the door as he entered and watched as he approached her. The green eye magnetized, mesmerized and stirred him. He remembered those eyes now. They scarred the half-forgotten past. Recognition, strong and forceful, vibrated within him. The reason for her silence slammed through him as his heart began to pound. She hadn't wanted him to recognize her in this state.

"Jyotafna," he whispered into the darkened room.

She smiled, her breathing shallow, her face twisted with the effort. Her lips moved stiffly as she tried to speak. Her breath wheezed like a faint whistle in the shrouds, almost inaudible. He bent his head near her lips and waited as she forced out her final words.

"Darling Rao…to be yours…to be your woman…extracted whole from the quarry of creation…*that*, I desired."

Rao gasped. He *knew* she'd recognized him. Weakly, she touched his head in farewell. He knelt beside her and wept.

5 FANTINE

The spider weaved and spun higher across the thick web of gossamer silk, and took shelter from the icy wind in the far corner of the dim street lamp. Fantine watched it and sighed. For a moment she envied the tiny insect hiding, shying away from the world behind the warmth of the light globe.

The narrow alley behind the patisserie was deserted but for two cats scurrying from one dustbin to another. The apartments were surrounded by several older buildings. Lights flickered in the dismal quarter. A broken window shutter creaked as it swung in the bitter wind and steam wafted from smelly drains.

In the bitter cold, Fantine shivered. She pressed her face into the softness of the old Angora scarf wrapped around her neck, the warmth of it covering her cold nose. She'd stood there for an hour...waiting. These were lean times for harlots tramping the seedy streets in harsh winter with unemployment looming. Only courtesans in the affluent districts were highly paid by wealthy customers.

Fantine thought about her daughter Monique, asleep upstairs. She was one week behind on payment for her singing lessons. The tutor was kind and patient. He understood the gift Monique possessed.

I should go, she thought. *No-one will come now.* Only fools—*pauvre diables*—would venture out in this weather. She turned and saw the silhouette of a man in the faint light. The sound of hollow footsteps made her hesitate. Fantine wrapped her cloak more tightly around herself.

Captain Moreau walked briskly through the cul-de-sac, restlessness overwhelming him. This was usually a popular rendezvous for trollops to parade, but not tonight. He felt empty. All his tomorrows seemed to drown in an endless labyrinth.

His shoes clattered on the cobblestones. He tried to cast aside his morbidity as he saw the figure huddled in the flickering lamplight. Moreau stopped, waiting with caution, watching the woman's lowered face, veiled with a scarf. A woman, he realized as the wind ruffled a mass of mahogany curls. He drew closer, shielding her from the easterly gust as he studied the brown eyes, speckled with green, the pupils like inky pools in the soft glow of light.

She nodded.

"*Bonsoir Monsieur. Mon Paradis de chaleur?* " she asked in an alluring tone.

Moreau's left eye twitched, astonished at the educated tone of the prostitute's words. How could he fathom the secrets hidden in those captivating eyes?

"Fantine *est mon nom.*" She smiled.

"*Capitan* Moreau." He kissed her gloved hand.

She turned. "*Suivez moi, sil vous plait.*"

He followed her to a large gabled house. Flakes of snow laced the darkness, covering the ground with a light blanket of white. The stairs leading to the front entrance were littered with broken bottles and empty cans. Old newspapers lay soggy and tattered, curled corners slapping in the wind.

From behind the closed doors Madame Gaston bawled furiously at her drunken husband. Phillippe, a street minstrel desperately seeking work, practiced his mournful singing.

Ah, there's loveable Babette, the crazy fortune teller, always swearing. Fantine smiled. Through the faded lace curtains, Moreau watched the silk clad woman chasing a monkey in circles around the room.

"Joujou! That was the last saucepan of milk!" she yelled. On the second floor, the bawdy L'Hirondelle roared with laughter as she told lewd jokes to the sailors.

"*Maison des larmes*," Fantine sighed, leading the Captain towards the aging wooden staircase. "There's never a dull moment here." She stopped and caught her breath, her cheeks flushed. "They remind me of rats trapped in their holes," she said.

The smell of garlic, onions and urine rose. In the dark corner, a tramp huddled with a whiskey bottle in his hand.

Suddenly, Phillipe swung open his door. "*Merde!*" He kicked a rat out the door and it scurried below.

The flight of stairs, riddled with dry rot, creaked beneath their weight as they ascended. He stood one step below and watched as she paused to test a loose step. Petite and pretty, her bearing was one of elegance, breeding and educated charm. Moreau was mystified. A deep sadness rose within him, emotions lancing his heart. He wished to swear like the minstrel, embrace Fantine and whisk her away from this squalor. She was an enigma to him.

"Have you lived here long?" he asked.

"Several years," she answered softly. He saw in her eyes a look of another season, another time, somewhere half-forgotten, half-remembered. They continued to climb until they reached the attic. The room was small and tidy. An oil lamp hung low from the ceiling attached by a long chain to a hook. The snow patterned the latticed window, slowly covering it. The glow from the coal fire cast red and yellow hues and warmed the room. Above the hearth, swinging on a rusty wire, a large copper kettle steamed. On the mantelpiece lay a treasure—the classic masters of French Literature—Victor Hugo, Emile Zola, Guy de Maupassant, Voltaire, Anatole France and the great French poets, Cyrano de Bergerac, La Fontaine and Charles Baudelaire. In the corner a young child slept on an iron bed.

"Would you like to take tea with me? It is so cold."

"Yes please, that would be very nice."

She approached her daughter's bed and tucked the frayed grey blankets around the little girl's legs.

Moving back to the table, Fantine poured the tea. She placed the large enamel mug on a small milking stool near him, and then curled beside the fire.

The captain's mind whirled. He had no right to be judge or jury. In the humble room, his compassion rose to new levels.

"You shouldn't have been out in this weather," he said

The child coughed and Fantine anxiously lifted her head.

"Will you be staying for a while in Paris?" she asked.

"Only a few more days then back to the Far East."

"It sounds so remote and romantic." She rubbed her itchy nose. "To what part of the east do you travel?"

"Malaya, Hong Kong, Macau, India, also Africa and the West Indies, then I return to Europe. I have a small, quaint house on the exotic island of Montserrat near the ocean, hidden in a cove."

He placed his empty mug on the stool and stretched his legs.

"May I pour you some more?"

"No, thank you."

He felt her warmth. She was a voice out of the wilderness. He was moved by her poverty and the strange emotions of this young woman. Moreau was nervous; almost afraid to disturb these secret feelings gently awakening in him.

"I presume you ship spices and herbs over here. What other cargo do you carry?" She smiled, a large dimple pressing into the rosy roundness of her left cheek.

"Yes, also timber, rice, silk, tea, hemp, rubber and so forth. Are you interested in the subject?"

She hesitated before answering, "I am an avid reader."

Captain Moreau laughed as she perfectly pronounced each syllable.

"Perhaps I could sail with you to Monserrat one day and walk along the golden beaches," she murmured. Her dark eyes veiled with longing, disturbed him.

"I would like that. The Frigate birds are beautiful. They have bright red collars," he said.

She uttered a muffled whimper. Instantly, he stood and held her in his arms.

"Hush now, I am here."

No one had ever hugged her. She clung to him with despair.

"Come and sit beside me." He clasped her hand gently. "The Frigate birds will wait for you." He brushed the curls out of her eyes.

"The places I love most are libraries and museums, and of course the theatre. Quite regularly I take my daughter to see a good play, preferably a comedy." She suddenly shivered "Ah! *Mon Dieu!* It is bitter tonight. When will you return to Europe again?"

"A year, maybe less. I run the west coast of Africa and the West Indies then alternate the following year between the Far East and Europe. It is a lucrative trade, I must admit." He took out his pipe.

She got up, picked up the coal scuttle and tossed a large black lump of coal onto the orange glow. It hissed and sent wafts of smoke in loops and spirals up the chimney as the wind increased.

"Tell me a little about you," he asked.

"I was a few days old when my mother left me on the doorstep of an orphanage. I ran away at an early age and was thrown into the world of thieves, prostitutes, pimps and other vermin. Monique's father—an artist I knew in Montmartre—disappeared after her birth. Somehow I learnt to survive in the gutter." She paused and brushed her long brown curls sideways. "I also wash dishes in the morning at a local restaurant. In my child, there is hope for the future. Perhaps people such as I are capable of building empires." She sighed deeply. "There...is a ray of sunshine." She got up and touched her daughter's flushed cheeks. "Do you have family here in Paris?"

He lit his pipe, puffing several times. "I come from a long line of seafarers. My father was a typical old seadog with a great passion for adventure. My mother adored him. He disappeared in Macau. Not a trace of him was ever found. Very mysterious."

The Captain watched Fantine go to the larder. She cut a small piece of fruit cake and placed it in front of him.

"Thank you so much, you haven't got much left for yourself."

"I'll bake another one tomorrow." She smiled. "Tell me more about your father.

"He carried varieties of cargo throughout the East, but made his fortune from opium. Sold the cursed stuff to underworld dealers." He paused.

"What happened then?" She rubbed her hands together in front of the coal fire.

"I sailed to Macau and Hong Kong several times. There's lots of money involved in such a rotten business. One has to be cautious and cunning when you deal with corrupt police and dangerous cut-throats. I tried for months and months to seek his whereabouts. He'd simply vanished. Mother pined for him. She did not wish to live without him.

He licked his finger. "That cake is absolutely delicious! Let's talk of happy things. I am sailing in four days from Marseille."

She gazed at him with sad eyes. "So soon?"

Fantine undressed quickly and slipped beneath the eiderdown. She snuggled against his warmth and purred.

That night Fantine did not sell her body. She gave herself with rapture to Moreau. Both soared to infinite heights.

Throughout the night the wind whistled, the kettle wheezed and hissed, and the little girl in the corner coughed. Towards dawn, Captain Moreau placed ten thousand francs on the mantelpiece. He visited her again the following evening.

"Please do not open this until I have gone." He tucked the small gift behind the old clock on the mantelpiece.

Fantine's heart swelled. She kissed his hands in gratitude. Never had anyone treated her with such kindness and sensitivity.

"No Fantine, don't cry," he said as she saw him out the door. He disappeared into the silence of the cold street. She ran to the window and rubbed the condensation off the glass. He was gone. Would she ever see him again?

"Moreau!" Her lips trembled.

She moved the rattly iron bed to the middle of the room. Half the springs were broken. With the end of a small hatchet, she lifted two wooden floor planks. A mouse scurried across the carpet from the hole.

Beneath the floorboards lay an old coffer. She'd hidden it there from burglars who prowled the destitute alley. The money would pay for Monique's medicine, warm clothes, a new quilt and food for the larder. A gift from a gentleman. She felt a tightness in her chest, tears on her cheeks. Trembling with excitement, Fantine prized the box open and placed the money safely inside. Having done that, she shifted the bed back to its former position.

* * *

The next morning, Fantine watched as the milk cart ploughed through the thick snow. The horse neighed and snorted, it's flared nostrils puffed wisps of warm steam as Monsieur Duval pulled on the reins.

"Come on, you stubborn old girl, you can make it."

Standing close to him, she saw her friend's red nose dripping with cold and the lobes of his ears had almost turned blue. His snow-covered black beret covered a bald head. Beneath it, a wrinkled and tired face hid, lined with the silent stamp of penury and years of hardship. His warm brown eyes were alert and twinkling.

Fantine waved at him and hurried across the street carrying her small milk can and jug.

"*Bonjour*, Fantine."

"*Bonjour*, Duval.

"I'll have a little extra cream for Monique today. I've got some porridge cooking upstairs so I can't stop to chat but promise to do so next time. You look frozen, Duval." She giggled.

"Ah! Fantine, it is the devil's work. Much too cold—even for Cocotte." He rubbed the horse's long ears. "Poor Cocotte, you are getting old."

"How is Solange these days?" asked Fantine.

"Happy and fat, getting fatter, especially after the last child." He chuckled,

95

revealing a mouthful of stained, uneven teeth from years of smoking and neglect. "Did you hear the latest news?"

"No, what is it?"

"I think it won't be long before Germany will be at war with us."

"Ah! Duval, politics, wars. I have my own war to battle against." She rubbed her nose. "I don't really understand any of them, forgive me I must go."

"I'll finish my rounds early today. *Au Revoir*, Fantine."

Having wrapped her daughter in a layer of woollies, thick muffler and red balaclava topped with a large pompom, she dragged Monique by her tiny hand towards Monsieur Flaubert's crummy restaurant. She dashed through the back door into the large steamy kitchen permeated with the pungent smells of onion and garlic. She settled the child in the corner with a book. With a sigh of resignation, she looked around at the disarray of the kitchen. Hanging up her coat and scarf, she huffed, and reached for the bucket and mop.

Flaubert kicked open the swinging doors, his hands full of plates, cups and cutlery.

"*Bonjour*, Fantine. What a rough lot we have today. At least they had onion soup to warm their bones. Don't bother to clean the floor now. See to the dishes—and scrub them well.

She could hear the men and women drowning their sorrows from running the gutters in search of work.

All morning Fantine toiled. Her body tired as she scrubbed floors and washed dishes, while Monique sat in the corner nibbling at crusty bread with cheese, and sipped hot milk.

"*Vóila*, Fantine," exclaimed Flaubert, pinching her bottom. "In your pay packet this week, I gave you a little extra for Monique. See you Monday."

"Thank you so much." She kissed him on the cheek.

At midday, Fantine and Monique left the restaurant. Once more, the snow had started to fall heavily. As soon as they entered their attic room, Fantine removed the coffer from its hiding place underneath the bed and placed the additional money in it. She lit the fire and warmed the split-pea soup on the kerosene cooker.

* * *

The depression years hung like a dark shroud over Europe. Fantine was disguised by her double life, the prostitute prowling the streets at night and working in the restaurant during the day. But she did it for Monique, her beautiful little girl with a talent that deserved to be honed.

Fantine's mind swayed back with bitterness to the years when she had worked as a librarian in the *Bibliothèque nationale de France* and her first brush with aristocracy, Baron Dubois. He'd entered the grand hall and approached her.

"I am interested in the life of the Roman, Marcus Aurelius.

"Certainly," she responded.

A week later, he visited the library again and asked if she would have dinner with him. She accepted. He'd arrived in a splendid carriage; they'd talked about history, hunger and poverty in undeveloped countries.

The horse cantered through the boulevard towards the elite restaurant where she watched the aloof man holding a cup of coffee, his little finger arrogantly in the air and listened to the cold tone of his voice as he ordered the sumptuous meal.

The bottle of *Beau Joie* made her stomach churn at the wasted expense. *Pompous ass!*

Returning later amongst the majestic trees on the avenue, Dubois stopped the carriage. He pressed himself against her, sliding his unwelcome hands between her thighs. With revulsion, she rejected his advances.

"*Arêtes, s'il vous plaît, Monsieur!*" Fantine pushed his hands away. "I am not some cheap *putain* who must be paid for services."

"So my dinner and wine bought me nothing?"

The incredulity in his voice angered her more. What had he expected? Had he thought because she was a mere librarian, she would be open to his filthy advances?

Fantine eyed him furiously. "The nobility, you of the *haute monde,* are despots! Through the ages they have held the reins of tyranny and power," she lashed out at him. "You unleash it on us, the ones you deem the lower class, treat us like animals."

"I beg your pardon?" The baron was stunned. No one had ever spoken to him in that manner.

"Have you ever had to crawl in the gutter seeking work? *La Bastille* was the last strength of the people," she said, her words aimed at him like a slap in the face.

"You ungrateful little *poule!* I have wined and dined you, and now you refuse me? That is why we treat you like the *bâtards sales* you are!" He argued back until the discussion escalated into unpleasantness unbecoming of a gentleman.

"Stop the carriage!" Fantine could take no more.

As the carriage drew to a halt he opened the door, pushing her out into the night, humiliating her further as he flung a few *sou* at her.

The following afternoon, the library's director gave her notice to leave. He would not explain, except to say he had received a complaint from a patron.

"*Cela va sans dire,*" muttered Fantine. There was no point in arguing. It was the baron's word against hers and she did not have the means to fight him in court.

Fantine never forgot the baron's behavior on that night. Unable to find employment again, she was dragged down into the abyss of prostitution to survive.

But that was the past, now was the future. All she desired was for Monique to follow her vocation and be crowned with the blessing of success.

* * *

Fantine choked with pride as her daughter's magnificent voice soared through the walls of Notre Dame Cathedral that night at midnight mass. She knelt and vowed that Monique's rare gift would one day delight the savage hearts of France.

At the end of the service, Fantine and Monique walked down the aisle between the pews. Father Lavergne stood at the exit.

"*Bonsoir*, Fantine." He turned to Monique. "You have grown so tall. *Le Bon Dieu* has blessed you with a heavenly voice." He smiled.

"When I can afford it, Monique takes singing lessons tutored by a struggling musician," said Fantine.

"I do know someone from the *Conservatoire* I can recommend," said Father Lavergne.

"Thank you, Father, I am most grateful. When do you think I could speak to the gentleman?"

"I'll see him this week. You look pale, Fantine. How is work at Flaubert?"

"Hard, but it brings in money regularly."

The priest's penetrating gaze made her feel uncomfortable. He was always distressed when he saw her on the streets.

The priest in his Divine goodness knew where her heart truly belonged. It belonged to God and not the godforsaken trade she'd had to turn to for money.

"Why do you drive yourself so hard?" he asked

"For Monique's sake, I must free her from this squalor."

Father Lavergne raised his face to the grey sky. "Never forget, Fantine, you are of my flock. Knock when you need me."

* * *

Two years had elapsed since Captain Moreau left. Fantine pushed herself to the limits of her physical strength and added another chest under the bed. She invested in gold bought on the black market. The seasons rushed in with great expectations and flew out with a sense of finality, and Monique sang.

On July 14, Paris celebrated *La Bastille*. The night was warm; the glow worms waltzed and showered the sky like meteors. Sheets of fireworks burst into greens, yellow, gold, purple, blue and scarlet against the dark sky. Accordions played along the boulevards and the people celebrated with abandon.

Babette, the fortune teller, stood gossiping with L'Hirondelle near the entrance to the large gabled house, Fantine prepared to go out with her daughter and join the people of France to commemorate that significant night. They wore blue dresses with large-brimmed white hats and red shoes.

Fantine and Monique made their way down from the attic. Babette's door was open. Fantine noticed a large copper saucepan simmering on the primus stove on a wooden stand. Joujou ran around the room in frantic circles. The terrified monkey scampered up the faded burgundy velvet drapes and pulled at the long frayed cords. She tugged at them with her sharp teeth until it snapped. The yarn got entangled around her leg. Trapped and panic-stricken she trailed the cord behind her and zigzagged blindly around the primus. It toppled and hit the floor. The small, dented lid opened and paraffin oil soaked the carpet. The naked flame caught on the oil and Fantine gasped in horror as the room was set ablaze. Joujou was soon overcome by the intense heat and thick smoke. She whimpered and then lay limp near the sink.

"Ah! *Mon Dieu*," Fantine heard L'Hirondelle cry out from below as flames licked ferociously at the drapes.

"Joujou," Babette clutched at her chest, crashing up the stairs. "Joujou!" She dived blindly through the furnace.

Choking on the acrid smoke, Fantine spotted her pet. The flames raced towards her. She was trapped. Babette picked up Joujou and ran to the window, screaming in agony, clothes on fire.

Fearing impending doom, Fantine yelled to Monique, "The chests! Come quickly, we must get the money." With lightning speed, they reached the attic. "Grab the small one, I'll carry the second."

With terror in her heart, Fantine watched the stairs as they descended. Monique started to cry.

"*Ma petite*, we can do it!"

The flames belched below. Gaston, still drunk, was dragged out by his wife. Phillipe looked up at Fantine, alarmed and confused. He bolted away leaving them to the mercy of the flames.

In the street, on the festival of *La Bastille*, the people looked on in horror as Babette clasped Joujou to her bosom, her hair burning like a torch and the monkey's long tail aglow. Together, like a shooting star, they plunged to their death.

Fantine and Monique dodged the flames lapping at the floorboards as they raced through the thick smoke to the front door. The old house groaned and collapsed. The crowds stampeded towards them. Duval was the first to reach Fantine.

"Take us to Father Lavergne," Fantine panted.

* * *

They sheltered at *St Joseph de L'Apparition* monastery for three months before Fantine started house-hunting and purchased a colonial style house with a large balcony, several spacious rooms and high ceilings. Patches of peonies, daffodils and cosmos filled the garden with colour. Nearby a small wood thrived with beech, spruce and poplar.

"The old lady who'd owned it had passed away," said Fantine. "Her son— an anthropologist—is planning to return to Borneo. I believe he wishes to stay there indefinitely…one of those eccentric types. He's dropped the price considerably. Sheer luck of course." Fantine laughed. "I love this place."

Father Lavergne stood beside her admiring the property. "Borneo, most interesting," pondered Father Lavergne. "The Ibans and Kayans—natives of the island—used to practice head-hunting. They were cannibals, did you know that?"

"No!"

"Indeed, yes. My dear Fantine, how can I be of help?"

"Well, I require a gardener to prune the trees, cut the hedges and shrubs, lawns and generally clear the mess. The house also needs painting. I shall purchase some furniture next week. First thing tomorrow morning, I am going to see *Monsieur* LaSalle, the lawyer, regarding the transactions of deeds and financial documents."

* * *

Autumn arrived, the trees had mantles of yellow and russet leaves. The rooks, jackdaws and crows rasped in the tall pines. Flocks of swifts and house-martins swarmed while wild geese honked in formation, bidding farewell to another season, many never to return.

By mid-autumn, wealthy gentry flocked to Madam Fantine's house, the most sought after courtesan in Paris. Fantine also purchased a small cottage on the outskirts of Paris, a home for both her and Monique. Her daughter never knew of her mother's secretive life.

Fantine snuggled between white, starched cotton sheets and tartan mohair blankets. She brushed her face against the soft pillow laced with frills.

A great longing welled insider her. She could hear Captain Moreau's voice and remembered the morning he left.

The moon peeped out from behind the fleecy clouds. A nightjar whirred above the silver birch. Fantine tossed and turned through the night until at last, she fell asleep, the yearning for her captain in her heart.

* * *

Monique attended the most exclusive school under the tutelage of Maestro Rambanini, conductor and composer, who trained her and paved the way to her success.

"I shall make you the greatest opera singer yet." roared Maestro Rambanini. "So sing, my nightingale, and tear at the hearts of France...Ah! Your mother's powerful words..."

The nightingale's name was everywhere. On the street posts, restaurants, concert halls, theatres and even on the retired old Duval's milk cart.

Captain Moreau crossed the semi-lit cobbled street. The skeleton of old charred oak beams loomed in the darkness where once had stood the gabled house. He shuddered. For a while he stood there. An emaciated mongrel cocked his leg and urinated on the street lamp post. The dog turned; his sunken eyes like black sockets as he peered apprehensively at the man. He sniffed the air then darted towards the dustbins. Captain Moreau followed the animal's direction. The pungent smell of garlic, onion and fried fish hit him as he entered the crowded restaurant.

Monsieur Flaubert noticed the immaculately dressed, tall Captain in navy blue uniform, studded gold buttons, blue cap and black shiny shoes. Such customers were rare.

"Good evening, *monsieur*, I wonder if you could tell me what happened to that building opposite." The captain stood before Flaubert, hat in hand.

Flaubert rubbed his eyes. "A terrible accident! The place caught on fire. Babette, who lived upstairs, ran to save her monkey but they were trapped. She held her pet and jumped from the window. Both were alight when they hit the ground."

"What happened to the other people who lived here?" asked Captain Moreau.

"Some escaped."

"I am looking for a lady. Fantine was her name and she had a little girl."

Flaubert looked at him, astonished. "Fantine…I haven't seen her since the fire. She worked for me in the kitchen."

"Any idea who would know of her whereabouts?"

"I can think of two friends of hers. Father Lavergne from *St Joseph de L'Apparition* monastery and Duval, the milkman. I am sure she kept in touch with Duval. He lives at the back of the old market."

"Thank you, *monsieur*."

"My pleasure, *capitain*."

* * *

The white-washed colonial house was the most unique brothel, the only one of its kind. The Parlor room was sumptuous. In the corner was a large damask antique oak table and on it a collection of decanters and flagons. The exquisitely designed parquet floor gleamed in polished shades of brown. The room was artistically furnished with Egyptian leather pouffes and Turkish brocade couches. In the adjacent dining room, the refractory tables and benches were made of yew, auburn tinged with yellow. On the high walls hung several magnificent Persian carpets and from the ceiling, several lanterns swung from solid brass chains. The boudoirs were in Fantine's favourite colours.

"There is a gentleman who wishes to see you, *Madame*. He wouldn't give his name. He seems to know you." The young courtesan stood at the door and smiled.

Fantine looked through the window and glanced at the leaves below beneath the dull sky. "Let the gentleman in."

She watched Captain Moreau enter the room and trembled. Memories awoke and stirred inside her. Melancholy veiled her happiness at seeing him again.

For the first time in her life, she wanted to purge the past and fly on wings of fate towards that which was ultimately good and clean. Fear surged through her, making her light-headed.

"Life has not scarred your face, Fantine."

She pursed her lips, fighting the tears that filled her brown eyes. "You haven't changed either.'

A single tear trickled and imbedded itself in the groove of her dimple. He brushed a finger against her cheek and gently scooped up the tear.

"I hope that's a tear of happiness," he whispered.

Suddenly Fantine looked up wildly. She wanted to eradicate the house, sink it into oblivion. Manacled to the filthy past, how could she free herself from its clutches? Life was a lousy game.

Only Monique was pure. Her voice was pure. Stricken, she looked into

Moreau's eyes, meeting his penetrating gaze. He was a magnetic force walking with her through the green valley, slowly ascending the hill with the rising sun.

Fantine was attacked by paroxysms of tremors and swooned. Distressed, Moreau caught her in his arms and laid his beloved on the bed. He sat beside her and sponged her feverish face.

* * *

"Let's go to my country house," she said to him later that afternoon. "Monique is away at boarding school and it will be peaceful there. Just the two of us."

"Darling, I can only stay for two weeks. I was instructed by my company to sail the ship back to Scotland." Moreau puffed on his pipe. "Trade between Europe, Africa and the Far East is extremely dangerous these days. U-boats lurk in the oceans."

"What will you do then?" Concerned, Fantine frowned.

"I have plans. Risky with close friends in Cherbourg. As you are aware, darling, Germany is advancing through Europe like a cancer. The bastards will soon invade France. It is not safe for me. I shall reside in Plymouth secretly. My comrades in France will deliver messages to you from me." He tapped his pipe in the ashtray. "They hide in coves with their small boats and sneak across the channel by night, barmy devils!" Moreau chuckled.

Impulsively, he knelt in front of Fantine, raised his sad eyes and whispered, "*Je taime*, Fantine, *mon coeur est brisé*. I don't want to leave you." He kissed her warm hand. "We will share our destiny together. The Frigate birds are waiting beyond the golden sands."

Fantine was enraptured.

* * *

On May 12, 1940, the Germans entered Paris. Fantine and Duval joined the French Underground. She played a double role as courier for the French Resistance and a Madam entertaining high rank German officers. Astute, fearless and daring, she infiltrated the core of the Nazi intelligence network through her liaison with the German officers, and supplied the French Underground with vital information about troop maneuvers, ammunition depots and factories in Germany.

Obersturmfuhrer Hans Shultz, a regular customer and *OberHauptman* von Shwerer, who had recently arrived from Germany, entered the elegant house. Fantine greeted them at the door in her gorgeous, turquoise dress, two blood hounds followed behind. *OberSturmfuhrer* Hans Schultz clicked his heels together.

"Good evening, Madam."

"Good evening."

"You look absolutely stunning." He removed his hat and gave it to the maid.

"Thank you." She smiled.

"May I introduce my friend, *Oberhauptman* von Shwerer?"

"How do you do?"

The prying cold eyes of the Nazi officer sent a shiver through her body.

"You have excellent taste, *fraulein*. The architecture, the furnishings... Ah!" he exclaimed, walking towards the hanging Persian carpets. "A masterpiece...my compliments."

"Would you like a drink first, gentlemen?" she asked. "We have excellent cuisine tonight."

OberStumFuehrer Schultz touched Fantine's hand. "I think we will first have a little schnapps. I went to the opera last night—saw *Il Travatore*. The soprano—they call her *The Nightingale*—she was superb. What a performance she gave. Have you heard her?"

"Yes, several times," Fantine answered.

"So young," he remarked. "In which opera did you see her?" he asked with curiosity.

Fantine sipped her wine. "The one I liked best was Mascagni's *Cavalleria Rusticana.*"

"I would like to meet her." He touched Fantine's hand again. "Perhaps she could give a performance of German music." He scrutinized her face for a few seconds. "May I take you to the opera one day?"

"I'd be delighted."

* * *

In the house of ill-fame, Madame Fantine sold her body but not her loyal heart. She shed tears of martyrdom; she plotted and conspired against the Germans, to save the people of France. Fantine harbored the men and women of the Resistance who slipped through the concealed passage in the wood. She transmitted radio messages from her cellar below.

Captain Moreau risked his life. He shuttled many prisoners of war in his small boat across the English Channel. With the help of the partisans, he succeeded to meet with Fantine on several occasions in the remote caves in the forests before escaping back to England each time. The hunter and the vixen played a dangerous game. *OberHauptman* von Shwerer saw the hate in Fantine's eyes; he did not trust her and waited.

"We are being watched," said Fantine to Duval. "I think you had better not come to the house anymore, unless it is imperative and then, only at night. I haven't been to Flaubert's restaurant for ages, perhaps we could meet there. It is less conspicuous."

OberHauptman von Shwerer, cordial but aloof, was always accompanied by his blood hounds. Concerned for her safety and Monique's future, Fantine decided to pay a visit to Father Lavergne, and entrusted her testament to him. Monique would inherit Fantine's properties, but all other assets she bequeathed to the church.

Fantine was under constant surveillance by *Oberhauptman* von Shwerer. The day she met Duval at Flaubert's restaurant he followed, then detoured and drove to her house with his two bloodhounds. They sniffed the scent to the entrance of the hidden trapdoor leading to the underground tunnel.

That night, Duval, Fantine and six other patriots of the Resistance drank a toast to freedom and sang the French anthem. It was then that *OberHauptman* von Shwerer stormed the concealed passage with a squad of soldiers.

The cellar was full of rifles, hand grenades, cases of explosives, radio transmitters and receivers, files and documents in code. After several days of interrogation under extreme torture, Duval and his friends were shot and Fantine's brothel was closed.

"And you, *Fraulein*." *OberHauptman* von Schwerer approached Fantine and traced his fingers upon her pale face. "What shall we do with you?"

She raised her eyes to the tiny barred window in her cell and smiled. "You cannot kill an idea. You cannot take away hopes and dreams."

"I am going to make you pay, *Fraulein*. Not with your life, that is much too easy." His left eye twitched nervously. "I shall let you live and throw you back in the streets as a pathetic human being. When I finish with you, I shall erase that smile forever from your face." He walked out briskly.

Dr Johann Gruber, the Nazi surgeon, poured the hydrochloric acid with great dexterity all over her face. Her screams reverberated through the walls of the prison. They dumped her on *La Place de Misericorde* and the officers laughed as their car sped away.

The corrosive acid ravaged her face, but by some miracle, the dimple on her left cheek was spared. Father Lavergne gave her shelter and nursed Fantine with great tenderness. She retreated to a small room at the back of the monastery and lay for hours on the iron bed looking at the Crucifix.

"Promise me, Father, that you will never reveal my fate to Monique. Let her only remember her mother died for France."

* * *

La Boheme was a great success.

The applause in the Opera House was sensational, electrifying. Many broke down and wept shamelessly.

Monique dined with *Obersturmfuehrer* Hans Shultz that evening.

"You remind me of someone I knew." He paused, studying her lovely young features. "She lived in Paris, you look so much like her, and the eyes, the mouth … it is incredible." He lit his pipe and gazed across the Seine where swans preened themselves on the smooth water. "She was rather strange and secretive, although educated and most intelligent. Perhaps, I might say, cunning. Would you like to hear more? I'd hate to spoil a lovely evening."

"Oh, please do!"

"I won't go into details but she was caught by the Gestapo for subversive underground activities. A high price to pay for patriotism."

He sent puffs of smoke into the air. "Fantine was her name—late thirties with sad brown eyes and a mass of curls. I can't get over the resemblance between you two."

Monique's face turned ashen. "You will forgive me but I am rather tired and would like to have an early evening. I'm afraid the performance tonight drained my energy."

"Of course, I'll take you home. May I call you again soon?"

"Yes." Monique's world had shattered.

* * *

"I don't know where she was sent," said Father Lavergne to Monique the next day. "She was whisked away with Duval and other underground friends. No one knows of her whereabouts. It is dangerous to meddle with the Gestapo. They must never suspect you are her daughter."

As the harsh winter swept across Europe, the war left its scar of death everywhere. Monique believed that her mother had disappeared like thousands of others, either kept in concentration camps or shot.

Fantine stayed with Father Lavergne until the end of the war, when Captain Moreau stepped into her life again. She sat near the window looking at the avenues of the poplars bursting with buds, her face covered with a black veil. A flock of starlings swooped down near a bed of crocuses and pulled long worms from the warm earth. Hearing the door open, she thought it was the priest, and turned. She uttered a piercing cry like the desolate howl of a wounded animal.

"No Fantine...no, do not cry...no more tears...I shall never leave you again, never."

He lifted her veil and brushed his lips over her scarred features. "Oh! I love this face more than ever now..." Fantine's tears flowed.

* * *

After a moving applause at the end of *Madame Butterfly*, the house was hushed. Fantine stood on the balcony and clapped her last *adieu*. Monique lifted her eyes to the unknown woman veiled in black and smiled. Fantine bowed as Captain Moreau led her away.

"Come, Fantine, let me take you home to Montserrat where the brilliant red frigate birds nest."

6 FLOSSIE AND THE BOWERY MOB

Downtown Brooklyn, in a place called the Bowery where drunkards and the destitute despaired, drowning their sorrows in the bottle, it cost less than a dime a night to sleep on a tattered mattress in the House of Alms. Many never woke from what would be their last sleep. A spark of divinity streamed the dark alleys where God's fingers touched the weary, forgotten humanity lying in the gutters.

Tucked away at the edge of this dismal place, stood a small house where an elderly woman dozed in her rocking chair on the porch, her tortoise-shell cat purring in her lap. On the leaning fence was a hand-written sign—*Room to rent*. Four young men, neatly-dressed in dark cotton trousers and grey jumpers, stood and looked around.

"This will make an excellent hideout. Perfect for our business. Let's go and chat to the lady," said Tiger adjusting his blue cap, his club foot dragging, tired from the long walk.

The Bowery gang followed him into the yard. The gate's rusted hinges squeaked and the cat scampered as the strangers approached. The woman lifted her head.

Lonie, Buck and Tango greeted and doffed their hats. Tiger moved slowly, limping up the three rotten wooden stairs. "Good morning, we would like to rent a room if it is available, please?" Tiger addressed her, his manners polished.

"Eh?" she muttered, and put one hand over her ear.

"She can't hear a damn word you say. Stone-deaf," Tango whispered.

"I'll raise my voice as loud as possible. If she can't hear this time, I'll scribble a note. You always carry pen and paper." Tiger stepped forward and repeated his request.

She watched his lips move, reading his words. "I'm Flossie, and you are...?"

"We are...contractors...buyers and sellers of merchandise. This is Lonie, Buck and Tango, and I am Tiger."

The lady nodded, rose and led them through the house and down into the basement. In the corner, a few dusty pieces of antique furniture stood haphazardly arranged, and a collection of photographs decorated the far-side wall. On the opposite side, a kerosene stove stood on a rickety table.

"You can use the back door to go in and out of the house so we won't disturb each other. Long ago, this district was beautiful and peaceful. Now it is a dark hole of slime. My husband drank himself to death. Times are hard." She puffed and blew all the way down the stairs to the damp basement. If the mice that scurried in the crevices could write on the wall, they'd tell of Flossie's years of loneliness, poverty and unhappiness.

The woman shuffled then stopped, took a deep breath and said, "At the rear of the basement is a bath, sink and toilet. The rusty chain doesn't always work. This door leads to the garden." There," she indicated to a large stone table and tap beside it. "You can scrub your washing and hang it on the fence, as long as it doesn't collapse." She laughed and waved towards the leaning pickets.

The four men warmed to her wit and humour.

"When I was young and strong, I used to pull the laundry out of a copper drum with a long pole. It's still there, hidden behind the oak tree. Once a week, the timber man used to deliver bags with logs to heat the water. He doesn't anymore so we have to heat the water on the stove or have a cold wash. I miss chatting with him. I often invited him for morning tea. He was so charming! I would like a weekly rent of $8. That's not too much, is it?" She chuckled.

Two small dimples carved her gaunt cheeks. Tiger touched her gnarled hands, gazed into her sunken eyes and said, "Thank you."

"You're welcome. I hope we'll be friends. It's lonely here."

Flossie was grateful, deaf to the world. The four men became a miracle in her life. There was food in the house again. The gallant brigands supplied all the groceries she required. She no longer retired to bed with hunger pains. When her crippled bones were too tired, they helped her with the chores, clearing the garden and mending the rickety fence.

One Friday morning, the four men milled around the crowded market. Buck and Lonie weaved across to the kosher chicken stalls. The two watched several women on the opposite side haggling over prices with the frustrated vendor.

The vendor argued back as he flung both hands in the air. "Bloody women," he muttered.

Buck and Lonie took advantage of his distraction and slipped two chickens under their coat and disappeared. They could still hear the silly women arguing as they walked away.

Meanwhile, Tango and Tiger filled their bags with fruit and vegetables and soon, the men escaped back to Flossie's in their rusty old station wagon.

Flossie played an important role in their lives too. She cooked their meals whenever she was able and captured their young hearts with the stories she told of her adventures long ago. The cat had gotten used their presence and no longer ran away when they came home. Lonie picked up the soft animal from Flossie's lap and cradled him. Startled, she woke and saw Buck swinging a chicken in each hand.

"Surprise, surprise," Buck shouted to the overwhelmed lady. Chickens were expensive, a luxury she couldn't afford. "To celebrate the Sabbath."

The banquet, cooked by the men was exquisite. Two roast chickens with stuffing, baked sweet potatoes, fresh parsnips, swede, pumpkin, turnips, carrots, leeks and gravy, and for dessert, rice pudding sprinkled with cinnamon.

Tiger sat beside Flossie, brushed her hand and said, "Put the leftovers in the larder. The food will be delicious tomorrow."

"Thank you all," she stammered, her eyes bathed in tears.

* * *

On the more affluent side of town, Judge Lawrence Montefiore strolled with his wife, Talia in the park. A stunning, graceful woman, the sun shone on her long, silky plaits. A boy ran towards them, holding the string of a kite. It glided, whirled then dived on the grass, landing at Montefiore's feet. He picked it up and handed the colourful toy to the youngster.

"Thank you, Sir."

The Judge stroked the child's soft curly hair and said, "Off you go. Try it again."

Montefiore had an obsession with hair and fur so obscure, so powerful he could not control it, rendering him giddy.

In his luxurious home in Manhattan, he kept three fluffy Persian cats and two huge, shaggy Saint Bernard. For hours, he brushed their coats and snuggled against them.

Every day, Talia accompanied her husband on a walk. Both loved the outings except for the rapacious insanity that scaled the walls of his mind. He'd freak and want to run his fingers through the children's hair.

Sensing his discomfort, Talia held his hand, trembling. "Come, Darling, let's go home."

Lying beside his wife, Montefiore untied her blue ribbon. Talia's shiny hair flowed onto her shoulders. The ivory teeth of his favourite dark brown comb, tinged with a deep red hue, weaved through her velvety blonde curls.

* * *

"We'll target Hymie's jewelry shop in the Bronx. He and his wife live above. Hymie is a simpleton, a schmuck," Tiger muttered.

"She is sharp. One has to watch her shifty eyes. They jump like a yo-yo. You can't tell whether she looks sideways or vertical. I've never seen eyes as weird as that woman's," Tango remarked.

"It's best not to show our faces as we have in the past, pretending to buy something. The Passover is next week. Orthodox Jews go to the synagogue for evening prayer. Good timing to fleece Hymie—the arrogant little man." Tiger sniggered.

Before returning home to celebrate the Holy Night of the Israelites' exodus out of Egypt, Lonie—expert locksmith and safe cracker—with his friends, plundered Hymie's loot. They sneaked into the back garden and slipped into the basement.

"We'll have to figure out where to hide the haul in here. The gold and silver is a worth a mint." Tiger scratched his head.

"I've noticed Flossie is not steady on her legs these days. We ought to buy her a wheelchair, a battery one. All she'll have to do is push a button or turn a knob. She could wheel herself to the park. We can demolish the front porch steps—they're unsafe—and build a ramp for her. I'm sure she'd love that. Listen to me talking like a soppy old bugger," Tiger said. "I can't believe how quickly we have become attached to the old girl, but she looks after us well."

"We've been living here for almost two years," Lonie remarked.

"Flossie's sad eyes remind me of my mother." Tiger blew his nose. "My father, the drunken bastard, used to beat her until she could hardly walk. I jumped on him once, but he flung me against the wall. Her lungs were weak and she was dying. Father walked out the door and we never saw him again, the slob."

"Remember when the four of us used to play in the street, growing up in the Bronx? You were always the gang leader," said Tango.

"Yes, I remember. Food was scarce on the table. Hunger pains bring bad memories. That's when we started stealing. We love Flossie. She is like a rainbow on the horizon and will always be there for us."

* * *

The following morning, munching on his hot dog, Buck stopped chewing suddenly and whispered, "Don't turn. Frankenstein and his henchmen are near the butcher's shop. They've spotted us."

As the racketeers crossed the street towards them, Lonie said to the vendor, "I'll have a hot dog as well."

"What are you doing in this neighbourhood?" Frankenstein scowled. "This is our turf."

"Having a hot dog and enjoying it. They're no good for your big gut. You're ready to pop," said Tiger.

Frankenstein was tall, square and fat, with dark hair, thin moustache, sunken eyes and a mole on his nose—an ugly fellow with a towering rage. He yelled, "I'll burn the lot of you, especially you, you club-footed mug— you'll sizzle."

Tiger growled, "You are a breeding nest full of maggots, threatening shopkeepers with your filthy protection money. Poor sods are frightened to tell the police in case you slit their throats or burn their shops. You bleed the poor buggers dry."

Suddenly the rivalry disappeared into the cold wind. Nervous, Frankenstein spotted a police car swerving towards them from the next street. "Cops!" he muttered and fled in the opposite direction with his scavenging gang.

* * *

In Autumn Tiger and his followers decided to meet with the black market gold dealer, Eisenstein, a brilliant businessman who sold and exported treasure to European customers.

"The dollar is rapidly losing its value. I think we might have to contact Eisenstein and sell our gold and silver from Hymie's haul. He never asks questions. A man loyal in his profession. I like that quality." Tiger chuckled. "Later, we'll plan our next adventure."

They placed the gold, packed in leather bags, under the seats of the station wagon and headed north to the wharf.

"There's a car trailing us," said Buck.

"Yes, I spotted Lucia's car. Tomaso, One-eyed Maggot and Frankenstein keep putting their heads out the window making sure they don't lose us," Tiger mumbled.

"We'll shake them off near the river, circle around the pillars. They must never discover Eisenstein's hideouts." Tango eased back off the accelerator. In the dim lights of the wharf, smog swirled, creating an eerie scene. "We'll drift in slowly and park, well-hidden, behind the two large containers," said Tiger.

Switching off the engine and rolling quietly into the shadows, they brought the car to a stop. Getting out quietly, Lonie and Tango crawled between the stacks of crates as Buck and Tiger buried themselves in the bales. Deep shadows sleeved in and around a looming crane. Whistling, a guard appeared on his rounds from the end of the pier. He saw someone running and gave chase with his flashlight. From the shadows, the Bowery gang watched as Frankenstein, Tomaso, Lucia and one-eyed Maggot crouched behind a container and waited.

The watchman froze for a moment. Cautious, pistol in hand, he moved, startling the dockyard cat that jumped out with a screech. The gangsters sprang out from behind the container and ran across the docks. Treading closely on their heels, the guard fired at the base of the crane where Tomaso hid. The bullet ricocheted off the steel, shattering Tomaso's groin as he screamed in agony.

Before the guard had a chance to reload his weapon, Frankenstein held a gun against his head. With only a moment's hesitation, he pulled the trigger. The guard slumped to the ground with a gaping hole in his forehead.

From his hiding place, Tiger watched the scene unravel before him. He gnashed his teeth. "He killed the guard! The poor man didn't have a chance. Let's cut them down."

Like the rats that roamed the docks, the two gangs dodged and hid, a barrage of shots zooming across the waterfront.

Detouring in semi-dark, Tiger slipped on an oil slick and crashed to the ground Frankenstein leapt towards him, One-Eyed Maggot and Lucia close behind him. Tango pressed his torch on, the strong light blinding their eyes. In that moment, Buck and Lonie mowed them down.

Tiger stopped, breathing heavily as he looked at the carnage, the macabre effusion of blood and said, "Let's throw the vermin in the Hudson." The next day, a pedestrian discovered the bodies floating in the river. Dock workers reported an abandoned car on the wharf and the body of the night watchman. .

Captain McLeary from the 23rd Precinct told the Press, "There are no clues as to who committed this crime. What we do know is they killed a big fish in the underworld that has been on our list for a long time. They were dangerous animals. There were no witnesses and the wharf was deserted except for the night watchman, who sadly became an innocent victim of what we suspect is mob warfare. This city is infested with these predators. Like moles they tunnel deeper and deeper, making it harder for us to catch them."

The case file was kept open, unsolved like many others. No-one claimed the bodies, except that of the innocent watchman. As news of more robberies and organized crime replaced the headlines, the mobsters were forgotten. In their paupers' graves, only the worms feasted.

* * *

In the sordid arena of the black market, Eisenstein stood his ground as a businessman and ranked a gentleman. Eisenstein, an Englishman now living in the Bronx, puffed on his pipe. "Bloody marvelous! You are a genius with sticky fingers. Congratulations."

He rummaged through the gold bracelets, rings, pendants, necklaces, armlets, antique repeaters with golden chains, and gold coins. "Bloody marvelous," he repeated. "I have an excellent Swiss customer interested

foremost in diamonds and precious stones. Anyone on the horizon, hmm?"
He guffawed as he adjusted his waistcoat.

"Maybe..." Tiger winked.

"I am a fair man—perhaps not honest but fair." Eisenstein opened his
briefcase. "This is your cut. You deserve it. The shoeshine boys on 42nd
Street will be our pigeons. We must never meet in the same spot. *Au revoir*."
He doffed his hat and disappeared under the bridge.

From then on, the cat burglars and the English crook met in cemeteries,
chapels, on beaches and in forests. The gallant pilferers hid their treasure in
Flossie's basement. Masters of ingenuity, they constructed partitions and
stored their wealth in tins inside the wooden walls and covered the sides
with Persian carpets.

Meanwhile the underworld hornets hounded Eisenstein, a slippery shark to
capture. They wanted their share and their noose was tightening. In a
shrewd move, he transferred his fortune to Switzerland and Argentina,
eluding their net. He disguised himself as a tramp, grew a beard and wore a
long dirty coat and black beret.

On a cold and blustery day in late November, he swiftly changed garments
and became the gentleman took a train and fled to Canada. Soon after
arriving in Montreal, he sailed on a banana cargo ship to South America.

* * *

The Depression hit the wealthy and the paupers, strong and weak,
spreading its ugly black wings. The stock exchange crashed. Bonds and
shares collapsed. Long queues trailed the pavements near bakeries with the
famished waiting to buy bread. Like a plague of locusts, vandals prowled
the streets and robbed. In a valley of despair, without hope, stripped to the
bone, many lost the will to live and committed suicide.

In Flossie's basement, Tiger sat with his mob as they sorted through their haul of the day. "It is dangerous to walk in the streets. People will skin you to buy food. They are desperate and hungry. The Depression has robbed us of our district. Our haul is getting smaller with all the other looters out there. We'll empty the merchant's shop beyond the shoe factory. I dislike the selfish man," he said. "We'll stock Flossie's larder, kitchen and basement. There won't be enough room to fill the station wagon. Gideon, the hunchback, lives behind the markets. He delivers fruit and vegetables and is always ready to help. We'll hire his horse and cart on Friday night and return them on Saturday at dawn. He'll be pleased with the extra money. Offer a year's income for a few hours."

With their plan in place and the strategy set, Flossie's basement became a connoisseur's delight as the mob stocked it with food stolen from the merchant's shop. She sat on the armchair beside Tiger, her head upon his shoulder in a rare show of affection.

"I love you all." Her weakened voice was almost inaudible. "Sometimes I fear death when I go to bed. The old ticker, pumping and pumping away, is very tired. Death is but a little sleep. How can I ever thank you for the happy years?" She turned and gazed at Buck, Lonie and Tango, then patted Tiger's hand.

"Flossie," said Tango, "You are a miracle in our lives. I am going to make a lovely pot of tea and we can have a little cake." He got up and wiped his eyes on a handkerchief. Flossie didn't hear. She'd dozed off.

"Paper money has little value at present, though the dollars we have will last us a lifetime. These oppressive days will pass. Remember Eisenstein's words—diamonds, precious stones, gold coin, concentrate on these. Ultimately, we'll find an avenue to sell the merchandise. There's a place not far from here that belongs to Judge Lawrence Montefiore. Word on the street is he's a cultured man, top of the ladder, although a tad supercilious and self-indulgent. He has a fortune in art, jewelry and collectables. Why don't we raid his place?" Surprised, his friends gaped at him. "We've never tried anyone of his position. At times I feel as tired as Flossie. We are like the tide, rolling and sweeping in and out." Tiger rubbed his eyes.

"He has two huge Saint Bernards. They run free in his garden," Buck confirmed. "They also have a pretty maid. I saw her feeding the dogs. What will we do about them?"

"We'll have to plan this one carefully and execute it this coming winter," said Tango.

At dawn, the fog lifted. Flossie stoked the fireplace and put the kettle on. Later in the morning, her devoted lodgers entered the kitchen and prepared breakfast. When they'd finished their meal, Flossie said, "Let's sit in the other room. I wish to confide a secret. Come." Slightly dizzy, she stumbled as she stood. Tiger rushed to help her and clasped his hands around her waist. "Now now, I am fine," she murmured. "I had two sisters, long gone, so is my husband—useless buck, never had any children. You came into my life like a rainbow. I am not going to waffle too much. This week—and I mean this week—I want you to find a lawyer. Take me to him. I'll make a will. I never needed one before. I am going to give you my house, a small but cosy home. The chimney is slightly crooked but you'll have shelter and never have to worry about rent or being thrown out into the Bowery gutters. I just love you," she sang out.

Tiger knelt beside Flossie. The silence was deafening except for Tiger's sniffles and the spit of crackling logs in the hearth.

"Your tears are my tears; your grief is my grief. It's best if I remain in the dark. Secrets get buried in the grave." Flossie blew her nose.

Tiger found the most prestigious law firm he could—Entrecasteau and Associates. He made an appointment for Flossie and themselves, scheduled for Monday morning the following week. They parked their car on the back street, out of sight of curious eyes.

Well-dressed, they entered the office and sat on plush, wide armchairs. On the walls hung three magnificent paintings—a sixteenth century Brigantine, a Schooner and a Cutter.

"Beautiful," Lonie whispered, his eyes riveted on them. "Bet they're worth a bit."

"Good morning," Claude Entrecasteau, the lawyer greeted. He was punctual and Tiger was pleased by that. "Please step into my office."

Tiger helped Flossie into a chair, her petite, fragile frame lost in the massive leather seat. Entrecasteau noticed Tiger's clubfoot but said nothing.

The lawyer spoke gently to the old lady. "Madam, your full name, please?"

Tiger interrupted with impeccable manners. "Raise your voice, please. She can't hear well."

"Flossie McVie," she answered.

"I understand you wish to make a will and bequeath your house to the four gentlemen present in this room?" He pronounced each syllable slowly and clearly.

"Yes, I do, most definitely," she cried out, a smile on her wrinkled face.

"Because of your age, you might need to bring us a medical report from your doctor before you sign the appropriate documents," he stated.

"Eh? A medical report? What for?"

"Well, you see, we need to have confirmation that you are of sound mind when you bequeath valuable property to non-family members."

"Of sound mind? *Well!* Let me tell you something, Mr Entrecasteau—" Flossie stopped and held her chest, her breath heaving in and out.

Tiger came to the rescue. "Calm down, Flossie, calm down." He patted her trembling hands.

"Will you excuse me for a few moments? I shall consult with my barrister. This is a vital issue," said Entrecasteau, and left the room.

Tiger attempted to calm the agitated Flossie, offering her water and rubbing her cold hands to soothe her. It seemed an eternity before the lawyer and barrister returned.

"Mrs McVie, do you fully understand your commitment, a most important decision?" the barrister asked.

Like a pack of wolves ready for the kill, Entrecasteau and his associate's penetrating gazes stung.

"I might be deaf but not stone deaf." She paused. "Old, yes, but my word is as good as yours. Do you think I'm daft? I don't lie and I haven't been to a doctor in years...don't intend to see one. This is my final answer, you two...bagels." Flossie adjusted her scarf and cleared her throat. "What a lot of *bobkés*. This is humiliating. There is nothing wrong with my mind." She flung the scarf sideways.

The room was hushed. It seemed even the walls closed in and listened. Flossie's words stabbed the heart. "Love is the greater gift. I love Tiger, Lonie, Buck and Tango, my true friends. My family vultures are all dead. Do you have any idea what it is to live in a silent world, afraid of the dark nights and lonely days with only a cat for company? The day we met it drizzled, and then the rainbow painted the sky with colours. These men are my friends, my rainbow. Before God, I swear in all sincerity and love, I wish to give my home to them. Now, let's get on with the will. It shouldn't take you too long to draw it up. It's only a tiny house on a tiny block." Flossie laughed.

"I like your sense of humour," said Entrecasteau.

"I have another admirer." Flossie's tears streamed upon her pale face.

The documents were completed, witnessed and signed. Tiger paid the lawyer a substantial fee for his prompt service and shook hands.

"Goodbye, Mrs McVie." Entrecasteau, always the French gentleman, kissed her cold hand.

* * *

Tango disliked the winter. Warming his frozen feet and hands near the fireplace caused him to develop chilblains. His toes and hands swelled. In bed they were extremely itchy. Before leaving, he rubbed some ointment onto his hands and feet.

The four took the subway just as it started to rain. A biting cold wind swept over the city. They hurried across the park, avoiding the street lamps and sticking to the shadows. Not a soul stirred in the houses beyond.

In the warmth of his fire-lit drawing room, Judge Lawrence Montefiore reviewed a bizarre espionage case. Page by page, he flipped through the file. Talia brought him a mug of hot cocoa then curled up near the hearth. Three Persian cats purred beside her.

"Why don't you go to bed?" Montefiore asked, his *pince nez* perched on his nose.

"I'll wait for you, darling. I am restless thinking of the dogs. It's freezing outside."

"Saint Bernards have thick coats. In Switzerland they withstand extreme cold temperatures. Don't worry; their kennels are sheltered from the cold weather." Montefiore sipped his drink.

"This is not Switzerland. They were born here." She chuckled.

"I can't concentrate. Let's go to bed," Montefiore said.

As he led his wife out the drawing room and up the ornate wooden staircase, Daisy, the housekeeper, switched off the hall light and returned to her quarters. In the bedroom, Montefiore combed Talia's hair enraptured by the blaze of golden locks.

Outside, in the freezing cold, the wind shrieked as Lonie, a genius locksmith, pried open the gate's heavy padlock. The robbers crept forward to the mansion.

"I hear the dogs. Quickly, before they sniff us out," said Tiger.

Lonie sprang the back door double latch and the men crept in. Tiger shone his torch towards the dining room. Cautious, he touched the pistol secured to his waist. In the middle of the room stood a tall sideboard. On copper hooks hung exquisite painted plates. Decanters, flagons and priceless antique ornaments decorated the wide drawers. A bookcase was tucked into the corner, making the room a cosy haven while outside hail showered down like white stringing balls.

The barking Saint Bernard pushed the door open, almost breaking the hinges. Like two bears in the forest chasing prey, their big feet pounded on the wooden floor boards.

Nervous, Tiger said to Buck and Lonie, "Quickly, escape through the unlocked door. I'll zigzag with Tango down the corridor."

The sniffling brutes were just behind them. One pounced on Tiger's back. Always prepared for unpredictable situations, Tango rummaged in his pocket, and found his pepper spray. A quick squirt in the burly Saint Bernard's face stung his eyes and he yelped in pain. "They'll be back in a while," said Tiger and stumbled blindly against a wall adjacent to the study and they hid behind it.

Upstairs in the room, Talia sat up, dislodging the comb from her husband's hand. "Listen, Tobias and Hercules are barking furiously. There may be intruders, darling. Please check."

Montefiore jumped out of bed, took his gun out his bedside drawer, and ran down the flight of stairs. Daisy, the maid, hearing the commotion followed closely behind Talia. Tobias hurled himself at Talia, stopping her from moving forward, his tail between his legs.

"What's wrong with Hercules?" Talia panicked as the dog approached slowly, his eyes swollen and red, and the fur around them damp with tears.

"The poor devil, I know what they've done. I smell the bastards," Montefiore whispered angrily. "Darling, crouch down beside the Devonport. Daisy, hide behind the curtains." Montefiore was drenched in perspiration. The brigands were armed and dangerous. His mind raced as he feared for Talia and the dogs.

Shivering, Daisy was concealed behind the velvet damask drapes, her night cap lopsided on her head. Hercules licked at her hand and she gently nudged him away with her foot.

Tobias snarled as he caught the strong scent of Tango's chilblain ointment and moved towards his hiding place.

In a panic, Tiger dragged his club foot towards the verandah. Montefiore heard the shuffling from opposite. He stood, aimed and fired, his bullet grazing Tiger's cheek. In the nick of time, the robber ducked, turned his head, pressed the trigger and fired back.

Like a phantom, Talia thrust herself on her husband. The deadly ball perforated her ribs and lodged in her heart. Numbly, Montefiore sank to the floor under her dead weight, cradled his wife, buried his face in her hair and wept. Daisy approached treading carefully towards them, kneeling beside her master and mistress. Tiger and Tango fled through the door to the balcony. The dogs' desolate howls flowed above the rain and followed them down the deserted road.

Flossie's bedroom light was on when the men entered the house. They opened her creaking door to find her fast asleep in the rocking chair. Tango picked up Flossie's favourite sheepskin blanket and covered her. The big clock chimed in the hallway.

* * *

The next morning, as Tiger prepared scrambled eggs for breakfast, their actions of the night before and the consequences it would bring down on them, played on his mind. He looked up as Flossie shuffled into the kitchen. "You must have slept well last night. Look at the time. It's almost ten. These eggs will build your muscles and make you strong."

"To be deaf is an advantage if I didn't hear a damn whisper," Flossie chortled.

Sensing Tiger's melancholy, Flossie watched him stirring the eggs. She mistook his deep silence for concern. "I will always be with you, Tiger. Like the eggs, your energy will flow in my old blood and help me shuffle along a bit longer."

Flossie unrolled her sleeve, revealing her shriveled biceps. "Look at those muscles, eh?"

She laughed at her own joke making Tiger want to laugh. Instead he wanted to cry. Destiny swayed in a storm.

Sitting in their car later, Buck flinched at the memory of the night before. "We nearly got caught. We could escape like Eisenstein did."

"Dumb, that's dumb. The roads, highways, and railways will all be blocked."

"What have I done? I never intended to kill her. So young…she appeared from nowhere…" Tiger hammered his fists on his head. "What are we going to do? We can't get caught. Flossie won't survive without us."

Tiger thought of his mother. He'd stolen to feed her, all these years, dragging his clubfoot around. Now he protected Flossie. She was old and trusted them, protected what hid in the silent walls of her humble home.

* * *

The tentacles of the law spread across New York, hunting for the fugitives.

"I see nothin' behind the curtains. I hear plen'ny shoot'n, jump'n peoples like popcorn. I scared, plen'ny scared," Daisy the housekeeper huffed.

"Hercules, he loony, pushin' and shovin', his big mouth on my backside. I pushin' the crazy dog."

Daisy rolled her eyes and kept repeating, "Loony dog, loony dog."

Commissioner Pascal Lombardi smiled and said, "Thank you for calling us, Daisy. You were quick and brave, thank you."

The house was armed with police, who stayed on the premises until the early hours of the morning. Demented with grief, the judge tightened his grip on Talia. He frothed at the mouth like a rabid dog, beyond reasoning.

"Get out," he yelled at the doctor. "I'll send you to the gallows. Don't touch my wife."

The compassionate physician and two male nurses restrained and sedated him. Lombardi patted the trembling Daisy on the shoulder.

"I'll post two policemen around the house for your protection. The judge will be in hospital for a few days. Do you have enough food for yourself and the two dogs, especially for the loony Hercules?" He smiled.

"Yes'sa." Her large, sad eyes were misty with tears.

The shameful and abhorrent crime ignited the newspapers, television, posters and radio. *Gangsters shoot Judge Lawrence Montefiore's wife.* The press swept the surrounding fence of the mansion guarded by the police.

* * *

Commissioner Pascal Lombardi was a close friend of the judge. They'd known each other for over twenty years. A few days after the murder, Montefiore reclined in the armchair, having been discharged from hospital.

"I am sure there were several of them," he said, gripping his pipe.

"I agree. I think it was the same gang who killed Frankenstein on the wharf with the mob. Unfortunately, the guard was caught up in the butchery. The sharks who came into your home have been thieving in different locations.

They've never been caught…very, elusive." Lombardi scowled.

"My dogs confused everyone, running from one entrance to another. The doors were wide open for the burglars to escape." Montefiore stopped as Daisy entered the room. "Good morning, Daisy," Montefiore greeted the devoted maid.

"Good mornin'. I bake cookies you like, Judge." She moved the flower pot to the right and placed the large teapot and biscuits in the centre.

"Thank you, Daisy."

She returned to the kitchen. The two Saint Bernards sprawled at the judge's feet and he stroked their thick, shiny fur.

"Any new leads on the case?" asked Pascal.

Montefiore shook his head. "Find my wife's killers…that's all I ask. I am tired now, and my body aches. Life without Talia is unbearable, forgive me." He walked the gentleman to the door. "Goodnight, Pascal."

* * *

The Bowery mob knew they needed a plan to lie low until the furor over the murder of Judge Lawrence Montefiore's wife died down.

"Let's go and see Sunshine, the fisherman. Selling fish to the market barely scrapes enough food for the family. We could go fishing with him, help the man financially. He lives down the coast which is several hours drive from here. The devil has a big heart. He'll be grateful." Tiger stretched and put both hands on his head. "I am almost afraid. For the first time, I would like to shape the course of our lives and pursue a good deed." He sighed. "We'll wait for a couple of days and drive along the isolated farms at night. Buck will drive. He has the eyes of a lynx."

A day before they left, Tiger knelt in front of Flossie. "We have to go away to close an important business deal. We'll be back in a week or two. Make sure you eat plenty of eggs." Tiger hugged her. "I love you, Flossie, my Flossie."

"Come back home safely, Tiger."

He cupped his palms on her tired face and prayed they would.

* * *

Eli Sunshine's wife took fresh bread from the oven and put it on the table next to a jug of goat's milk.

"What have you been doing since I last saw you?" Sunshine queried.

"Export, import—that kind of stuff," Tiger stated.

"The old tub still battles the waves, needs tucking here and there. You helped me cork the leaks last time." Sunshine chuckled.

"Yes, I remember. I miss those golden days. Should have been a fisherman and joined you. I hope what we propose will please you and your lovely wife." Tiger watched her smile. "How about a break from work? We need one too."

"Captain Sunshine, your wife, daughter and the four of us could navigate south along the coast and anchor in the coves. I can't think of anything more exciting than an extended fishing trip," Tango blurted.

"Lonie and I have experience with sails," Buck chirped.

Tiger stood and tapped Sunshine on the back. "Don't get a shock and don't ask questions. Miracles do happen. We will give you an advance for the loss of income, stock the boat with provisions, and travel all expenses paid, plus we'll leave you ample cash to restore the tub. This you could do when we return from vacation."

"Be careful, though. You must refurbish it in stages or suspicious, rolling tongues might bombard you with questions. Simply say you've saved for years," Tango suggested.

"Now, let's toast with some more goats' milk. Do you keep goats?" Tiger asked.

"Yes, at the back. A nanny and billy."

"Some kids we keep for breeding, a source of income." Eli poured more milk in everyone's mug.

"Who will milk the goats when we are at sea?" Buck asked.

"My father."

Tiger unbuckled several leather bags filled with thousands of dollars. "This is our secret. It cements a bond of friendship for life." Tiger murmured.

"Best place to stash the money is in your old milk cans," Tango said.

* * *

Bonds, shares and stocks became obsolete. Demand for gold, diamonds and priceless jewelry was staggering, so was the looting and racketeering. The value of property plunged while debt soared. The destitute and hungry begged in the alleys. Stray cats and dogs prowled between empty dustbins, and the City wept.

"I do not trust anyone these days and asked you to come over. Important issues plague my mind. Do you mind if we discuss them?" said Montefiore.

"No, not at all. I'd be honored," Lombardi replied.

Slobbering, Hercules tried to untie the Commissioner's shoelace.

"Funny dog has peculiar habits. Daisy calls him Loony. Now, to another subject. How is the pursuit of the hyenas?" Montefiore rasped.

"They leave no stone unturned. Someone, something will dig the ferrets out. I shall hunt them. They will have no place to run." Grave-faced, Lombardi frowned.

"Daily I grieve for Talia, like a dagger in my heart. In the future, at the appropriate time, I intend to sell the house. Half the proceeds of the sale I wish Daisy to have." Montefiore was emphatic. "Yes, to Daisy. She has been with us for many years. Loyal, pure beyond all praise. Her mother lives in Harlem and cares for an invalid son. My married brother in Long Island is most comfortable. With the remaining half of my estate, I shall get off the stage and wander. Here is my will. There won't be much left."

Pascal was silent. He realized Montefiore was lost in the recessed corridors of his dark world.

"Perhaps one day I'll find Talia riding through the fog in the aspirations of my twilight years. Do I confuse you?"

"No, I am overwhelmed. You have a noble soul." Lombardi blew his nose.

"Please, protect Daisy from the vultures. She will need your help. I trust you implicitly. My sincere gratitude, thank you."

* * *

June was the hottest month on record. Temperatures soared for days. Flossie lit the small kerosene stove. She wanted to cook two hard-boiled eggs for breakfast. Unwell, her hands shook as she lifted the enamel saucepan.

The heat rendered her dizzy. Her blouse got entangled in the stove's dented handle. She pulled, over-balanced, tugged again and fell backwards, dragging the stove with her. The loose cap came off, spilling the kerosene. The flames licked her clothes and hair as she screamed Tiger's name. No-one heard. Within minutes Flossie's body was alight. Her roasted flesh oozed on the floor. The devouring fire belched through the wooden house like a furnace, down to the basement. The walls and beams tottered, tins filled with jewelry and money hidden in crevices, buckled from the intense heat. The wind rose. Ablaze under the boiling sun, the house crumbled. Black smoke spiraled across the saddened Bowery, Flossie's last *adieu*.

Bizarre case—old woman burnt in house fire. Jewelry and money hidden in the walls.

The newspapers whirled and stormed the city with shock. Entrecasteau, the lawyer, read the morning paper over breakfast. Half a toast in his mouth, he picked up the telephone.

"May I speak to the Commissioner, please? It's most urgent. Claude Entrecasteau, the lawyer. I'll be brief. I am referring to the strange case of the old lady who died in the fire. I'll be in the office all day. *Au revoir.*"

That evening at the mansion, Daisy prepared a savory dish for the Judge and Commissioner.

"We are closing in on them, Lawrence. We have to snare them. We know there are four. One has a club foot and limps. They are shrewd and know which way the wind blows. I am convinced they will not approach Entrecasteau or the insurance company. I doubt the house was insured." Pascal sipped his red wine. "To keep the ball rolling, I should put a poster in the newspapers about the club foot. They are slippery like eels and move fast. In the sewers one can obtain false number plates, passports and identities with a little money."

"Yes, maybe they purchase old bangers and keep changing. The blackguards are endowed with a gift for survival," Montefiore agreed.

Daisy brought a large custard bowl laced with cream.

"Delicious, thank you, Daisy. Give some to Tobias and Hercules. There's plenty for all."

"Yes'sa, I give 'em plen'ny."

"According to the lawyer, there was a heart-stirring bond between the lady and the 'Robin Hoods'." Pascal stroked Tobias head.

"Most interesting evening. It's late," said Montefiore.

"You'll hear from me soon." The Commissioner waved to Daisy.

* * *

A fortnight later, the fisherman's boat moored in the bay close too Sunshine's home.

"How can we express our gratitude? Worn out, battered by years of work, you gave me a once in a lifetime happiness. Like a singing lark, you are." Sunshine's laughter pealed with the wind.

The four returned to the Bowery. Tiger's blood turned cold, shivering as he spotted the cordoned-off area around the land where Flossie's house had once stood.

"Flossie," he stammered. "We'll drive around to the back of the cemetery. Perhaps the priest will tell us what's happened."

Pulling up at the church, Tango got out the car and rang the church bell. The priest came out.

"I wondered why the streets are sealed off?" he asked.

"A tragic accident. The old lady who lived over there perished in the fire. The cat escaped. She is with me now. I don't know the details. There is an investigation."

"Oh...thank you," said Tango. Stunned, he turned and walked back to the car.

The man of the cloth watched as they drove off in the station wagon.

"Flossie, my Flossie—all alone. I wasn't there when you needed me." Knots of anguish churned Tiger's insides and he retched, doubling over in pain.

The story petrel, a bird of ill omen rode upon Destiny's wings.

"We need a place to hide. I'm sure Gideon will let us bunk in his shed," Tango muttered.

"We must avoid the police on the roads. We'll be in a pickle should they follow us," said Lonie.

In the evening, Gideon—milk of human kindness—spread straw and hay on the muddy shed floor and brought his guests supper.

Heedful, the four men crossed the street the following morning and bought bagels and pies. Leaving the baker's shop, Tiger spotted the hot dog vendor.

"I love hot dogs."

They rushed towards him.

"Four please, plenty of mustard."

"I haven't seen that mean lot of gorillas since that day you nearly came to blows. The city is unsafe with vampires," the man stormed.

"They vanished! See you next time. Your hot dog is the best in New York," said Tiger gratefully.

Through the years of living in the Bowery, Flossie never attended Mass. To the priest she'd said, "My God is not in a House of Stone. I walk with Him everywhere."

The man of the cloth was suspicious when Tango asked about Flossie's home. He had spotted them in their car on several occasions, concealed under the oak tree, its branches swollen with acorns and spread like arms in supplication.

The Christian traitor sold his soul. He informed the police about the station wagon. He had no right to judge.

A soon as their car swerved around the corner near the tall hedge on the fence line of Flossie's property, a tidal wave of police surrounded them in ambush. The four were unarmed. Tiger did not stir. Lonie, Buck and Tango dived into the bush from the side door. For a split second, Tango turned.

"Bye, Tiger."

The massacre began. Like wingless butterflies his men dropped. Tears trickled down Tiger's cheeks.

* * *

Weeks of prolonged investigation, cross-examination and interrogation began. Claude Entrecasteau, Tiger's defense lawyer, handled the case. There was a hush in the court room except for the rasping of the crows in the trees.

"Under mitigating circumstances, in self-defense, I sentence you to five years imprisonment."

Tiger raised his head. The judge's eyes were veiled with desolation and loneliness. "Thank you, your Honour. Forgive me." The judge's grief was Tiger's bitter sorrow. He covered his face with his hands. "Forgive me," Tiger sobbed.

* * *

Over the three years that followed, Montefiore received a brief note from Tiger each month. "Forgive me."

The judge decided to sell his house and appointed Pascal, the Commissioner, to assist Daisy into her future investment.

"Please don't cry, Daisy. Some things are difficult to explain. Since Talia died, my heart strings are torn. I am going away. Perhaps one day I'll find peace. I have provided for you and your family. You'll never go hungry. Contact the Commissioner, a man I trust. He will assist you with your affairs. My brother in Long Island will take Tobias and loony Hercules. He loves dogs. My three cats are good company for your sick brother. We will leave the house the same day. Now, let's have hot chocolate." Montefiore sighed.

"Yes'sa," she sniffled.

Tiger's letter from prison returned the fourth year. Restless, the judge rented an apartment in Manhattan. Prey to melancholy, he bought a bottle of whiskey. Thoughts of the court flooded his mind, cases where he'd sent offenders to the gallows. Montefiore took another swig. Somewhere in the labyrinth rose the false perjurers, swearing under oath. The wealthy, arrogant society disguised in borrowed plumes and colours, toasting their drinks. Drowning in his sorrows, Montefiore slumped on the table, his bottle nearly empty.

* * *

When Judge Lawrence Montefiore's letters returned to Tiger in prison, he decided to contact Flossie's lawyer, Claude Entrecasteau.

Dear Sir,

I'll be most grateful if you could help me find the whereabouts of Judge Lawrence Montefiore's maid. I would much like to write to the lady and ask her forgiveness, make my peace with her. I shall pay you for your services when I get out.

Thank you,

Tiger

* * *

In his nomadic existence, he grew a beard. Montefiore had never been to the Bowery. Magnetic instinct pulled stubbornly. He rented a room close to where Flossie's burnt house used to be. Daily, he passed the vacant land, searching the shadows for his dead wife, madness stealing his alcohol-numbed mind. The stubborn yet majestic oak tree was still there on the plot that now belonged to Tiger, the man who had stolen her life.

Montefiore gave a mute cry. "Talia, Talia, where are you?" Then he rushed back to his refuge and opened a bottle of rum.

The seasons came and went. Spring burst with colour the day Tiger stepped out of prison, the gates closing behind him. He gazed up as a flock of geese honked, flying in formation.

Gideon welcomed him when he arrived at his humble home. "Stay with me as long as you wish. I bought another horse. The old one died. You can help me in the market."

Later that afternoon, Tiger strolled through the park. A bearded man sat on the bench wrapped in a heavy overcoat and woolly cap. Tiger walked on, not recognizing the judge. In his increasing madness, the judge never recognized Tiger either. Shivering and with bleary eyes, Montefiore stood and trudged back to his hovel.

For half an hour he searched for his beloved dark brown comb tinged with a deep read hue. The one he'd once used to brush his Talia's golden hair. He looked inside his drawer and found the cloth he wrapped it in, creased and adorned with strands of different colored hair he'd collected over the years. The thought he might have lost it frightened him.

Beads of perspiration accumulated on his forehead. Shadows of memories from the past haunted him. He withdrew more and more from the outside world to the dark cocoon of his room.

He hardly touched his meager food supply—a slice of mildewed bread, a few sardines and half a peeled onion. His starved body longed for the release of death. Obsessed with finding his comb, he sifted through the contents of the room. His cherished comb…all those years…it couldn't be gone.

On the table lay dusty books and an album. In panic, the frail Montefiore lifted the flattened mattress. His comb was not to be seen.

In the foggy arena of his mind, he was carried to a remote distant time. Montefiore visualized his wife's hair falling upon her shoulders like a golden halo. She thrilled him, her lips open and moist. He explored her body, blood pulsating through his veins. Time slipped away…

It was almost dark. With a demonic shrill, he stumbled towards the door. A few clothes hung on rusty nails. Tears ran in furrows on his sunken cheeks. Convulsive laughter attacked the mad man. A sudden idea struck. There was one hope, one last outpost.

Perhaps the comb was on the bench in the park where he used to wait for the children, brushing their paradise of locks which aroused a maddening sensation in him.

Montefiore coughed, spitting red phlegm, clenching his fists against his chest in pain. To one side of the window, a mirror hung on a nail, its silvery surface dull with dust and age. What was it he saw? *Talia*! He reached for the mirror, staggered and fell through the window.

The first streaks of light broke. Dawn. The fog lay heavy on the Bowery. Judge Lawrence Montefiore was found dead on the pavement outside the window, the comb gripped in his hand.

* * *

Claude Entrecasteau, now slightly grey, was moved to see Tiger enter the office. They shook hands.

"A good time to sell the plot. All the very best, Tiger." Entrecasteau handed him the title deeds and Daisy's address in Harlem.

"Thank you so much for your help. Have you any idea of the whereabouts of Judge Lawrence Montefiore?" Tiger asked, his face veiled with sadness.

"Judge Montefiore abandoned his affluent position and disappeared. He was found dead this morning. The poor man was consumed by his madness, fell through his window..." Entrecasteau shook his head as he saw Tiger out.

The sale of the land was swift.

"Thank you, Flossie, for this gift," Tiger whispered. "I will use it to buy a fishing boat and sail wherever the wind takes me."

He took the bus and travelled to Sunshine's place, who helped him purchase a boat. He painted Flossie in red on both sides of the splendid boat, now his home.

A month later, he wrote to Judge Lawrence Montefiore's maid, Daisy. She responded promptly. He bought a station wagon and paid her a visit where she still lived in the same house in Harlem with her invalid brother, Amos. Their mother has passed away two years before. The judge had bequeathed half of his money to Daisy, so she had enough funds to build an extension. Sun streamed into the room where he watched the birds and trees from his bed near the window.

Every two weeks, Tiger took Daisy and Amos sailing for the day.

"I bake cookies for you. The judge liked my cookies." She sighed.

Sitting on deck, Tiger touched Daisy's hand. "I ask your forgiveness for what happened to your mistress." His sad brown eyes were moist and she felt his sorrow.

* * *

The years came and slipped away. The month of May was warm. Terns dived into the ocean, seagulls cackled above them, perched on the deck sails. Schools of dolphins dipped playfully in and out of the ocean.

Daisy looked pretty in her red and white polka dot dress, and a white ribbon in her hair. Tiger stood beside her and wrapped his arms around her shoulders.

"Marry me, Daisy. I would like you to be my wife."

She turned and glanced at Amos, who smiled and nodded. "Yes, yes, yes!" Ecstatic, she laughed and cried. Tiger gripped her waist, lifted her in the air and did a quick turn.

They were married in a small chapel in Harlem, the ceremony conducted by

Daisy's priest and attended by Sunshine and his family. The *obligato* rose above the chorus, her blissful voice rending Tiger's heartstrings. He clasped his wife's hand and knew he was forgiven.

Daisy sold her property in Harlem and gave the proceeds to the community. Tiger, Daisy and Amos moved to their new home in the ocean. When a seagull splattered a dropping on his head as they boarded his boat, he took it as a sign of good luck.

Tiger, the happy fisherman, loved the sea and would spend many years sailing and fishing with Sunshine. He sailed it into his old age, enjoying the freedom of the waves until the day he sailed beyond the sun. One day— many happy years later—as dusk cloaked the ocean, Tiger rested his clubfoot on deck. Beyond time and space, there was no pain as he entered the musical realm of the spheres.

7 HAMACCABEE AND AURORA

Hamaccabee and Aurora glided side by side above the ocean in search of food. For twenty years, they'd soared across the vast seas, flying hundreds of miles, always returning each year to the same remote, windswept island in the southern ocean where they built their home. This was the pair's haven. In life and death, they were united. In life and death, they were parted.

As the sun rose, Hamaccabee said, "My Aurora, spring is here. Your time to give birth to another beautiful egg is near."

Aurora was happy to be beside Hamaccabee. That was all she desired. He was her rhapsody. "Look at the pod of dolphins surfing the waves. Such intelligent creatures. Here is the true breath of life. Freedom!" she trilled.

"Yes, free…free." Hamaccabee waved his brilliant white twelve foot wingspan. They rose towards the breathtaking panorama of flaming red sky lancing the dark blue sea. "Beware of the devil." Scanning the water with apprehension, Hamaccabee hissed and arched his chest. "Long-line fishing is man's evil way…most cruel."

Concerned, Aurora watched him. She brushed the tip of her wings against his and guessed what he was going to say next.

"Dear Aurora, they are deadly. Albatrosses, other birds and fish perish, attracted by the bait on their hooks. The victims bite and are dragged behind the boat. The hooks sink deep, lodge and rip out their throat. They drown. It would be a far, far better world without humanity!" Hamaccabee's anger pealed with the wind. He swung his long beak from right to left.

The view from above was spectacular. Hamaccabee and Aurora navigated along the island's distant beaches. Sea lions basked in the warm sun. Giant bull walruses fought over females. The pups between them were almost trampled. Mating season was, at times, fatal. Steering south, elephant and leopard seals crowded the rugged coves. At noon, the mist slowly lifted like a parasol. The rainbow of light that replaced it, streamed upon the lonely wilderness.

Morning slipped into her gown of indigo. Hamaccabee, the great Albatross, hovered gracefully above Aurora's nest. A magnificent sight was he as Aurora turned the egg beneath her splendid white breast. Wrapped in her warm plumage, she sheltered from the cold wind behind a large rock.

"I'll be back soon, krill are plentiful but your favourite squid becomes less," said Hamaccabee.

Under her wing, Aurora cherished her embryo. Hamaccabee disappeared and dived towards the expanse of blue. Aurora looked around and sighed. For centuries, multitudes of Albatrosses had come to nest on the isolated island, but today so few remained, each protecting their single egg they laid a year. Incubation period lasted between seventy and eighty days before the fledgling hatched.

Aurora was restless. She gazed at the grey sky. The weather had changed. The fair wind stirred a woolpack of cirrus clouds. She thought of Hamaccabee, whom she loved dearly. He was her anchor, hope and elation. Hamaccabee had only been gone a few hours and already she ached with longing for him.

Engraved in her memory was the first time she saw him. Memories of their complex ritual dance so long ago on the same island, near the same rock, overlooking the endless horizon and stark blue ocean.

The days passed slowly. Aurora grew tired alone in the nest.

Through the years, whenever Hamaccabee left her in search of food, her heart fluttered, always anxious with waiting. She wondered how far he flew to get the squid she relished.

"I must stretch for a while." With caution, she raised one leg at a time and stood beside the nest to preen herself. The breeze ruffled her soft feathers. She spread her brilliant white wings, gingerly turned the embryo and clutched on the nest egg.

She thought of Hamaccabee. Of late it was dangerous to skim above the oceans. The nets spread like tentacles barely concealed below the water. Humans were an abomination, the worst predators. Like maggots they devoured their prey. Aurora shuddered.

She needed Hamaccabee beside her to protect with his shield of warm plumage, the unborn. Nervous, Aurora turned the large white egg once more. She lifted her head and heard Hamaccabee's call from afar. The excited Albatross was relieved. Happy she uttered a clicking noise.

He flew above her, flapping his magnificent, powerful wings. Gliding in beside Aurora, he brushed his beak against hers.

"Beloved, I love you."

They alternated sitting on the egg. During the incubation, Hamaccabee stayed away for brief periods.

On the seventy-ninth day, Aurora heard a faint crackling. Elated, yet anxious, she peeped beneath her feathers. The eggshell had split to reveal a fluffy head.

Racing through the strong winds, exhausted by the flight, Hamaccabee arrived to see the fledgling emerge. He approached, bent and opened his long beak. The tiny, noisy male fledgling swallowed the regurgitated fish. Fascinated, he watched the little one.

"He is lovely, like you. Look at his little wings. Amazing how beautiful," said Hamaccabee.

"Rest now. You are tired, my beloved," Aurora hushed.

She swiftly left hunting for the next meal. The newborn fell asleep against his father's warm chest.

For the first few weeks the chick was never left by himself. Hamaccabee and Aurora took turns taking care of him. Without food or warmth, he would die. First Hamaccabee, then Aurora would brave the scourge of nets, always on guard. It was a hazardous and difficult task to feed the ravenous young and themselves. They had to fly for miles to catch Krill and squid for their offspring, a battle these days.

"The oceans are becoming empty. Many fish have disappeared. I blame the humans. They leave destruction everywhere," said a frustrated Hamaccabee.

"I remember when flocks of white and black winged Albatrosses glided on the waves; their happy sound rang at sea and on the islands. The breeding seasons were full of hope for our survival. Now the flight of the vanishing Albatrosses is silent, a dreadful silence." Aurora murmured, watching Hamaccabee's melancholy face.

"Overfishing is disastrous for us. The sweeping, wide nets…another curse. A calamity raking thousands of fish, all kinds and sizes. Once on deck, the very small die quickly before they are thrown back into the ocean. Livid,

Hamaccabee turned in circles stamping his feet. "We are threatened with extinction. It is too late. The damage is done. Too late!"

Shivering, Aurora fluffed her feathers. "What happened to the world we flew, on wings of freedom without fear? The one egg females lay do not always hatch, often the shells are broken or brittle. Some fledglings are born deformed and the mother abandons the little helpless one.

Aurora's sad eyes tore at Hamaccabee's heart. "Beloved Aurora, man pollutes the oceans and ships dump their rubbish. Most of it sinks deep, some floats and is swept by the current to the beaches, littering the coasts where seals breed. Fish are contaminated by poisons unknown to us and we eat them. Others get trapped in suffocating bags. There is so much we don't understand. This has a catastrophic effect on all life."

Hamaccabee risked his life on several occasions diving for tuna and other fish while white sharks lurked. The growing offspring waddled around the large rock and sat waiting for his meals.

"I think it is safe to leave him in the nest for brief periods," said Aurora one day.

Ten months had passed since the young Albatross had hatched. The chick grew quickly in size with a ravenous appetite. He stood tall and strong as he stretched his magnificent, glossy white wings and flapped them enthusiastically.

A small black feather tuft marked his chest. The dazzling bird raised his long neck and approached Aurora. She brushed her beak against his.

Hamaccabee appeared not long after, his crop filled with succulent krill. The hungry Albatross swallowed the regurgitated fish hungrily.

The young bird kept flapping his wings and followed Aurora. "I think the restless spirit is ready to fly," she said.

The eager young Albatross gazed at the endless blue and cried out, "Such a long way down to fly."

"The rising air will suspend you. Constant swing from side to side and soon you will reach the sea. Look at the other birds," said Hamaccabee.

"It's frightening." The nervous bird waved his strong wings and followed his parents to the edge of the cliff.

Aurora coaxed and encouraged him to take his first flight. "Keep your wings moving and you won't fall. Watch me. I'll be below you," she reassured him but still he hesitated.

She hovered over the thermal and Hamaccabee soon followed.

"Fly," she hailed.

The graceful young Albatross reached the edge, stretched his wings and took off. Triumphant, the three flew below.

Free in the air, the grand offspring glided above the spindrift with radiant energy and glanced back in farewell. Gracefully, he rose to the blushing horizon and disappeared beyond the rays of the rising sun

Winter had arrived. Of late, Aurora felt a strong premonition of impending doom. The nest was abandoned and the lonely island was wrapped in a white blanket. Ferocious storms swept across the cold continent and so the turbulent season paved the way to a gentle spring crowned with colours. For weeks Hamaccabee and Aurora wandered north rushing below the clouds with the fair wind, unbound over the timeless high seas.

"I love you, Hamaccabee. I've loved you from the dawn of time, my warrior."

Airborne for long distances, skimming above the waters, they rested for a while to drink and refresh.

A fortnight later, a ship sailed in the offing. Aurora froze. She recognized the vessel from the past and knew what this meant. Several years ago the whalers spotted two leviathans through the fog. The cunning mammoth's eluded capture, maneuvered with skill and escaped the executioners.

The savaged...killers...had returned. Hamaccabee and Aurora flew above the whale they pursued. They watched in horror as the frightened mammal avoided the swishing harpoon by diving deep and circling beneath the swell. The gloating captain leered at the cries of the Albatrosses.

"I can't bear this. He is so helpless and we have no hope to save him," Aurora cried out.

There was no escape for the whale. He'd come up for air when the first harpoon pierced his side. Bleeding profusely, he writhed in agony. The second harpoon was lethal as it perforated his neck. Aurora uttered a heart-rending cry.

The proud giant, who'd once bounced freely in his domain, was thrown aboard the foul ship and sawn to pieces.

The captain on the poop deck gave orders to the crew below. He did not notice Hamaccabee charging with breathless speed towards him. For a split second he looked up, but it was too late. Hamaccabee struck. His eight inch, powerful beak punctured and tore out the captain's right eye.

Hamaccabee and Aurora surged back to their howling wilderness as the captain crawled on his knees, the pulpy eye hung over his cheek.

The following season Aurora did not lay an egg. Loving Hamaccabee was a comfort. He understood. The whale haunted her. She feared death daily and never let Hamaccabee out of her sight.

"The island is our refuge from man. We must keep at a distance from the troubled waters." He stroked her head with soft feathers.

"The season's pattern has changed." Aurora sniffed. "Spring comes earlier, summers are longer with frequent violent storms and it's remarkably warmer on the islands."

Autumn arrived late. At dawn, the sky was covered with birds. Ebenezer, the skipper of the trawler, brushed his grey beard. *Plenty of fish today*, he thought.

Petrels, gulls, terns skirted noisily, among them the Albatrosses

"Don't go too near the nets," Hamaccabee worried.

"There's a good catch below," Aurora called excitedly.

The clanking winch with a steel cable around the drum hauled the nets onto the trawler. Cloud formations gathered. It began to rain gently at first, then strengthened and became torrential. The winds howled.

Impulsively, Aurora aimed at a big fish. With full impact she dived. Her right wing became entangled in the mesh of the net. Aurora struggled to free herself but her injured, ripped feathers were wedged tight.

Hamaccabee panicked, terror in his heart. He outstripped the wind and flew above her.

"Hamaccabee."

Her eyes were veiled with tears. Innumerable trapped fish leapt on top of each other, covering Aurora. Gasping beneath their weight, she drowned. Hamaccabee hovered in circles, his wings weak. Desolate, he was unable to save his beloved.

Ebenezer watched the king of the sea birds and felt he was a bad omen. Hamaccabee's eyes burned with hatred as he stared down the terrified skipper. He loathed the useless worthless man below...the abomination of the detestable trawlers...and nets...

The ship rolled from side to side. Ebenezer ran amok on deck. The savage wind shrieked above the rising swell. The nets jammed the winch. They whirled and swiveled in knots, then broke loose. The sixty foot monster wall of water swept up the boat and tumbled it violently. She dived vertically into the sea, broke her back and sank, swallowed by the undercurrent.

Tormented, Hamaccabee plunged once more into the foaming flood, his heart wrung with sorrow. He bid a plaintive adieu, rose above the waves and returned to his hermitage. The great Albatross sat beside the large rock. He no longer wished to live. His life ebbed away. Hamaccabee wished for release from this world. Free…free…beyond time, beyond space, he soared to Aurora he loved. In life and death they were united.

Five years later, two Albatrosses built their nest on the same remote windswept island. The splendid male stood near the corner of the large rock. Beside him were Hamaccabee's scattered bones. His offspring gently turned them with his beak and his forlorn call echoed across the island.

8 MARCUS AURELIUS

"In my youth and at present, the battles still rage between the legions. Once, the fields were dressed in full bloom with flowers. Alas, the warm earth is now covered with corpses. Wars, Wars...power, greed and hatred."

Marcus Aurelius paused and looked around at his loyal friends. His mouth twitched and he stretched his six legs, for Marcus Aurelius was a large shiny black cockroach. With his two long antennae swaying, he sniffed from side to side, his sense of smell sharp and his bulging eyes alert. Unforeseen danger abounded.

Cleopatra, his beloved, was enormously fat, slowly sidling beside her champion. At night when the humans retired to their beds, hordes of cockroaches slipped through a maze of crevices. Amongst them were the two lovers at their rendezvous, attacking the household kitchen. Man was their worst predator.

"People are filthy, disgusting—like rats. They collect so much rubbish. No wonder they are plagued with diseases," Aurelius rasped.

"And they think we are a pest—vermin—trying to exterminate us with their dangerous weapons." Cleopatra brushed her wobbly body against him.

During the day, they lived in the attic with battalions of cockroaches and other insects as well as field mice. Marcus built a cosy nest for the two in a large copper bucket filled with paper, straw and rags.

"The little ones are due any day," said Cleopatra, caressing him.

There was a hush in the attic when the legendary General Marcus Aurelius spoke. "This meeting is of great significance for the future survival of our species."

On his right stood Julius Hanoratus, the Tribune, and to his left the impressively handsome Titus, chief captain with his officers.

"Humans have concealed an arsenal to eliminate us. Do not touch any devices under cupboards or other furniture as they are lethal." The general's raucous tone sent a chilly premonition to his audience. "At present the attic is a safe haven, nevertheless it is vital our builders dig additional tunnels in case we have to escape in a hurry. The enemy is everywhere."

Julius roared passionately, "We outnumber the devils. This is our strength. We'll slip through every conceivable hole, raid and plunder their stocks on the docks, in the warehouses, and run along the ships' thick ropes to sneak into the galleys. Spies informed me that men possess a new weapon—a deadly spray." He clicked his legs together.

"Attack the bazaars in the cobbled alleys but beware of the rats. Let us send an envoy to Governor Brutus Philipanus and put forward the plot to him. Spread the message across the Kingdom of cockroaches. Rise! Rise against the tyranny of humans!" Julius' antennae shivered as he shouted.

Marcus glanced at Cleopatra. "Remember when we lived beneath the thick bark of the oak tree? King and Queen of the forest were we. Curse the human race! They crave more and more land. Stripped the entire forest when in full bloom, a day I shall never forget nor forgive. I wept for every fallen giant." Marcus's chest heaved lividly as he brushed his legs against his beloved's. "Now it is a sad place—row upon row of ugly houses for hideous two-legged monsters."

Bitterly, Cleopatra cried out, "Our planet laced with the splendor of creation is dying. I hear the earth rumble with a sigh. Diabolical machines rip up its bowels wiping away everything living and leaving the beautiful land in ruin and desolation." She trembled as she snuggled against Marcus.

Enraged, Titus flicked his antennae to the side. "Thousands of us have been slain. The forests where colourful butterflies danced from tree to tree have disappeared, and too few lizards, dragon flies and rabbits are seen these days. Even the wild flowers and long-legged insects I liked to munch on have vanished. Worse still are the deadly sprays. Men fumigate our hideouts, forcing us to die a terrible, suffocating death. Tragically, even the seasons have changed." Despair hung heavily in his voice.

* * *

Downstairs, an old man and woman sat chatting.

"We haven't been up to the attic for quite some time," the woman remarked.

"Mmmm," her husband mumbled.

"We have several antiques and oil paintings up there I intend to sell. They should fetch a good price. The hurricane lamp is broken, so we could use two candles," she stated.

Together they walked upstairs to the attic. The man opened the creaking door unaware of the lurking cockroaches crouched at their garrison posts ... waiting.

155

"I'll go right, you turn left," the man said.

The woman paced a few steps and tripped, dropping the candle.

"Attack!" roared the general.

From all corners the colonists charged. The cockroaches pierced the woman's eye with their sharp pincers and she screamed.

The man groped around in panic. As the invading mass crawled over them, his candle hit the dry timbers. Shooting flames spread and hundreds of cockroaches leapt blindly into the inferno while others escaped through the gaps to swarm towards the garden, trampling and crushing each other.

* * *

Birds showered upon the moving prey without mercy and a massacre ensued. Gasping, Cleopatra, the general and a limping Julius reached the refuge of the barn with those who had survived.

The fire engulfed the roof of the house and the structure collapsed.

"Nothing lasts, all is futile," Cleopatra whispered. "All our treasures, our people now ashes."

Marcus' heart ached. How he loved her. He feared for his wife's life. To lose her would be unbearable. "Is there a safe place where no-one will hunt or hurt us?" Marcus stroked Cleopatra's face tenderly with his antennae.

"Perhaps beyond? There look up at the brilliant lights," she whispered.

At noon three days later, the inspiring and wise, eagle-eyed Titus stood on the hill surrounded by his army. He gazed at the spectacular oasis across the valley. The hot wind sent whiffs of dust between the mounds of sand, small shrubs and molehills. As he waited, millions of baby cockroaches hatched from their eggs and darted forward.

Titus raised his hand. "There is our bond and power. Tomorrow we go to battle, a full scale, and victorious invasion against the enemy."

"I know of a concealed stone wall ideal for our nest and young, sheltered from the wind and rain. Come with me! We'll head to the field on the far side," said Marcus. He caressed Cleopatra's swollen abdomen. "Remain here until I return from battle."

"Titus is a great leader," she murmured. "He will keep you safe."

* * *

A year passed. In the isolated field the stone wall, overgrown with weeds, sheltered the elderly Cleopatra and Marcus. They huddled together for warmth.

"Humans haven't hanged. They still slaughter each other in wars for greed, power and hatred," Marcus murmured.

"I love you, beloved Marcus. You are my dawn, my dusk, and the seasons in my life, always beside me."

"Oh Cleopatra." Marcus clasped her close, his emotions close to the surface.

"What is it?" She watched his melancholy face.

"I kept silent; I didn't want to distress you about Titus. One of the survivors told me what happened on the ship."

"What ship?" she stammered, baffled.

"Long after the great victorious battle, Titus and his warriors ventured an assault on the wharf. They scaled and stormed the docked ship, swarming the kitchen when the rats appeared from the hold. The rats tore the cockroach army to shreds. They fled on deck surrounded by hundreds of furry black beasts. Trapped, Titus and his heroes jumped into the water and drowned."

Marcus wiped his moist eyes. The solitary night owl's hoot burbled across the hill.

"Marcus, my weak leg has been painful of late. You give me strength. You light every step I take. Hold me close, I am cold."

Their antennae entwined as above the stonewall the wind whistled.

9 THE ALBINOS

Several years had passed since Arusha, former head of the Dookoo tribe, was stricken with the malaria that ravaged entire villages. He was a compassionate and merciful figure, often sitting in his hut with Doombala and Chingola, the Albinos. He considered them wise and joined in conversation concerning the welfare of his people, talking about important issues, tribal laws, speaking of gathering food for survival and hunting when food was scarce.

Destiny, the age-old betrayer, sealed their fate when Arusha died. King Mansa, surrounded by his witchdoctor and elders, decided to expel Doombala and Chingola from the village. Mansa believed their white skin was the curse of demonic spirits.

Doombala was mortified. His large pupils flitted and shifted nervously in his pink eyes. The humiliation was unbearable. The Albinos with their white skin, crinkly hair, long eyelashes and pale brows were ostracized pariahs to be abandoned by humanity. Doombala's heart turned to stone. Lovingly, Chingola gripped her husband's hand. He howled like a wounded animal. They were neither white nor black—misfits amongst their people.

The giant trees, like parasols, swayed with sadness. The gentle couple glanced at the summit of the mountain. The waterfall rushed over the steep rocks below. A mantel of pearly spray cloaked the prismatic colours of the rainbow.

"So beautiful," Doombala murmured, his chest tight, taking it as a sign of better things to come.

Chingola carried a wide bag with clothes and food on her shoulder. Doombala slung bows and a long pouch of arrows on his back, strapped a knife to his waist and carried a machete in his hand. Inside two gourds, sealed and corked, were medicinal herbs extracted from plants and tree residue.

Lotions of white milky sap from the cassava roots, brewed with pounded garlic and salt, were used against insects' bites, poisons, wounds and infections. The Albinos expertise in African survival methods was exceptional. Above all, they were skilled hunters.

The outcasts trekked through Rwanda's pristine forests and followed the shallow part of the river east. Weary after a day's travel, they came across a clearing among the trees.

"It's sheltered here, a good place to rest for the night," said Doombala.

In a small calabash, Chingola placed kola nuts and black beans. She said, "We're like a leaf in the wind. Someday we'll find a safe sanctuary." Chingola lay beside her man and listened to the cicadas and bats.

For several weeks they shuffled deep into the jungle festooned with gigantic ferns, thorny vines and looping lianas hanging from branches. Far away beyond the trees, wild bull elephants blasted like trumpets.

Doombala whispered, "I hear voices. Quick, hide in the undergrowth."

As they crouched low, two columns of slaves trailed past, followed by guards, overseers and poachers. The porter slaves carried ivory—tusks and horns—leopards skins, cheetah and golden-maned lion heads.

The gruesome sight of the butchered cats chilled the Albinos' spines. Chingola shuddered. Livid, Doombala watched with horror as the drivers lashed their whips at the file of battered porters laden with food and heavy chests containing stolen gold.

Concealed by the reeds, Doombala and Chingola followed the travelers some distance until late afternoon when they stopped to camp for the night. The slaves lit a fire.

A repulsive, skinny guard with a porcupine quill piercing his left nostril and weepy, infected eyes sat cross-legged and gulped a swig of rum. "We have to reach Zanzibar before the heavy rains and avoid the tribal wars in Rwanda and the Congo." He spat.

"Yes, yes," said the head overseer sitting next to him, rattling the baboon and hippopotamus teeth around his wrists and ankles. "Dangerous territories, many escape to Zanzibar." He stretched his legs and yawned.

"Hassantee, that sly fox trader in Zanzibar, will sell our merchandise to the white man who ship most to Europe. It's a filthy business."

The lure of money and power provided the strongest impetus for the poachers to ply their trade. He slumped on the ground with a grin on his face. The full moon sneaked between the trees, and a pack of hyenas prowled.

In the reeds, the Albinos planned their attack. "I'll get the drunk," said Doombala. "Hold the pouch."

Inside a small clay pot, the white powder from the seedlings of the poisonous liana plant mixed with the bark resin created a deadly onaye—a paralyzing poison.

Doombala strung his bow. The arrowhead hissed through the air, piercing the guard's temple. The poison had quick effect on his heart and nervous system. Within moments, the man's tongue hung from his frothing mouth and he'd stopped breathing. Next to him, the gang leader gave a harrowing scream.

Doombala whispered, "Let's hide behind the pile of ivory tusks. This will confuse them." They zigzagged screened by thick foliage. "Easy to pick them from here," he panted.

The slaves had put the fire out, reducing the light. Doombala could detect a broken twig, crushed insect or bent leaf but primarily, he used his keen perception and sharpness of ears and scents. With eyes of a lynx, Doombala's arrows zoomed at his victims with accuracy. Eerie suspense hung in the air and turned the blood cold. The disarrayed and panicked guards started shooting blindly at flitting shadows. It was hard to discern who slew who between the drivers, overseers and poachers. Bewildered the slaves fled and hid behind the trees.

Doombala put his fingers on his wife's lips. "Ssh, I can smell someone."

The head overseer crawled along the forest floor on his belly. Doombala and Chingola crept forward. Startled, the man looked up. "Albinos," he stammered.

Doombala swung his knife at the gang leader with full force. It perforated his chest and he screamed at the searing pain, coughing blood. "Albinos." His red tongue lolled as Doombala cut off his head.

It started to drizzle. Towards dawn, the palm nut eagle vultures swooped below and ripped chunks of flesh from the corpses.

Doombala's voice rose above the giant trees to call out to the slaves. "We won't hurt you. Come, take the gold. We do not wish to have any. The tusks and pelts, bury them deep in the earth. They belong to the merciful Great Spirit. Do not ever kill animals, small or large, for profit. No one escapes from the Mighty Spirit. Come in peace, our hearts are united."

Huddled in groups, the slaves emerged, their eyes shining with hope. Leaving, the Albinos looked back and waved to them.

Doombala sniffed the air. "We must be approaching the Savannah. Big cats are fighting. We'll keep to the edge of the forest."

The large trees had buttresses at the bases of their trunks where animals sheltered in deep recesses.

"Wonderful refuge," said Chingola.

They crawled inside the maze and saw a glint of white in the dark.

Chingola whispered, "Bones—a carcass—a cheetah's."

Doombala inched forward. "There are two holes in the fur below the neck, shot by the poachers, the barbarians," he said and gnashed his teeth.

"She came here to die." Chingola sighed.

The orange-red ball of the sun glowed on the plains dotted with Acacia. In the distance a pride of lions and cubs sprawled lazily under scattered trees. The hungry Albinos surveyed the grazing Thompson's gazelles with their young. Swiftly, they speared a fawn and tied its legs to a pole with vines, resting it between them on their shoulders. They roasted the tender pieces on a small open fire, interring the skin and bones when they were done.

Gazing at the sky, Doombala said, "Ever since we left, my mind is in a storm. I must follow my destiny. I'll never have peace until King Mansa pays for casting us out. The Sacred Spirit will pave our way. His light shines. If we go west all along the rolling mountains, the forests stretch for miles. Eventually we will reach the Congo border undetected." Doombala watched his young wife peeling wild berries. "You understand what I must do?"

"Yes," Chingola murmured.

"Meanwhile, let us rest here for a while."

Doombala got up and helped her with the fruit. In a flash, Doombala saw a female cheetah spring across in front of the massive tree, followed by a cub. Seconds later, a lion chased the young cheetah and grabbed him by the throat. The cub struggled helplessly. His mother swung around and with a tremendous leap, sunk her teeth into the wild cat's hind leg. They fought, ripping at each other. The cunning cheetah lured the lion into the thick bracken to spare the cub, never to be seen again. Immediately the couple lifted the injured cub and laid him inside on a bed of ferns. He snarled.

"We must stop the bleeding." Concerned, Doombala shook his head. A deep gash perforated the cub's lower belly, his throat and chest badly torn by the lion's sharp claws.

Chingola prized open a gourd and dabbed the milky cassava sap on the lesions, covering the lacerations with a thick layer of leaves. Every two hours they packed a fresh poultice of pounded garlic on the wounds.

"I'll sleep on his right." Chingola snuggled next to the cheetah cub. "He's like a child."

Throughout the night the cub whined, his nose dry. Compassionate, Chingola sponged his feverish face with water.

"I'll give him bitter herbs to drink to ease the pain," she whispered.

For days the cub's body raged with fever, as they devotedly administered medicines. The sky was dressed in pink with the rising sun when the cheetah finally awoke. He growled, showing his tiny teeth as he saw the Albinos sitting opposite him. Weak, the cub tried to stand but staggered and fell. Traumatized, he called for his mother. Chingola covered her face and wept.

Like a whirlwind, Doombala spun out onto the open Savannah. Within two hours he returned carrying an impala on his back. He sliced the liver, heart and lungs into shreds then placed the calabash beside the beautiful cat. The alarmed cub snapped, mistrustful of the Albinos, and turned his golden head from side to side. Too ravenous to refuse the offering, soon the food was gone.

"He is recovering." Doombala laughed. "Later, I'll give him some more."

Satisfied, the cheetah groomed himself then yawned and slept for most of the day.

The young animal got used to Chingola's presence. Daily, she rubbed his coat with oils extracted from vegetable plants. His wounds healed slowly and he grew in strength. Within a month, Doombala took him for brief walks across the Savannah.

The bond between man and animal was unparalleled. Far out on the horizon, the rainbow crowned the earth with its brilliant colours and Doombala took it as another sign from the Great Spirit.

"We'll call him Rainbow. It suits him," said Chingola with enthusiasm, rubbing her face against the purring cat.

"He's not limping anymore," Doombala remarked, smiling.

The graceful animal was ready for his first hunt. The couple watched him with fear in their hearts that he might not come back. He did, with a baby warthog. Proudly, he flung his prize at their feet and gorged himself on his prey.

In the following months, Rainbow became an excellent hunter while Doombala speared small game and Chingola gathered wild fruit, edible plants and tubers. She often rested her head on the tame cat's warm chest. Rainbow was magnificent, long and lean, rippled with taut muscles as he sprinted like lightning, his splendid markings dotting his beige fur.

Almost two years had passed since they'd rescued him.

"The Powerful Spirit will protect us on our own dangerous journey. We thank the Great Spirit who brought Rainbow into our lives. Tomorrow we depart with the big cat beside us to pursue and destroy the wicked ones," Doombala shouted lustily.

They left early. Puzzled, the cheetah waited a few minutes near the lair then, loyal to his people, followed the Albinos. They covered long distances in dense jungle. Camouflaged, Rainbow skulked high in the trees along the branches, his prey the monkeys.

"Delicious monkey brains for Rainbow." Chingola's laughter rose with the breeze.

Low clouds cluttered the sky. At the edge of the village, disguised in the undergrowth, they waited in the dark. Bats circled. King Mansa, the witch doctor and three elders sat on the ground drinking.

Doombala's heart burned with vengeance. He bit his lip. Rainbow felt the tension. He sniffed the enemy's scent, and flicked his tail. Trained to kill, he watched the Albino's every move.

Mansa got up to urinate behind the hut. Doombala stroked Rainbow's head, and then imitated the call of a cheetah. Raising his right hand, twice opening and closing his palms, he pointed. The intelligent cheetah leaped on the chief and broke his neck.

"I must go and check. Maybe the chief drank too much," they heard the witchdoctor mumble.

Doombala pressed his face against Rainbow's and signaled twice with his palms again. Like a monster, the splendid cheetah landed, tearing out the witchdoctor's throat. Moments later, the two corpses were discovered by the guards.

Stampeding villagers shrieked with terror as the guards ran towards the river. "Big cats! Run!"

The three veterans scrambled after them, screaming a war cry. Doombala held his machete. Rainbow and Chingola followed him. Trapped, the men retreated into the rushing water.

Doombala grappled with the first who saw the machete hurling down on him. The Albino slashed a vicious blow and severed the man's left foot. The current swept him away.

Rainbow swam towards the second and dragged him under the water. Boldly Chingola eliminated the last fat one as she sent her knife flying to bury in his chest.

Lightning flashed above the giant trees and thunder rumbled like cannons. It began to rain gently at first, and then strengthened to torrential.

Doombala raised his voice. "The Everlasting Spirit is pleased. He will lead us to a new beginning filled with goodness. My heart is released from vengeance. We are liberated."

Doombala lifted his head. He loved the rain on his face. Gently he brushed Rainbow's brow and kissed his wet nose. Chingola uttered a hushed cry.

They swung west to the Congo. Exhausted, Chingola lay down and whispered, "On wings of freedom, the leaf in the wind will rest when our child is born."

Speechless, Doombala knelt. His tears trickled on her belly.

The lofty peaks of the Ruwenzori Mountains, shrouded in mist, loomed in the distance.

"What splendor of creation," Doombala cried out.

They arrived at the vast wilderness a week later. Chingola trembled with happiness. "Here is our hermitage."

Clumps of trees and shrubs fringed the base of the elevation. "We'll only climb to the ridge." Doombala pointed. "Steep and high, further up are alpine bushes and rocks."

They discovered a massive cave, screened by coils of hanging creepers. Inside were two tunnels hewn like domes.

"Our home." Chingola wrapped her arms around her husband. She watched Rainbow with amusement as he purred against them, happy with their choice.

The magnificent cheetah loved his new territory, the plains below abundant with game and above the rugged cliffs roamed smaller animals.

At daybreak Chingola went into labour. Her contractions became stronger and more frequent. Drenched with perspiration, she flung her head back and shrieked. Doombala sponged her face. Her cervix gradually dilated revealing a small tuft of hair on the infant's head. The baby was born dark ebony, and his mewl shivered against the pillars of mountains.

Stunned, Doombala sobbed with happiness. "He's not albino. He is black!" His body shook with spasms as he chanted, "Black, black ..." and cradled the little one at Chingola's breast. "The curse is lifted."

With the birth of the baby, the cheetah's own primordial instincts awoke. He suddenly disappeared for a week, reappeared then vanished for months. The hot winds and thick dust blew across the wilderness and still there was no sign of the cheetah.

"I'll be back late this afternoon." Doombala kissed his wife. He looked at his son suckling, emitting faint gurgles. Chingola understood his need to search for Rainbow.

He walked for a long time through the tall, dry grass then sat beneath an Acacia tree. Alert, Doombala listened. He thought he saw something move, and dived for cover.

Through the shimmering heat they emerged; Rainbow, four cubs and their mother. The female pricked up her ears and snarled. Doombala kept still. The mother sensed the imminent danger, the threat to her young and was about to pounce when Rainbow swiped his powerful paw at her. She crouched submissively. The frightened cubs scattered. The loyal cheetah followed Doombala's scent. He purred, rubbing his body against him.

Doombala kissed the loving Rainbow and whispered in his ear. "Chingola's little one is black, not albino."

Rainbow licked Doombala's face with his rough tongue. The ordeal was over. The cubs ran to their mother when she called. Sad, Doombala watched the golden pride recede into the distance.

Often during the following four years, Rainbow prowled above the escarpment then vanished.

"I miss him," said Doombala, stoking the small fire.

Chingola paced to the cave's entrance. "Rainbow, Rainbow." Her call veiled the timeless arena. Chingola's heart rained with tears of longing for the golden, purring cheetah. Somewhere in the wilderness Rainbow roamed, never forgotten.

In their hermitage on the Ruwenzori Mountains, the Albinos and their child lived free.

10 THE CONQUISTADOR AND KALANEET

The Amazonian tribesman watched his wife squat to give birth on the river bank. As soon as the infant was born, she cut the umbilical cord with her teeth, made a knot and lay on the warm earth. The father picked up the crying baby, bathed him for a few seconds in the water, and then cradled him at the woman's breast.

The sun seeped through from above the massive shrine of trees as the child fed. Some distance away, screened among the thick foliage, a jaguar cub played with his mother's tail while a second cub brushed himself against her face. The Amazonians were a familiar sight to the animals of the jungle.

That night, the man and his family took refuge below the giant trees. The tall Indian stroked his sleeping wife's hair and listened to the baby's soft gurgles. The Jaguars prowled beyond. The tribesman felt safe among the graceful creatures.

At dawn, the couple trekked back to their bamboo longhouse, wide and high, and thatched with layers of ferns and raffia. The top was secured by intertwined branches and joined to numerous upright posts, well insulated against torrential rains. In the middle, a small fire burned to repel mosquitoes. Whiffs of smoke escaped from the opening in the roof and narrow door.

Surrounded by the Xanaparadoo tribe, the village headman's inspired voice rose. "Today we shall celebrate the birth of the son of Pardess, the great hunter and his wife, Kalaneet."

Drums beat with abandon. Moved, the proud father approached the patriarch and rested the child upon his knees. The chief clasped the newborn to his chest and hailed. "He is our future warrior. Xanaparadoo mothers, it is the fertility season, give birth to heroes who will protect us against marauding enemies. Preserve our forests, animals and mighty river."

The long beaked toucans screeched as the Elder continued. "It is a time for hunting and storing. Woman of the Amazon, gather cassava, seeds, plants and fruit. Pardess, swift as an eagle with your braves; follow the trail of the anaconda and flush them out for succulent meat."

Pardess blurted out, "I suggest soon, before the rains. Men and boys, spread wide nets in many areas to trap tapirs, they multiply this time of year."

The inimitable patriarch wiped the sweat off his brow and added, "Another source of delicious food is monkeys. Nature must be balanced," he paused. "Monkeys have a charm of their own, most intelligent. Do not aim your bows and arrows at suckling mothers or mature breeders, only at the number of older ones, they are past being handsome. Our beautiful women love their brains; that's why they are so clever." He raised his hands towards the sky and laughed.

171

Throughout the night, the dwellers of the jungle rejoiced and feasted on tender tapirs, monkeys brains cooked on open fires, cassava dumplings dipped in honey, succulent fruit and legumes, and an intoxicating drink made from fermented yellow wild flowers. The call of the splendid male Jaguar shivered on the pillars of the forests as the magnificent female followed his scent.

* * *

The expedition left Spain in the early spring on the *Marqueza* with one hundred occupants on board. "We should reach South America in six to eight weeks depending on the trade winds. Avoid the doldrums," blared the Captain, puffing his pipe.

Raoul, a man of authority and directing the expedition, adjusted his stomacher against the morning chill. "Yes, yes, how could I forget? Not a breeze for days, unbearable heat. Yes, yes," he repeated and turned around.

"Good morning," Dr Navaro greeted the two men. He wore a white shirt with ruffled cuffs, an embroidered waistcoat over it and a brimmed hat decorated with flamingo plumes. He drew a deep, long breath. "Ah to be a bird, what freedom," he exclaimed, watching ferns and gannets dive.

The physician was also a scholar and read omnivorously. He studied ancient civilizations, predominantly the Kingdoms of the East. Philistines, Amorites, Canaanites and Phoenicians fascinated him. On the *Marqueza*, his first concern was the health of the conquistador. He instructed the sailors to put hot shot in buckets of vinegar and still it everywhere on the ship. Noxious fumes killed virulent diseases.

The wise doctor introduced cats to eradicate vermin rats. Daily, he checked the kitchen and hold where food was stored. He believed implicitly in blood-letting and amputations when ulcers and chronic sores on the extremities became life-threatening.

The captain commanded a nor' west by North. The wind filled the *Marqueza's* white sails as she cruised to the open sea.

Raoul watched the shores of Spain recede. He had no regrets leaving his homeland having lost both parents during a smallpox epidemic. His uncle, a prominent figure entouraged by nobility, had raised him. Raoul was endowed with an elite education and granted a privileged, high position to join the Conquistador on several expeditions. A restless soul, his heart rebelled against the Spanish Monarchy who had supreme dominance and power. They exploited and financed their explorations from people upon whom they imposed heavy taxes, as well as the Conquistador's brutal piracy in the high seas. Holding the cross, the victorious Spanish—in peaked helmets and shiny cuirasses invaded new lands. Francisco Pizzaro, the tyrant, conquered the Incas, and Cortez defeated the Aztec. They pillaged, savaged and enslaved both empires.

Bitter, Raoul's mind was shadowed by the inquisition's centuries of ruthless terror. A chill ran down his spine. His country was an abomination. He vowed never set foot on Spanish soil again.

The driftwood followed the magnetic force of his destiny. Towards noon, master and explorer were standing on the poop deck. "Look," said the captain, "two brigantines in the offing race towards Africa hunting for slaves."

"I don't believe in slavery. Spanish, French, Dutch and English are all to blame in this horrifying human trade, evil and tragic," Raoul stormed.

The captain stared at him, surprised at his daring openness. It was dangerous to meddle in politics, so he changed the subject. "The ship holds well before the wind, dolphins and flying fish are escorting us in both sides, it is lunchtime and I am famished." He chuckled.

Weeks later, the sailor in the crow's nest cried out, "Land!" It had started to drizzle. The captain scanned the coast of South America rising through the mist with his glasses.

Raoul leaned against the rail, the salty ocean spray on his face. "Spectacular wilderness," his voice rang above the galloping waves.

The captain surrounded by his officers, perused the chartered map and stated, "We shall steer south towards the mouth of the Amazon. My calculations indicate there are coves in which to anchor, we'll navigate the widest channel to the interior."

A lonely albatross glided above. She followed the *Marqueza* for hours before arching her splendid white chest and soaring up, she disappeared.

In the afternoon the weather changed. The nervous captain paced the main deck with quick strides, concerned as he directed his eyes to the north where ominous dark clouds formed. The wind rose. "There's a storm approaching very fast," he alerted the first mate and the crew. "Reduce sail immediately, batten down the hatches and check the ballast in the lower hold."

The sky turned black and heavy rain came in sheets, lashing the ship. Mammoth waves sixty feet high threatened to swamp and overturn the *Marqueza*. Panic ensued as soldiers and sailors scrambled in all directions. Raoul darted to the poop deck. The savage winds had flung the captain sideways and he'd tripped. Raoul spotted Dr Navaro bending over the screaming master, whose leg was caught between the twisted timbers of a support mast. Alarmed, he rushed across to help and both men tried in desperation to pull him out. To their horror, a spike perforated the captain's thigh. Raoul carried a small blunderbuss, at all times. His mind raced. "Hopeless! We can't save him. Look up." He pointed, fear in his eyes. The main mast groaned as it swayed, almost ripped from its base. Raoul knelt beside the captain and placed the pistol in his hand. "God Bless."

The two men sprinted to the bulwarks. The captain's lips turned pale, shrinking at the devil hurling down. He pressed the trigger to his temple as the mast descended and crushed him.

The gigantic wall of water slammed once more. The *Marqueza* careened. "Dive now, now!" Frantic, Raoul shouted orders. The ship, strangled by the raging sea, sank vertically to the deep, dragging with her all on board. Raoul braced himself on a broken spar. Eyes of a lynx, he saw the doctor clinging to a floating chest. The young conquistador cried in helpless frustration. Eventually, the storm subsided and the outline of the shore emerged.

* * *

Coconut trees lined the isolated cove on the extreme far right of the delta. The high tide rolled onto the beach bringing with it two large water bands and a keg containing salted dried meat. Some distance below, deep in the swampy mangrove were three long boats engraved *Marqueza*.

Raoul rummaged a small pocket compass from his shirt. He held it in the air and raved with excitement. "A treasure in the jungle."

Through the turbulent passage, the longboat surged. Navaro riveted his gaze on the daredevil Raoul in front who ploughed the oars against the chopping white horses, fearless and bearing a westerly direction. To their relief, they reached the calm of the river. Gaudy-colored toucans and scarlet macaws shrieked. There wasn't the slightest ripple on the shimmering water as they moored the boat in the narrow cleavage of the river's bank. Both gazed with delight at the birds perched in the lower branches.

"Timeless splendor," Raoul said in a hushed tone.

In the deep recesses of his mind he remembered another time, another season he'd loved and somewhere remote for which he longed.

* * *

Pardess and several tribesmen cut branches from the clump of saplings, splicing and shaving them to make wooden spears and arrows. Hours later they tied the stacks with raffia and headed back.

Pardess suddenly stopped and thumped his fists upon his chest. A warning signal. "I smell something, strange smell," he whispered and sniffed the air. They all imitated him. The group threaded in silence when they heard voices.

"There's movement opposite, prowling beasts," said Raoul. Pardess thought the voice was young but the language was foreign to him.

"Where does one run, so remote and wild. Definitely not swim, nor climb." This time the voice seemed older to Pardess. "Can we catch fish?"

"No, there could be dangerous crocodiles submerged here," answered Raoul.

"Notice the monkeys? They love berries and other fruit. We could scout for edible ones. Risky though, many are poisonous," Navaro continued his musings.

"So are plants, mushrooms. I don't recognize the fatal ones. At least we have water and meat left." Raoul shrugged and placed a hand above his eyes to scan the banks.

The natives trudged between the tall reeds. Struck numb, they stared. "They must have come from the spirit world!" The tribesmen shivered in fear as Pardess stammered, "Yellow spirits! Go and alert the headman."

The tribe crossed the shallow part of the river and formed a circle surrounding the Spaniards. With caution, they advanced. The spirit visitors seemed astounded at the sight of the stark natives.

"Smile, they've never seen a white man. There must be other Indians

176

scattered over hundreds of miles. Smile," said the physician as he studied the many pregnant women. Others had padded raffia girdles across their waist and braided between the legs. The doctor assumed they were menstruating. "Ingenious hygiene," he chortled, as his observation turned to the tall males' wiry physiques. "Take note, Raoul, they are hairless and walk with a sprinted gait."

Kalaneet, heavy with child, stepped beside her husband. Pardess, holding his year old son, followed the chief. "Yellow spirits," the dazed leader muttered. Pardess' unwavering loyalty reassured the wise man to trust him and said, "They are peaceful creatures wherever they came from and mean no harm to us."

The two nervous explorers approached, smiling. Raoul wiped his sweaty brow and touched his head. "I...Raoul, he...Navaro," he said, pointing first at himself then to the doctor. The jungle headman nodded. The Xanaparadoo tribe sealed their bond with the aliens.

Kalaneet stood close to Raoul. Trembling in disbelief, and with bated breath, she lifted her hand to touch his blonde hair, travelling to the bushy beard and thick hairy chest. An ominous premonition welled inside her. Bewildered, she turned and buried her face on Pardess' shoulder.

"Dialogue will be somewhat difficult. We can use pantomime gestures, like a clown. I'll sketch a simple story of our journey, Navaro," Raoul stated.

"Brilliant," Navaro chuckled.

Raoul knelt and started drawing on the soggy mud. The natives converged, stupefied. "Indeed a simple story, but they understood, tracing their eyes on your fingers at the doomed ship."

Outside Pardess' house, the explorers slept on hammocks lashed between the trees. At night cicadas clicked, owls hooted, Kalaneet's cradle song echoed between the gallery of giants, and the overture climaxed with the jaguar's call. Kalaneet gave birth to a second son, and Pardess— with the villagers—built a small hut for the foreigners.

"I feel like a clown," said Raoul. A wide plaited raffia cord encircled their waists. Below the navel, a fibrous, soft twine protected the penis and strung between the buttocks cheeks.

"We're almost covered, like the scanty gear of the women during their monthly period." Navaro couldn't stop laughing and held his sides.

Raoul gnashed his teeth and complained, "I can't get used to walking bare feet. My soles blister and my big toe has a nasty ulcer."

"I have a lotion that might help. You realise, comrade, we will never leave this jungle. I see Kalaneet bathing her son," Navaro called.

Raoul winced in pain. Pardess was chasing a pet monkey around the compound when he noticed Raoul limping. He gestured both men to follow him. In the centre of the village stood a massive shed. Inside, it was divided by three partitions. The first horde was piles of arrows, spears, bows and slings. The second contained plants, seeds, dried fruit and vegetables. The last and most distinct were row upon row of clay pots, bottles and jars. Raoul and Navaro were lost in amazement. Dried ground specific plants and leaves were bottled in different receptacles for medicinal purposes. A range of jars were filled with a white powder, oils extracted from vegetables were preserved in pots and the paragon bitter herbs sealed in bottles.

"Life saving, every conceivable sickness of the jungle has symbols, an apothecary," Raoul exclaimed, enchanted.

Pardess indicated a small jar and gave it to Raoul. He showed him where to apply the dark paste. "Their methods, though they may seem primitive to the white man, are more effective than our ways. The bitter herb's therapeutic properties are extraordinary." The physician remarked and continued, "I think the white powder is a repellent against insect bites and infections, and so are the oils. I am baffled by the illustrations of snakes and poisonous crawlers. Maybe they daub the powder on punctures, and use ligatures and wooden clamps displayed here, or bleed with leeches preserved in jars. They must have ingenious knowledge of antivenin. Malaria is the worst killer, victims are the young."

Within weeks, both men and the Indians learnt to communicate with impersonated hilarious sounds, grunts, gestures, mime and laughter. A lofty, spirited camaraderie blossomed.

* * *

The night was wild. Forked lightning flashed through the forests, followed by roaring thunder and torrential rain. Raoul heard a chilling scream. He woke Navaro. They saw Pardess running towards them, flinging his arms. "Son, son," he cried.

Navaro grabbed his bag. Something dreadful had happened. Flashes embedded in his mind of the man he could not save on the last expedition. With his heart racing, the doctor made a sign of the cross across his chest as he and Raoul followed Pardess back to the longhouse. Kalaneet was in hysterics as the child gasped for air. After examining the boy, Navaro delivered his diagnosis. "He has diphtheria. The swelling is fatal. I need to make an incision in the throat so that he can breathe," Navaro said.

Kalaneet's face was veiled with despair. Pardess watched the doctor holding the knife over the flames to sterilize it. Raoul stared at the confused Indian, who did not comprehend the implication of the surgical instrument. Threat hung in the air, but there was no time to explain. Heedful of the threat, Navaro nodded and tipped his head towards Pardess indicating to Raoul that he should stand behind the concerned father. The situation was tense, every moment was life threatening. Knife in hand, Dr Navaro stooped over the child.

Raoul was on edge as he fixed his eyes fixed on Pardess who was about to spring on the physician. Like a panther, he pounced upon the father to keep him back, and they fought with rage. Swiftly, Navaro punctured a small opening in the air pipe, the boy's chest rose and fell with gentle breathing. Kalaneet knelt near the doctor, kissing his hands. For a split second, from the corner of his eye, Raoul saw Kalaneet laughing. He flashed his hand towards them and Pardess turned his head. Raoul loosened his grip and the dazed Indian staggered to Kalaneet and his son, his dark eyes moist.

Kalaneet glanced at Raoul and drew close to him. She brushed her fingers upon his large hand, turned it upward and hid her face in his palm, sobbing. The Indian Kalaneet of the timeless Amazon splendor ignited past embers. He remembered another season; another he'd loved, snatched from his life. Raoul's throat felt dry, his chest tight. He wanted to hold Kalaneet, but how could he?

The devoted doctor lay all night beside the child. Every hour, he trickled a few drops of bitter herbs into his mouth and rubbed eucalyptus balm on the chest to ease the air flow. Around the tiny aperture on the throat, he spilled a thin layer of white powder. Kalaneet sponged her son's face with cool water. Pardess and Raoul rubbed the boy's body with oils.

At dawn they hastened with more medications and soothing lotions from the apothecary. Nahar, the headman's daughter, carried wild honey and placed it near the exhausted Navaro. He watched her face recede as he fell asleep. The villagers brought food and sat cross-legged around Pardess' home, humming. Within a few days the youngster recovered. He romped in circles chasing his father and Raoul.

* * *

The mating Jaguars prowled. Navaro heard faint rustling. Nahar approached and sat beside him. Above the shrine of trees, the rhythm of the night pulsated. Navaro dedicated his day to the sick. Raoul, in the past leaving the shores of his country, had vowed never to return. At present, a threat hung over him like a dark shadow and preyed on his mind. He was convinced Spain would send another expedition in search of the *Marqueza*. The isolated paradise was a hermitage to the Indians of the Amazon. With a burning heart, Raoul pledged to clip the wings of the predators.

"It is imperative we tell the chief and Pardess of the menacing danger. With every drop of blood in my veins, I shall defend and shield the people of the river," Raoul's fiery eyes flashed.

Staunchly, Navaro replied, "I agree. I am assured the conquistador will relentless pursue the stretch around the mouth of the Amazon. Entranced, the tribe squatted facing the legendary headman. To the left stood Pardess and Raoul. Emotional, the chief said, "Pardess speak, Raoul speak."

As visionary, Raoul broke the silence in simple but profound words and Pardess translated. Raoul waved his hand across the forests, his words soul stirring. "Trees, animals, birds, river, your heart is there. Protect them with your life. Forests belong to you. Bad people come from far, big ships. They hurt your women, they bring ugly devils with fire in them, shining spears, knives, hurt your body." Raoul flung his arms. "Attack your spears, bows and arrows. When danger, hide women and children in forest. When safe, come out. Your warriors will protect you. Hide all canoes in reeds. Proud heroes of the mighty river, my spirit is with you. I help. Look at picture." Open mouthed, they followed Raoul's hand. He outlined small groups of Indians in canoes, others hidden behind trees and bushes.

With a heart of oak, Pardess drew their attention and flared, "When you see, hear enemy signal call of the macaws, when you see, hear friends call of the toucans."

The rebel Raoul brushed his beard and stipulated, "Tactics, war games are essential against invaders. The Spanish ships have big guns and destructive weapons; they could wipe the entire tribe out, a catastrophe. The natives' advantage is the jungle, fast small canoes, silent bows and arrows, and our strategy's help."

* * *

Raoul's predictions were accurate. Almost three years had passed. The rains came and so did the Spanish Conquistador. Splendid *Larquitta* with one hundred and fifty on board anchored in the sheltered bay on the extreme right of the delta. The westerly breeze filled the ships' wide sails. Through the channel she sped, close to the wind, racing across the wild swell and leaving behind a trail of spindrift as she glided towards the primitive jungle.

"The Amazon!" Captain Garibaldi cheered.

Pardess and eight Indians paddled the marsh. Raoul and Navaro led the second team of canoes. The heat was stiflingly humid and beautiful butterflies laced the trees. Pardess was disturbed by monkeys' behavior. Primarily he used his keen perception and sharpness of eyes and ears. He leaned and listened. His face touched the bronze water. Prudently, the Amazonian detected impending danger and imitated the macaw's shrill. Raoul responded and the code was mimed to the Xanaparadoo braves all along the river.

Larquitta's commander was aware of dangerous navigation amidst shoals and mud banks. "So still, not a ripple on the river," he growled, wrung his hands and then called at the top of his voice to the midshipman on the crow's nest. "Watch out for tributaries!"

The ship drifted a kilometer downstream. Frightened birds screeched when the anchor dropped with a tremendous splash. Captain Garibaldi took out his fob watch and said, "At dawn, I want three long boats to survey the interior. Myself and my first mate shall accompany. The remaining crew and soldiers stay on board. There is no sign of life except birds and monkeys." He guffawed.

The davits were set up to swing the long boats down. The soldiers descended a wide rope ladder, the ends of which swished in the brackish water. "Shoulder the muskets," ordered the captain and looked at his compass.

Concealed, between the winding tributary Navaro and Raoul treaded across to Pardess. The tall Indian whispered, "Once the soldiers reach the bend in the far corner," he indicated, "We'll trap them."

The first barrage of arrows zoomed at the long boat in the rear. "I can't see a soul. They hide in the undergrowth," shouted a terrified soldier. Alarmed, the conquistadors fired blindly when another discharge of arrows fatally wounded four. The boat swayed and rocked. Terrified, the Spaniards lost balance and dived. Within minutes, hungry piranhas swarmed. Their jagged teeth ripped open the flesh and like a shredder, they devoured the victims.

Garibaldi heard the agonizing screams. He signaled to the first mate in the second boat. "Row fast, wait in the bush among the dense foliage." He broke out in a cold sweat, spotting a canoe weaving in the shadows. Instinct and a split-second decision prompted the man of the seas to swing the boat and escape the breadth of the river in the opposite direction.

The conquistador ploughed the oars with accelerating strokes through the weedy slush for cover. As the blushing sun was setting, the Indians crawled like predatory cats, the jaguars snarled at the smell of an unfamiliar scent, and the soldiers crouched in fear above the mud bank.

"Wild beasts," muttered a soldier, with chattering teeth.

"I hear something close by. Makes the flesh creep," said the first mate, his pulse racing.

Leaping Indians lunged their long spears and the officer was impaled to a tree. The conquistador sprayed continuous lead shots at them. Blood and fury breathed revenge.

A graveyard hush pervaded in the jungle. Defiant, Pardess exposed himself and pursued Garibaldi. His men fired at the Indians, but missed. The small canoe swerved in circles. The captain, camouflaged in the reeds, hissed, "We have a slight chance if we split, confuse them. Four of you sneak into this dark hole. Make your way back to the ship." He took his compass out. "You will need it."

The Xanaparadoo drove the fleeing invaders deeper to the perils of the swamps. The conquistador shrieked, chilled to the marrow as they struggled before being sucked into the quicksand.

Captain Garibaldi and three soldiers trod warily through the long grass until, exhausted, they fell asleep. Nimble as a squirrel, Pardess skulked along the lower branches. He hurled himself upon the captain with powerful fists. Gasping for air, the master felt the ground sliding from underneath him. His neck broke like a twig.

Pardess fumed and spat again. "Our blood and heart is here. This is our forests, our river, our animals and birds, our woman and children, our warriors. You are the worst predators, enemies, invaders, poison." He frothed at the mouth and stamped both feet on the ground, a signal the natives recognized. Pardess whistled, the village was deserted. Kalaneet remembered the tune from childhood. Behind the trees and sheltered hideouts the tribe emerged, perturbed.

Kalaneet, like a fawn, sprinted across the compound into Pardess' arms. "Kalaneet," he whispered. The Xanaparadoo's jubilation was electrifying. The headman approached and hugged Pardess. Behind him stood Nahar, her face was veiled with melancholy. We must leave early tomorrow and join Navaro, Raoul and our heroes near the big ship. The enemy will never leave, never." Pardess' eyes blazed. He turned and touched Nahar's hair with tenderness. "I'll bring Navaro back."

Kalaneet snuggled beside her husband as their older son dreamed, the baby gurgled, owls hooted, and the jaguar purred around her male.

* * *

Life throbbed in the Amazon as it had for thousands of years. An oil lamp suspended from the side of the ship shone upon the bosun as he alighted on the quarter deck. He cast his eyes to the dark.

"War of nerves," said an officer, approaching with rapid giant strides.

"I wonder how far downstream the three boats steered. We've been waiting and waiting," the bosun snapped.

"It'll be a relief with the rising sun," the officer mumbled.

Power of strength, Pardess and eight tribesmen waded through the marsh, always watchful for lurking crocodiles and predators. Pardess thought of Kalaneet. He ached for her. The forest's wilderness was their sanctuary and conquistador vermin had shattered their lives. Heaving, Pardess mimicked the trill of the gorgeous toucans again and again...

"He is back. Not far from here. What a breed of man," Navaro laughed, exultant.

Raoul tapped Pardess shoulder. "She is trapped from every angle," he remarked. "I sailed in those ships before on expeditions and know them well. We should burn it," he spat.

"How?" Pardess stammered. Raoul explained, "We must plan with the tribe. It is vital, most important, to target the main magazine. The assault on the ship has to be coordinated at the same time."

Navaro watched eagle wing Pardess. He'd come to love the Indian and virtuous people of the amazon.

"I promised Nahar to bring you back. The captain and his soldiers will never return. Many of our warriors fly now with the spirits." Saddened, the hunter gazed at a flock of birds sweeping above. The jaguar's forlorn call echoed beyond as canoes amassed around the *Larquitta*. The natives clambered into the dark hull of the ship like rats.

"I hear the savages," A second officer yelled, frantic.

Soldiers and crew rushed with muskets and swords. The agile Pardess and several Indians crawled along the bulwarks as more canoes streamed out between the reeds.

"Number one, run out your guns," bosun rasped.

The gunners poured the grape and canister. Like fire ants, the Xanaparadoo stormed the *Larquitta* and scaled her sides. To the death and fierce with veils of wrath, the Indians lashed into fury. The air was filled with the acrid smell of cordite. Raoul grabbed an oil lamp hanging at the entrance of the dry hold. Navaro and Pardess followed him inside to where barrels of gunpowder, numerous leather cases and bags were stored. Swiftly, they filled some of the bags and spread the gunpowder in an unbroken line, ascending the staircase to the main deck. Raoul smashed the oil lamp on the gunpowder and the three sprinted toward the poop deck.

Pardess raised a rallying cry, "Jump, jump off the ship, now!"

A Spaniard hid behind some bales and aimed his musket and Pardess staggered under shooting pains. The soldier swung back and dived. As he came up to breathe, an arrow perforated his jugular vein.

"We'll lower Pardess on the rope ladder," said Navaro in panic, a chill running down his spine. Like a raging bull, he bellowed, "Paddle faster! Away from the ship, get away from the ship!"

Within minutes, a tremendous explosion erupted as the magazine detonated. The ship rumbled as blazing fire belched in all directions, licking the oak beams and rigging. Trapped in the inferno, their clothes alight, the soldiers jumped into the river as the arrows showered at them. Bodies scattered among timber fragments drifted downstream. Crippled, the Larquitta groaned and sank.

* * *

The breeze rolled in, Toucans and Macaws screeched, and monkeys swung from tree to tree. The braves rowed towards the village as the forest sighed around them. Raoul bent over.

"Destiny is written in the wind," Pardess voice was faint. "Kalaneet."

Raoul howled like a wounded animal. Navaro wept and touched Pardess' face as he was seized by an uncontrollable spasm. The silent warrior could not keep his promise to Nahar.

In despair, the doctor sobbed for all the dead heroes floating in the Amazon. His tears were shed for the noble people of the jungle who'd sacrificed their lives. Navaro was ashamed of his ancestry, ashamed to be called a Spaniard.

Raoul, Navaro and two Indians carried Pardess on a raffia stretcher, covered with ferns and reeds. They placed him at Kalaneet's feet. She swooned and collapsed. Tragic with desolation, she grieved, and did not leave the house for several weeks. Raoul watched and cared for her sons. Nahar, Navaro and the villagers cooked.

"This is a favourite dish my mother used to make. It seems so long ago," Raoul said as he caressed Kalaneet's flushed cheeks. Kalaneet's eyes were bathed in tears. "The children are asleep. Come Kalaneet, let's go for a walk. The owls and jaguars miss you."

They sat beneath the trees and listened to the rhapsody of the night. Raoul felt tightness in his chest and said, "Destiny is written in the wind. Those were Pardess' last words. He called your name. Perhaps destiny is written in the wind with you, Kalaneet. Every breath and step I take, I shall love and protect you for the rest of my days." The doleful hoot of the owl pervaded above the gallery of trees as Kalaneet lay on the warm earth. Gently, Raoul ran his fingers upon her beautifully carved features. Tormented, Kalaneet thought of Pardess and emitted a faint cry. Raoul drew her into his arms to comfort her.

* * *

The following year, the headman blessed the couple in marriage. Raoul loved Kalaneet. She was the crowning fulfillment in the arena of his life. The driftwood followed the magnetic force of his destiny and anchored above the riverbank in the sanctuary of the giants. Kalaneet gave birth to a third son, named Pardess as the call of the splendid male jaguar shivered on the pillars of the forest and the magnificent female followed his scent.

11 ZEBEDEE THE EUNUCH

Zebedee, personal slave to General Hadrian Maximilian, was a tall eunuch with the strength of a powerful bull. He watched the orgies in the auditorium with revulsion.

The Roman dignitary sprawled on the cool marble floor, totally inebriated, saliva dribbling from his open mouth. Between his thighs, a naked woman peered up at Zebedee, leered and broke into a hyena's laugh.

The hall reeked with intoxicating spirits, foul sweaty bodies, semen and spicy food. The female crawled like an animal and slithered down Hadrian's lower legs. She swilled more wine from a decanter, mocking the giant slave, and spat the liquid at him.

The humiliation was more than flesh and blood could bear. Zebedee wanted to wring her white neck. His throat dry and tight, he wanted to scream. Transfixed, he stood above the despised general, his eyes blazing with hatred. That night, the eunuch vowed never to be trampled under the wheels of the Roman Chariots.

Erect, Zebedee walked out to the garden and leaned against the olive tree. He sighed with relief at being out of the stifling den of iniquity. He drew deep breaths, inebriated by the sweet scent of the frangipani that filtered into his nostrils. The fresh, clean air filled his lungs. His muscles were stiff and aching. Spotting two shadows below, he waited and remembered. Five years had passed since that abominable day.

* * *

Ben Zvi, the leader of the Jewish heroes, Zebedee and the patriots hid in a maze of caves in the sandy hills spread across the arid Judean wilderness.

Loaded with arms, the Romans—*Corps d'Armée*—hunted the enemy.

The rebel Hebrew visionaries were flushed out with fury from their burrows like angry hornets, their weapons spears, bows and arrows as they cried out their distinguished code—*War to the death.*

From dawn to dusk, the buzzards' shrieks meant advancing Romans. At night, the eerie jackal's call signaled danger.

The general and his infantry of two thousand men advanced on the hills. "Set fire to the dry bushes in the east and west! We'll dig them out like trapped animals," Hadrian screamed.

Flames belched forth and black smoke camouflaged the Zealots who flitted between the jutting rocks and scrambled to higher ground, legendary in their escape.

With relentless aplomb, the general and his ambuscade pursued the clusters of combatants. Below the summit, the bold and audacious Ben Zvi and his comrades hid in narrow hidden labyrinth—a refuge for jackals.

Determined to confuse the soldiers, Zebedee and his men sprinted and zigzagged like gazelles defiantly sacrificing their lives and, with unswerving loyalty, fought the Roman infantry into retreat.

The wind changed.

"Skirt around and trap them on the lower side," Hadrian thundered.

Outwitted and exhausted, Zebedee watched with stark horror as the Romans' noose closed in. There was nowhere to run. He shuddered as dark thoughts of dungeons and torture flooded his mind, tied to the wheel while his bones were crushed by an iron bar at their cruel hands.

As the captured Jews were executed, Hadrian stood over Zebedee, whom he'd stripped naked. The long, magnificent peacock plume of his galea stroked against Zebedee's chest and travelled below his navel.

"I will not kill you. It is much too swift. For the rest of your days, you will serve me in total silence." With a slash of his sword, he castrated Zebedee and then cut out his tongue.

* * *

Zebedee longed for the days of his youth, running through the olive cypress and frangipani trees with Ben Zvi. More than ever, the eunuch—once rhapsodist— missed laughter, Ben Zvi, singing, and playing his lyre.

Indeed, music seduced Zebedee's soul and soothed his savage heart.

Zebedee waited under the ancient olive tree. Blood surged through his throbbing temples. The couple in the shadows of the white marble pillars spoke in whispers.

"Come with me, Cardenia. Leave your husband, follow your destiny of freedom," said Fabian Oratorius, the handsome Centurion.

"You speak in riddles." She nestled her head against his chest and he brushed her mass of golden locks.

"The despotic Roman Empire is crumbling. Greed and ruthlessness will ultimately cause its final destruction. I never wish to return to my country of birth—never." Fabian gnashed his teeth.

"I carry Hadrian's child," Cardenia whimpered.

"I will protect you and the child." Fabian kissed her flushed cheeks and ran his fingers through her hair. "The powerful Roman legions broke the spirit of the Jewish people, destroyed their Holy Temple in Jerusalem, plundered their vessels, butchered and enslaved thousands. The fugitives fled to the wilderness." The centurion paused as she listened. "I cannot let them destroy us too. If they find out about us, General Hadrian will not hesitate to execute us both. Zebedee will be here soon. He'll join us on our journey. The gentle giant is familiar with the desert."

Cardenia despised the Romans as much as Fabian did. When Hadrian went away, the centurion secretly showed her the abominable pits of horror containing the painful torture devices.

Cardenia bitterly deplored the starved cage animals released into the arena to savagely maul their victims while the Romans watched and cheered.

Her heart had turned to stone when her father, Pliny Augustus disappeared a year after Zebedee's tragedy. She grieved for both.

Surrounded by senators, tribunes and counselors, Pliny Augustus was the power behind the board, but Hadrian had jealously disagreed with him on many issues and, months later Pliny Augustus had vanished.

One morning, Zebedee had taken Hadrian's black stallion for a morning ride to keep it in excellent form. Two hours later, he dismounted near a tall cactus hedge to rest the horse. Partially hidden in the sand, Zebedee spotted a Roman gold coin. His keen eyes had traced tracks to an old dry well screened by weeds. Augustus's skeleton lay there, clad in white robes, his empty eye sockets peering unseeingly at Zebedee.

They'd kept the secret between the three of them—Zebedee, Fabian and Cardenia—as they dared not speak of it to anyone. When spies lurked in the dark, it was dangerous to meddle in politics.

Cardenia knew it was Hadrian who had killed her father but there was no proof during the prolonged investigation. All lips were sealed and Cardenia had to protect her unborn child at all costs.

Vendetta burnt inside Zebedee, Fabian and Cardenia's souls. She seethed with hatred against the virulent Romans who abused female slaves every day, sharing them with the beastly, predatory soldiers.

She was aware Hadrian copulated with many slaves and the abdominal filth made her scream.

Fabian clutched her to his chest. "I am here. Under my wings, I'll protect and provide for your child, our child. With every breath and step you take, your centurion will be near you. Zebedee is the limb to our freedom. He will guide and lead us, a true manna in the wilderness. I trust him implicitly. He will love your offspring."

Cardenia's sad thoughts returned to the gentle mute. How he must suffer living in a silent world.

Nimble–footed, Zebedee stepped out from the shadows. Fabian hugged him.

"Greetings," said Cardenia, nervously. She saw the honesty in the eunuch's brown eyes and trusted him. On impulse, she reached up to wrap her dainty arms around his broad muscular neck. He smiled.

"We must make haste," said Fabian to Zebedee. "I took the general's black stallion and secured behind the thick cactus hedge. It's packed with provisions and garments to blend with the land, a precaution in case we are ambushed." Fabian frowned. "We might be lucky to find date trees and hunt wild deer. I have experience launching spears with accuracy, so does Zebedee." Fabian chuckled.

"Zebedee, go to the stables and bring back Hadrian's two white stallions. If the guard is suspicious, do what you have to. We'll wait, be quick. Thank you, my friend."

The eunuch nodded and disappeared.

The sentry often saw Zebedee feeding and brushing the horses. Nonchalantly, he paced to the water trough. Zebedee nuzzled the magnificent animals. He decided to distract the man and raised his voice. "Bring me the red jar immediately. There's a swelling on the horse's hind leg—looks like a nasty bite. The general will be furious."

The guard jumped up with the medication, and bent to place it near the giant. Swift as a cheetah, Zebedee twisted his neck.

The centurion sighed with relief when the eunuch and stallions came into sight. He tapped the mute on the shoulder.

"What we are to do, Zebedee, is the worse punishment on the evil Hadrian. An eye for an eye—the tyrant will never see his wife again." Fabian wiped his sweaty face and turned to Cardenia. "He knows you carry his child. Nightmares will haunt him."

The centurion gazed at the stars. "Cardenia beloved, you will raise your offspring amongst the proud Jewish people and ride the white stallion. Like a wounded animal, Hadrian will grovel on the ground, chasing his Roman Centurion, Zebedee and his three stallions blindly until death snatches him from this humiliating execution." Fabian held Cardenia in his arms. "With total devotion Zebedee will shield you from harm and watch over you for life."

The eunuch wiped away his tears and the three rode into the night.

* * *

Ben Zvi stepped outside the cave and scanned the rugged mountains. Spirals of dust rose from the valley as three horses came into view. He mimicked the buzzard's shriek. Within minutes, groups of warriors emerged from their hideout.

Ben Zvi murmured, "They are definitely not soldiers but ride magnificent horses. From the distance, I do not recognize their garments. The ravine beyond is deserted. Secure it for me. No killing."

The horses cantered to a stop at the foot of the cliffs and Ben Zvi saw a giant of a man scan the cliffs with hawk eyes. He indicated to Fabian the man on the horse next to him and dismounted before helping the third rider down.

Ben Zvi and his men approached slowly. His heart pounded. From spies, he'd learned Zebedee's fate. He knew his friend's familiar face well and cried out with despair, "Zebedee!"

Ben Zvi flung his spear aside and ran towards the mute giant. Zebedee uttered gurgling sounds of recognition. The leader knelt before him and kissed Zebedee's hands and the hem of his robe. The eunuch gently lifted him, shook his head then wrapped his strong biceps around the weeping rebel.

Cardenia touched her belly, where her unborn child kicked, knowing they had come to the right place for protection.

* * *

Hadrian—deranged, fuelled with hate and revenge—savaged the land, spreading terror across the southern territories. He frothed at the mouth like a rabid dog and the blood boiled in his veins as his battalions marched in files, pilfering and destroying, searching for his wife, the traitorous Centurion and the eunuch.

Hadrian never suspected Cardenia would dare ride a great distance because of her pregnancy. The irony of fate leered at him. In the north, clusters of Hebrews dispersed in hidden labyrinths and pockets of swamp, ready to ambush the enemy.

* * *

Ben Zvi watched as Zebedee beat his head on the magnificent cypress tree in frustration, his face sad. The mute was trying to say something. The rebel's heart ached for his friend. He touched the eunuch's trembling hands. "There is a Roman garrison near Lake Tiberius. To the west is a pocket of swamps—a good place to hide. Galerius Marcello, the barbarian commander in charge of Northern Judea, relentlessly follows our shadows, fighting against his destiny. Last year the butcher captured one of our heroes. For hours he flayed his skin, and then dumped him in the valley, still alive. The jackals soon appeared, smelling the blood."

Zebedee covered his face, shaking. A tower of strength, he stood and paced up and down, slashing his hands across his throat.

"Yes, Zebedee my friend, we'll garrote the lot of them", Ben Zvi rasped. "We must steer far north beyond Galilee, and below to the border of Tyre. Olive groves and massive cedar trees line the mountains there, a breathtaking arena. I know the route. It's a hazardous journey we must make before the Romans discover our tracks. We are united, branded together for life, my brave Zebedee. We'll crush the virulent Romans forever."

* * *

For several weeks, they travelled.

"We are short of provisions. Cardenia is weak. I suggest before we head to the marsh, we steal food from the Roman camp. It's too risky in the day but tonight, we go. From above the ridge, we'll watch their movements and when it is safe, we will sneak in and take what we need."

Later that night, darkness hooded the Roman camp. A few lamps shone inside the tents. The melancholy call of a jackal echoed across the valley. To keep the horses quiet, Fabian kneaded his fingers through their splendid manes until they settled and the jackal quietened.

The two crouched in the ditch. Leopard-like, they skulked and crawled through the darkness towards the kitchen scent. Not a soul was inside.

Ben Zvi lifted a canvas bag and filled it with bread, grain, goat cheese and goatskin bottles filled with milk. Zebedee indicated towards a whole cooked goat in the copper drum. Smiling, he slung it on his back and they fled.

The brave, weary men lumbered towards their destination—the swamp—where patriots crept out from the quagmire to greet them.

* * *

That evening, Galerius Marcello strolled down the path to Lake Tiberius. He listened to the crickets and croaking frogs. He'd suspected for quite some time, where the invisible feral animals, the Jews, were harbored. He schemed.

* * *

"The Romans are brewing something. Our spies surveyed a cavalry of horses galloping towards us." Ben Zvi was concerned. "I've had a dreadful premonition the troops will follow our tracks shortly."

Zebedee bit his lip. He knelt and drew a battle scene in the mud with quick fingers. On the left and right he drew the rebels standing, a wide gap between them. He showed how the Jews could spread simultaneously on both sides, circle in opposite directions, surround the Romans and drive them deep into the swamp.

"Brilliant Zebedee, brilliant!" Ben Zvi peered excitedly at Cardenia and Fabian. Solemnly he said to them, "We are not in fertile Egypt amongst the tall reeds in the Nile any longer. Here, the swamps are infested with mosquitoes, snakes and quicksand's—the perfect grave for a Roman burial. We'll confuse them and our rebels will trap the cowards in the perilous quicksand."

"An eye for an eye! They'll choke and die slowly," Fabian spat.

Cardenia embraced Ben Zvi. "You are a remarkable breed of man."

The warrior wiped away her tears with his index, then turned to Zebedee and laid his hand on the gentle mute's shoulder. "There are none like you, Zebedee," he whispered.

Suddenly alert at the sound of galloping hooves, he swung back and rapped out, "The messenger has arrived back. No doubt he will inform us the Romans are converging. Zebedee and Fabian, I want you to take Cardenia and the three stallions up the hill and hide in the pine forest. Throughout the night, our groups will skirt the perimeter of the cliff and lie in wait for them."

At dawn the enemy rode in and dismounted. Ben Zvi whispered, "They are advancing on foot."

Breast plate, steel helmet and plumes, Marcello the Louse, headed his troops. He lashed out with fury, his voice echoing off the cliff. "Slaughter the lot!"

The rebel warriors ran out from their cover at full tilt with a hue and a cry. Pandemonium ensued. In disarray, the Roman infantry gave chase. The zealots lured them in circles through the tall and thorny bush, and into the boggy marsh. There was nowhere for the Roman army to escape to.

Between the reeds, concealed men strung their bows and arrows. Innumerable Romans fell, mortally wounded in the squashy morass.

Ben Zvi stalked Marcello with caution. The commander panicked, rushed to the right and made a sudden leap. He shrieked as he landed in the hellish mud. Slowly and silently, the quicksand swallowed him as he gasped and struggled until he vanished.

Esprit De Corps, Jewish fighters, spirited the army's horses between the tall cypress trees and ransacked the camp from which Marcello's troops had fled.

* * *

Marcello's death reached General Hadrian's ears through a spy.

Rome's *Vin D'Honneur* granted Hadrian's request to be Governor of Judea. Rome was aware the Jews were a threat to the powerful Roman Empire. Hadrian played a most significant role in the stage against their enemy.

Cardenia gave birth to her son in the large tent under the cedar. The bulbul sang on the swaying branch. Three months later, Governor Hadrian arrived in Galilee with his infantry of two thousand men. They camped a fair distance from the deserted garrison.

Late one night, a scout scaled the stone wall to Hadrian's bedroom, his face disguised by a mask. Deftly, he flung a leather pouch through the open window. Inside was a brief note…. *Cardenia has a son.*

Shattered, Hadrian slumped to the marble floor. "My son…my son" he stammered. His stomach turned into knots of anguish. "I shall dip the eunuch, the centurion traitor and Cardenia in boiling oil!" He retched.

* * *

The wise patriarch, Boaz, sat cross-legged near the tent. He gazed at the splendid panorama of cedars.

Ben Zvi, Zebedee and Fabian ascended towards him. The three reclined against the massive gnarled olive tree. The scholar watched Fabian's face. "To survive we must constantly weave and move, avoid capture by Hadrian and his horde." He brushed his long grey beard.

"They trample on every single blade of grass, overturn stones and snuffle. For days my mind whirled in a violent storm and then a solution sparked...Spider's Cobwebs."

The three gawked, perplexed and open-mouthed, Ben Zvi asked, "Spider's cobwebs?"

"Yes, this daring guerilla warfare must be executed as follows...before dawn, throughout the day to sunset, and that particular night."

The ageing philosopher smoothed his moustache. "The vicinity surrounding Hadrian's garrison and beyond, is a sprawl of cacti hedges bearing excellent fruit—ones you can peel the skin with needle-sharp thorns. Camels and mules relish them," he chuckled.

"The army has pitched their tents in the valley. A wide gully cuts between the camp and the hill on the opposite side. You approach from the rear of the hill and descend halfway down. Start digging holes, then weave back towards the summit. You'll be screened from view by the thick, tall cactus. Boaz smirked. "With your swords, start digging holes and slash the middle blades of the cactus into the cobweb of pits, then seal them with layers of twigs, leaves and earth. Weave back towards the summit. You'll be screened from view by the thick, tall cactus bushes."

Intrigued Zebedee stared at Boaz and clapped his hands.

Tired, Boaz rubbed his bloodshot eyes and said, "This game of deceit is to lure and snare the soldiers in the cobwebs and, to attract the attention of their troops, and our men will imitate the prolonged wailing cries of the jackal."

Fabian scowled. "We'll provoke the infantry," he roared. "Exposed to full view above the summit, I will be the torch bearer. They will watch me in disbelief as I hold the flame high in the air. Rebel groups against two thousand mighty Roman swordsmen—such audacity! Hadrian will go berserk as he gives us chase."

"Yes, gallant Fabian, a good move. Dangerous perils, but knights like you, Zebedee and Ben Zvi are rare. Riding, you will destroy with ruling passions. The troops will clamber blindly and turn into the spider's cobweb. The unexpected will befall them with horror. The sharp needles of the cacti are painful. They can cause acute inflammation and swelling if they are not pulled out immediately. There are thousands of them on each cacti blade."

Fabian blurted, "Fascinating, how deep and wide are the openings to be?"

The revered thinker said, "From foot to waist deep, and approximately from ankle to knee wide. Make sure the traps are not too close. This must be well-coordinated until you reach the highest level and wait for the night." He stared at Zebedee, "As long as Hadrian the viper is alive, with savagery, he'll butcher us. We need to get to him first. Let me know when you are ready."

Humbled, Zebedee knelt before him and kissed the hem of his white robe. Boaz touched his head. "Rise Zebedee, you will be loved and remembered for generations to come."

Boaz addressed the warriors. "It is imperative to abandon the sanctuary on the mountain before the onslaught, ride the horses to the refuge in the cypress forest on the fourth hill, then proceed on foot as planned." He turned to Zebedee. "With the herd, take Cardenia and Samson, then wait until the men return from their master stroke."

"There are fifty of us on this mountain and fifty guarding the second peak," remarked Ben Zvi. "We outnumber the horses. Some riders will mount the geldings and mares, holding the reins of the second one and gallop forth. We will split into groups of ten. Zebedee, Fabian, Cardenia and her son with fifty braves will drive the horses and reach pastures and refuge well before the Sinai Desert. I shall follow behind with my division." Ben Zvi paused and brushed his beard. "We are fortunate to possess several magnificent stallions," he stated.

* * *

A week later the weather changed, the rain came down in sheets.

A spy directed Fabian and Zebedee to the goats' pen on the far side of the Roman camp. Not a soul was to be seen. Worming themselves between the posts, the men tied a rope around the bleating nannies' necks and slipped out.

Twice a day, Zebedee milked the goats. Everyone shared in drinking the rich white manna. Above the valley, the cavalry of horses stolen from the Romans grazed on the lush grass and munched shooting young plants. The fighters hunted the abundant stock of game for food.

The earth was carpeted with bright red flowers called Blood of the Maccabees, cyclamen, and poppies.

Migratory birds flocked from Africa, the bees hummed and the pine needles whispered. Spring pulsated and gave birth to new life. Revenge and death consumed Hadrian's heart of stone.

Under the shadow of his wing, the meek and devoted Zebedee protected Cardenia and her son, Samson. He slept outside her tent. The three were inseparable. When the infant gurgled, the happy mute answered with his own burbling sounds.

The scholar listened to the chorus of bulbuls perched on the magnificent cedar, heaving a sigh.

Boaz turned to Zebedee, with emotional appeal he said, "Your eyes speak. I follow your thoughts and share your ravaged, pining heart."

Zebedee kissed his hand.

Darkness cloaked the land as it has since the dawn of time. The breeze stole between the cedars.

Ben Zvi roasted ducks on the open fire. He stoked the small chips of coal, and then sat near Fabian, holding sleepy Samson on his knee. He glanced at the patriarch. "We are ready. Our plan is scheduled for the end of the month."

"Yes, I feel it in my ailing bones."

Cardenia shivered. She wrapped her shawl around her shoulders. Stiff, Fabian stretched his legs. Zebedee, fresh as a lark, lifted the boy and cradled him on his warm chest, kissing his wriggling toes.

"Thank you, dear Zebedee."

Ben Zvi kept turning the delicious birds on their backs. Knife in hand, Ben Zvi slit half a duck. Laughing he gave it to Boaz, and then served the others.

"Succulent, tender," Boaz chortled, licking his fingers and drew their attention. "A day's journey to the east, not far from the Valley of Heroes, nomadic tribes and their camels move with the seasons." He wiped his lips. "I've known Sheik Tawfik for many years. A fascinating character, he is an astrologer of the desert who roams with the beast of burden. I often sat with him in his spacious tent, surrounded by his wife and sons, drinking sweet black coffee, brewed slowly in a Finjan. A poet as well. They leave soon. I miss my days of wild youth. For weeks the caravans will steer towards the Jordan River."

Ben Zvi cut in, "The soldiers never hinder them."

"Quite right" Boaz nodded. "On occasions the nomadic desert dwellers barter young camels' meat in exchange for food." He paused and brushed his head. "Twice I crossed our land with them to Beersheba. Spectacular, like a painting, the curtains rose, orange red sky. Sheik Tawfik rode the king of the desert, followed by the train of golden camels to Beersheba, the most popular and largest market in the region."

Boaz watched Zebedee's eyes veil with sadness. "I can't stay here. Hadrian and his henchmen will shroud the entire area. I'll be safe milling in the herd, wearing the same garments and speaking their language—a perfect disguise. The young are skilled; weave beautiful pouffes with large strips of soft leather, filled with camel's hair. They fit them in front of the hump. Also expertise in rope ladder entwined in the animal's sides as they crouch down, making it easy to mount." He turned to Ben Zvi. "Please, take me to the Sheik early tomorrow. The mule and cart are at the back. You should be back in three days."

Zebedee had never ridden on a camel. He marveled at their powerful stamina, roaming the desert for days without water until they reached an oasis. Zebedee placed Samson on Cardenia's lap.

Boaz kissed her forehead and stroked the boy's golden curls. "Goodnight, Cardenia."

"We'll all meet in the Sinai Desert," Boaz sang out as Zebedee hugged him.

* * *

Julius Octavius, second in command to the governor, rushed forward with giant strides. Short winded, he puffed, "I saw a flash of light over there...on top of the second hill." He waved a hand across the panoramic view. "The constant jackal howling bewilders me. It sounds different. I think we have to check."

Hadrian listened. "The rebels prowl above like animals, unpredictable. Assemble the troops at once." He lashed with fury.

With two beatings of the drums, the army skirted the valley.

In high spirits Fabian, the torch bearer, stood on the summit. "You'll never capture me, not beautiful Cardenia or my dear friend, Zebedee. You are doomed," he yelled.

Hadrian recognized the centurion's voice. Seized with hysteria, he raved, "Kill the traitor!"

The soldiers ascended the hill and within a short while, the first victim stumbled and fell into the Spider's cobweb. The harder he struggled to get out, the deeper the cactus thorns penetrated.

"Get them!" Hadrian's raucous screams pealed across the landscape. Hundreds of disoriented Romans were trapped in the holes between the hedges.

The spiny and painful needles punctured the soldiers' arms, hands, necks, legs and faces, and most agonizingly...their eyelids. Pinned in the holes, the troops tried to crawl out. The knees and palms of their hands were raw with spikey spurs. Paralyzed with fear, their harrowing cries echoed in the surroundings.

Ben Zvi, knowing the topography stage below, roared, "Now!"

A blanket of barbed arrows showered the infantry. Again and again, they pelted with a hiss, leaving a trail of Roman bodies.

The zealots fled back to the cypress forest to get their horses. Zebedee carried Samson on his back, his eyes streaming with tears as Cardenia was swept into Fabian's arms and they headed south.

A solitary eagle ripped the chest open off a body. Between its long, sharp talons, the raptorial bird carried chunks of flesh and flew. Buzzards and hawks swooped.

"Bury the dead in a deep large pit, use pitchforks to lift them," Julius ordered.

Hadrian paced up and down the corridor and entered the sumptuous hall. His officers stood to attention and saluted him. Hands behind his back, holding a map, he glanced at Julius. "They are invisible and strike anywhere," he stormed. Flustered, he walked to the table and unfolded the parchment, then summoned the men to approach.

With a goose quill, Hadrian marked a circle. "We haven't surveyed this remote northern part. The cliffs and cedar trees are perfect sites for men and horses to blend between the rolling mountains."

"With your approval, Sir, may I select the most proficient swordsmen?" Tense, Julius waited.

A few seconds passed. "Certainly, we leave a day after tomorrow. We'll be gone for quite some time."

The commander raised his hand as Romans did. "Thank you."

The sun was rising as Hadrian sat on the bed. A lizard scurried near his toes. He missed Cardenia. It was almost two years since he last saw her. "My boy...my boy...he must be walking." His tortured mind raced. "Where do they shelter? In caves, tents, holes?" Shattered, Hadrian covered his face. Nausea overcame him. He poured the pitcher of water on his head and chest.

The army column left.

The summit was deserted. A few wild goats roamed. Animal bones and feathers were scattered beside abandoned open fires. Horses' hooves stamped the valley and slopes of the mountains where a hoopoe pecked grubs.

Hadrian spotted a small tent on the far side. A massive cedar's swaying branches shielded it from the cold wind. He sprinted towards it, Julius behind him.

Breathless, Hadrian tore open the flaps. It was empty. Two little boots mocked him.

Hadrian shrunk and dug his teeth deep into his left arm. Crazed he crawled, clawing through the mud, rambling. Delirious, the governor grabbed the child's shoes and inserted them in his top pocket. For a long while the two

Romans sat silent. "Cardenia chose to follow Fabian and the fanatics. They will drift with the wind, fighting alongside the rebels. I see Cardenia riding her white stallion. Someday the restless driftwood will find her magnetic sanctuary."

Julius paused and gazed ahead. "Cardenia is at last a free lark. It's her destiny." He watched the broken Hadrian. "The invisible enemies have many horses, strong and united, they vanished in all directions. Pointless staying here, I'll wait for your decisions."

* * *

One hundred horses, a caravan of camels, shepherds with goats and sheep flooded around the oasis.

Cardenia wore a flowing blue dress fringed with brilliant sequins. Fabian strolled beside her, and Samson, his little hands tight on Zebedee's muscular neck. Milling through the bustling crowd, Cardenia was ecstatic. The colours, the strong scented perfumes of Arabia, the aromatic coffee and sweet smells of spicy food, roasted sheep and goats on open fires were intoxicating.

"I am so happy." Cardenia brushed her body against Fabian's.

Zebedee tapped the centurion on the back and pointed at where Ben Zvi and Boaz hastened towards them.

"Greetings, lovely Cardenia," said the scholar and kissed her hand. "We are invited to Sheik Tawfik's tent."

The Sheik was captivated by his audience—the tall handsome Fabian, Ben Zvi with the imposing figure and eyes of a hawk, ravishing Cardenia, her son and Zebedee, a face he would never forget.

Soul stirring, he approached him and touched the mute's lips with his thumb. "You live in our hearts. Now we feast," Tawfik claimed.

They dipped their fingers into large copper bowls filled with rice and topped with succulent goat and slices of mutton.

The women baked flat bread. Tawfik's wife served black coffee, dates and figs.

"It took us longer to travel this time. You cannot hurry camels. We'll stay here a week or two. Water is essential," said the Sheik.

"In which direction are you heading next?" Fabian queried.

"Egypt, Pearl of the Orient and a busy market. Merchants flock there from great distances. We'll sell some of our male camels as there are too many of them. In spring, the females are due to calf. We must retain a healthy balance to keep the blood life of these strapping creatures." He paused and sipped his coffee.

"Do snakes ever strike them in the scorching sand?" Cardenia frowned.

"On rare occasions. An asp once attached between the toes of a young camel's cushioned foot. The animal did not survive, the poison spread quickly. He was only nine days old. These navigators of the desert provide us with milk, meat, hide and cover. They sniff the air and foretell the stress of hot, gusty winds. During the sand storms, they crouch down and we shelter between the loyal beasts."

Sheik Tawfik puffed on his *hookah*. He inhaled the smoke from a tube; drawing through water contained in a clay vase and held it out to Fabian. "Would you like to try this?"

Tawfik watched Fabian's face with amusement. The centurion breathed in, exhaled, and coughed hoarsely. Cardenia burst into laughter and so did the Sheik.

"Too strong for my throat and lungs but it calms and soothes the mind," said Fabian.

"But it calms and soothes the mind. What are your plans?" Tawfik asked.

"We'll scout the Roman's movements around the Dead Sea. Their shadows lurk in dark places. They are a disease. Our only way to freedom is to wipe the parasites from the earth." Fabian rubbed his eyes, fatigued from their journey.

Zebedee raised his hands high in the air, his palms cupping the sky, as in prayer.

"If at any time you are in need of help, food, a place to stay, our home is yours. Share our tents. They are well cushioned." Tawfik chuckled, puffing on his *hookah*. "A gift for you, Zebedee, to keep you warm at night." The sheik handed him a camel blanket.

"You are a peaceful man. We are grateful for your hospitality and generosity. All things must pass. The sun will rise again. *Salaam,* Sheik Tawfik," said Ben Zvi.

The night teemed with life. Snakes, lizards, scorpions and ants sheltered and raced on the undulating sand. At dawn, they buried deep in the holes. Zebedee made Boaz a soft saddle from camels' hide and hair, to enable him to ride in comfort. Gently stroking his black stallion, he lifted the scholar and sat in front of him. Boaz leaned forward and clasped his hands round Zebedee's waist.

Riding on the crest of the morning sun, they left on their splendid horses. The cavalry receded in the shimmering heat. Only the shepherds with flocks of goats and sheep remained for a few days.

* * *

Julius Octavius was a disciplinarian. He followed orders. During the past three years of Hadrian's seditious rule, he witnessed unimaginable atrocities. Julius abhorred brutality. He raked up the past and remembered. In spring the swallows had gathered on the roof of his beautiful home as he stood on the balcony.

The two estate guards were chasing a peasant carrying a stolen pheasant.

The shaking man pleaded, his pregnant wife and children were hungry. They whipped the man without mercy until he bled, then he was cuffed and whisked away. Julius had never forgotten his face nor the man's sunken eyes now etched in memory forever.

A more sinister tableau fogged his mind, hunting wild boars with the aristocrats. It was their feigned laughter that Marcello despised most. The poor animal had struggled to get up. They stabbed it again and again, gloating and cheering. Marcello did not partake in the sport again.

The mutinous officer rebelled silently against the rule of the Roman Empire. Julius, the traitor, a spy who knew the rebels had left weeks before. Hadrian trusted him but the officer despised the powerful tyrant. Risking his life, his heart beating high, the errant knight decided to betray Hadrian.

"I have heard from reliable sources that the Jewish rebels are in the region of the Dead Sea. I suggest we leave without delay." Julius pouted.

It was never conceivable to Hadrian's mind that his three most cunning, ingenious fugitives would break the tight net and dare slip back to the vicinity of the desert. Hadrian, his cavalry of fifty horses and ten mules loaded with provisions, arrived a month later, to the desolate wilderness. The heat was intense.

Julius saw two shepherds with their flock and approached them. "Water, water." He mimed licking his lips. "Water for horses," he indicated.

They understood. He followed them to a well beside the shady mountain.

With towering rage, Hadrian bellowed like a mad bull. "Not a soul…. Cliffs, caves and flies." He splattered one across his face.

"Where are they, my officer? Vanished again? Your predictions, your timing?" He smirked.

Julius bridled. "No Sir, they are smart—in fact extremely intelligent. I am acquainted with the entire region and to the north of the Jordan River. We must think the way they do. Fabian is a brilliant fox. I will find them, that I vow," he snapped and paced forward. Abruptly he stopped. "Yes, they were here." Julius picked up a child's coat and gave it to him.

Hadrian's eyes twitched, his body attacked by paroxysms of uncontrollable shaking. He screamed, "Get them, get them. I'll gouge out their eyes and hang them for the vultures."

The officer was drenched with perspiration. The deceptive game was paramount. Cautious, Julius played his role tactfully, "Forgive me sir, may I speak to the men? A subject of great interest, you understand?"

Hadrian nodded and huffed.

"Thank you." Julius turned and walked towards the exhausted troops. "Take the horses to the water, sea salt is good for their hooves and kills any mites on them. There is sparse vegetation to graze, even wild flowers and small bushes grow in this barren desert."

Julius paused, captured by the stark glimmering Dead Sea. "The Dead Sea lies in the bed of the Rift valley at its deeper point. This is also the lowest point on Earth below sea level. The Jordan River constantly flows into the basin. The evaporation is due to high temperatures. Never dries." Fascinated, ear strained, they stared at him. "No form of life exists in the water, too salty. One can only float because of the density of the salt. It is fifty miles long and fifteen miles across."

Weary, Julius shuffled back and sat cross legged beneath the cliff where Hadrian was battling the flies. "I'll rest my horse in a day, and then follow the hornet's scent on my own. I'll move quick and silent, undetected, tether my horse and shelter in caves. I will return in fourteen days."

"I am off to cool in the water. Damn flies, snakes, scorpions and exasperating heat," Hadrian coughed. "This land is swarming with the cursed enemies of the Roman empire," he roared. His fury rumbled above the elevation.

Julius followed the Jordan River for a few days then swung east. He found traces of dry horse dung. At night, through the yawning gully, he rode and continued to the next creek. He let the horse drink, and then steered up the hill, winding in between the thick bramble bushes and fichus trees. Blindly, he fumbled against a huge hollow rock. Julius tied the gelding to a tree and nested inside, still as a stirring mouse. Hearing the hum of men's voices, he froze.

* * *

Dawn…the dew was heavy. Ben Zvi walked outside his tent. His lungs were filled with the crisp morning air as he stood there for a few minutes. "A horse, there's a horse down there." He sniffed and stumbled back. Zebedee and Fabian rushed to him.

"Ours are above the hill, well-guarded. This snorting came from below me," he whispered.

"Zebedee, you go down first. I will cover the right, Fabian the left."

The Roman knight errant, riding his destiny with courage, crawled from the hole and leaned on the tree, stroking the horse's mane. Zebedee leapt in front of him but he did not attack the man. In disbelief, he stared at Julius who rubbed his face against the horse's head. Ben Zvi and Fabian appeared. The leader, sword in hand, pounced, about to slash Julius's neck. Swiftly Zebedee intercepted, tapping his fingers upon his own ears suggesting they listen to the enemy.

"He is right," cried out Fabian.

Ben Zvi stepped aside with breathless impatience and stood near the gentle giant. "Thank you, Zebedee. You are a gift in our Jewish blood."

Julius's chest felt tight.

"Fabian, summon all our fighters immediately. Zebedee, take the Roman and his horse. Follow Fabian."

Frantic, Cardenia hearing her centurion's raucous voice, ran with her son towards him. He held her in his arms, and then kissed Samson. "This meeting is of great significance. Don't be alarmed. I love you, beloved."

Tired, Boaz reached the arena of warriors.

Ben Zvi's voice cloaked the loftiness of the pine forests. "Julius, second in command to Hadrian, is here. He came on his own."

The silence was terrifying. Struck numb, Cardenia shivered and nestled her head on Fabian' shoulder as he kissed her hand.

"Zebedee, bring the Roman out."

Chilled to the spine, proud Julius of noble breeding, walked erect, head held high. The breeze sighed, the pine needles whispered.

Boaz lifted himself, and stared at the elite officer of the Roman Empire. Paralyzed with hate and fury, he swooned. Zebedee jumped up. He cradled Boaz, uttering faint gurgles.

"What I wish to say are words of truth. There is no greater elevation," said Julius. "Hadrian pays handsome amounts of gold for spies. No one followed me. His troops converge near the Dead Sea. I told him I'll return with the new moon. He has no idea whatsoever where you are. Life is a paradox, inexplicable at times, a magnetic force. I would like you to trust me and wish no more to live like an animal. You are inspiring predators, fearless and noble. I would like to join you." Julius paused and rested his eyes on Zebedee and Boaz.

"Insanity drives Hadrian to capture you, Zebedee, and Fabian, but predominately his wife and son. It will be an honour to help you in any way I can."

Zebedee propped Boaz against a gnarled stump and stood beside him.

"The paradox is written in the stranger's fiery eyes. He is one of us." Boaz was elated. "Zebedee, let our guest share your hideout." Ben Zvi laughed. The riders took a short route. Ben Zvi dismounted. Folds of barren mountains loomed, spectacular grey against a red orange sky. The sun was dipping in the horizon.

"Further up, there is a long tunnel hewn from the bed rock, accessible to horses. Like a furrow, it stretches almost to the base of the steep third elevation. Inside, cool water drips from the walls and collects in a small basin. Shelter for thirsty creatures. Nature's phenomenon. No one has discovered this perfect secret," said the leader and glanced at Julius. "No one," he repeated. "The best time to attack is when the sun blinds them from the west."

"Darling, you stay in the tunnel with Samson. Boaz will keep you company, tell you stories of long, long ago. I am sure they will captivate you." He leaned his body against Cardenia. She thrilled with rapture for her centurion, softly whispered, "I'll wait for you beloved."

Fabian swung young Samson in the air. "Take care of your beautiful mother," he chanted. "Boaz, it is the golden season of life. Tomorrow we will ride on Destiny's wings."

Fabian hugged the scholar and left. The horses thundered, galloping down to the left to the shore.

"Split in two, half towards the bathers in the sea, the other half to the cliffs," Ben Zvi bellowed.

Panic stricken and semi naked, the troops scrambled out of the water. The fierce sun stung, blinding their eyes. Ben Zvi and his division mowed them down, leaving a trail of gory corpses on the scorching sand.

Stunned, Hadrian spotted Zebedee and Julius stampeding with the others towards him. His blood ran cold.

The soldiers near the cliff feared for their lives, mounted their horses and escaped. They were not pursued.

Trapped, Hadrian climbed the rocks, holding a long sharp knife. Ben Zvi, Fabian, Julius and Zebedee ascended in a semi-circle. Zebedee indicated he was going after him.

Nimble footed, he suddenly stopped, lifted his head and sniffed the air. The governor's vile body sweat revealed his presence.

Zebedee crept upon him and dragged Hadrian from his hidden cave. The Roman fought hard and stabbed his knife into Zebedee's shoulder.

"Eunuch, I should have taken both your eyes out as well."

The mute wrapped his powerful biceps round the despot's back and pulled both his arms out of their sockets. He shrieked. Like three goats, Ben Zvi, Fabian and Julius leapt beside him. They opened Hadrian's mouth like a vice. Zebedee cut out his tongue. Blood filled Hadrian's throat and he choked. Zebedee flung the knife as far away as he could.

The four descended the cliff. A solitary buzzard glided then dived, tearing at Hadrian's eyes and neck with his long beak.

* * *

Fabian married Cardenia. Boaz conducted the Jewish ceremony. The choir's voice veiled above the Judean Mountains, and streamed through the curtains of fleecy clouds. Unrelenting, the visionary warriors roamed the land and fought the enemy.

Cardenia never complained. Fabian, Zebedee and Ben Zvi were always beside her in their home in the wilderness. Julius, watching Cardenia gathering wood for the open fire, chortled, "Indeed, you are a lark...free— those were the exact words I said to Hadrian. He was peeved."

"I think you'll like my cooking. We're having a wild goat for lunch." She laughed.

The magnetic force pulled the driftwood to the unknown.

* * *

A year later, Cardenia was in labour. At dawn, the first streaks of light filtered between the trees. Zebedee carried water to the tent, Fabian wiped Cardenia's face and arms, and Ben Zvi cut strips of cloth. Cardenia rolled her head from side to side, her chest heaving.

"I am here, darling. The little one is nearly out," Fabian murmured, kissing her hand.

Boaz, leaning on his stick, shuffled as he approached a mare and foal. He stroked the young animal's magnificent shiny coat and whispered in its ear, "I am tired." The foal pushed his head under his mother's belly and suckled her teats. Boaz's aching joints creaked. He curled himself into a ball, and lay on the ground beside them.

At twilight, the baby's mewl pervaded above the valley. Fabian wrapped the newborn in a soft blanket and cradled him at his wife's breast. Exhausted, she fell asleep.

Excited, Zebedee sprang up like a wild goat and disappeared to tell Boaz.

"Zebedee has been gone for quite a while," said Ben Zvi. "Let's check."

They found the mute shaking, rocking the patriarch upon his knees. Devastated, he kissed Boaz eyes, clasping him to generate warmth into the stiff body. Ever so gently, Ben Zvi wiped his tears.

"We'll bury him near the favorite olive tree he loved."

Zebedee plunged into sorrow. For days he walked around the olive tree while Fabian and Ben Zvi brought him meals.

"It's a lovely day, Zebedee. Listen to the birds." Cardenia sang with the morning breeze. "My dear, dear Zebedee, I haven't decided on a name for the baby. Please scrawl in the earth what you wish the boy to be named."

His trembling fingers cut into the warm soil.

"Now you can hold Noah," Cardenia soothed.

In a seduction of the soul, Zebedee cupped Noah in his large palms.

"I'll survey the Roman camp tonight. The bloodhounds are after our scent. They were brought from Egypt recently," said Julius.

"The new commander will not rest until he captures the four of us. We are his main targets. Soldiers …. bloodhounds," Ben Zvi blurted and gnashed his teeth.

"Horses are easy to spot and noisy. Bloodhounds sniff and will follow great distances after them," said Julius.

Ben Zvi paced up and down, his hands folded behind his back as he pondered which steps to take.

"Whispering grass treads on our heels. I suggest we should let the entire herd of horses go free, except for a few, ride and spread them in different areas across the land. This will baffle and confuse the Roman army. Survival for us is vital. By foot, this is the answer." Ben Zvi stomped his boot.

"The predator and the hunted. Silent, cunning, relentlessly we'll smite the devils."

"Cardenia, the children," Fabian murmured.

"They are in our hearts, constantly on my mind." Ben Zvi wrung his hands. "A day's journey from here is a small village, tucked on the slope of a hill, isolated. Roman soldiers hardly ever pass through there. We'll ride tomorrow. I'll speak to the headman whom I've known for years…a charming character. He will give you shelter. Fabian stay beside your wife, protect Samson and Noah. Your sons are the future. They will crush the oppressors to perdition." Ben Zvi's eyes were moist. He then brushed Samson's mass of golden curls. "A good place to raise children."

"Paradise hidden in the wilderness," Cardenia chortled happily, strolling with Zebedee who cradled Noah on his wide chest. He kissed the infant's face and wriggling toes. Samson picked wild mushrooms beside his mother.

"When we meet again, we'll go down to the stream and swim with the children." Zebedee nodded. Cardenia whirled around like a butterfly.

A week before leaving, Julius knelt before Cardenia and said, "The raptorial Romans will never destroy your nest, never."

"With one blood we will defend those we love." Ben Zvi lifted Samson, hugging him. "Mighty, mighty Samson."

Dizzy, Cardenia sat cross legged on the warm earth. Fabian held the baby. Fabian felt a dark premonition and gazed into Zebedee's trustful eyes. The mute rubbed his cheeks on Noah's toes.

The wind rose between the trees when they left. The three covered great distances through yawning gullies, creeks and narrow gorges.

"The village where Fabian and his family are must never be known. Their lives depend on our secret. We cannot return to see them. Vermin spies crawl everywhere. We'll head towards Bethlehem hills and join our brothers.

For two years the war cry roared. Romans on horseback and bloodhounds hunted their prey. The zealots with bows and arrows skulked from caves, forests and cliffs, attacking with savagery.

The carnage was macabre. The sky turned black. The earth was stained with blood. Birds of prey carried limbs of Romans and fallen heroes.

In the opposite direction, soldiers pursued Ben Zvi and Julius. Zebedee climbed the steep hill. A solitary bloodhound followed him. Julius slumped as the sword pierced his chest. Zebedee turned. The bloodhound pounced, digging his pointed canine into his thigh, pulling and ripping. Zebedee's powerful muscles opened the beast's jaw and broke it. He flung the dog over the cliff.

In excruciating pain, bleeding profusely, Zebedee dragged himself higher and found a cave. He heard Ben Zvi howl like a wounded animal. His plaintive echo called above the peaks. Men like him never died; instead they rose with the mist.

Despaired, Zebedee wanted to save his dearest friend. He clutched his dry throat longing for his childhood in Bethlehem, running with Ben Zvi between the trees. He loved listening to him sing and play his lyre. The lonely mute wanted to cry, uttering faint burblings. He tunneled inside. Trembling in the lair, Zebedee scooped large and small stones, sealed the entrance and buried himself.

In the dark, he shivered. The mute saw Samson riding on a white stallion. Through the fog, little Noah appeared, wriggling his toes. Zebedee wanted to touch him.

Zebedee closed his eyes. His magnificent voice flooded the land of the heroes.

The driftwood floated in the stream and finally anchored on the bank, between the massive roots of the old olive tree.

THE END

ABOUT THE AUTHOR

Hadassah Pomeroy was born in Tel-Aviv, Israel. She served in the Israeli Air Force for two years. Hadassah speaks four languages. She also resided in Singapore working as a freelance translator and found Singapore to be an exhilarating place to live.

Accompanied by an anthropologist, a doctor and a cameraman, she navigated up the mighty Amazon River in an old tug boat on a memorable adventure to meet with the South American Indian tribes.

Hadassah also spent time with the four-foot pygmies in the forests of the Congo and found them thrilling people. In addition, Hadassah roamed with the Bushmen of the Kalahari Desert, hunting for food.

She now lives retired in Perth, Western Australia.

www.hadassahpomeroy.wordpress.com

Made in the USA
Charleston, SC
17 August 2015